Almost Heaven

To Candice,
My Forever Friend,
With love & Special Blessings

Lydia B. Miller

Almost Heaven

LYDIA B. MILLER

TATE PUBLISHING
AND **ENTERPRISES**, LLC

Published by Tate Publishing & Enterprises, LLC
127 E. Trade Center Terrace | Mustang, Oklahoma 73064 USA
1.888.361.9473 | www.tatepublishing.com

Tate Publishing is committed to excellence in the publishing industry. The company reflects the philosophy established by the founders, based on Psalm 68:11,
"The Lord gave the word and great was the company of those who published it."

Book design copyright © 2016 by Tate Publishing, LLC. All rights reserved.
Cover design by Lirey Blanco
Interior design by Richell Balansag

Published in the United States of America

ISBN: 978-1-68352-877-7
Fiction / Christian / General
16.08.03

To Rex and Laura

with all my love

in loving memory of

Megan Whitney Estrada-Miller

1986–2007

Where we leave off, we begin
The continuance of life never ends
And from as far back as our distant cosmic origin
We are, what we have always been
We are as one, you and I
For we are of the earth and of the sky…

—Lydia B. Miller

Acknowledgments

I would like to thank God first and foremost for including me in His creation story. One of the things I am most grateful for is the gift of potential. Each morning this precious gift arrives anew at my doorstep wrapped in unlimited opportunities and sealed with God's blessing and love. It would be impossible to recount all the gifts and favors my Heavenly Father has given me over the past 63 years, but high on the list of favorites is not only a gift, but a trait that I inherited from Him. It is the *need* to create and the joy that comes from sharing my creations with others. This *need* is central to who I am. Being able to express myself with words fueled by my imagination and guided by the inspiration of God has given my life meaning and purpose.

Thanks to my family and friends for your love and support, and for always providing encouragement and much needed prayers at just the right time. Your contributions to my life have made all the difference.

Last, but not least, I want to thank my husband, Roger. Words seem inadequate in light of all you do. I am especially grateful and appreciative for the gift of time you have so generously provided so that my life-long dream could become a reality. I will be forever grateful for all your sacrifices during this long process.

1

Gethyn Fields was not a bird. She did not have wings and was never meant to fly, yet in the end her spirit rose and soared to heights unimaginable.

While the young woman was slowly making her way up the steep, winding mountain road in the foggy predawn hours of Easter morning, her parents slept soundly in their warm feather-down bed, unaware it would be the last good night's sleep they would have for a long time to come. The day had been long, and now thoughts of sleep occupied the redhead's mind. John Denver's classic song "Country Roads" was playing softly on the radio, and the girl sang along in an attempt to stay awake.

> *Almost Heaven—West* Virginia
> *Blue Ridge Mountains—Shenandoah River*

Life is old there—older than the trees
Younger than the mountains—blowing like a breeze

Country roads—take me home
To the place—I belong...

Gethyn (rhymes with *Beth* and ends with *en*) had spent a productive day with her fiancé, Dave, checking out potential venues for their wedding, which was in the beginning stages of planning. Their future looked bright and full of promise so there was no reason to believe the sun would not come up tomorrow.

The young woman was so close to home. Another half mile and she would have been safe, but it wasn't to be. Gethyn's eyelids had grown increasingly heavy, until little by little she succumbed to sleep's powerful persuasion. At the precise time the SUV became airborne, she was having a vivid dream about a baby hatchling tumbling from its treetop nest and was even caught up in the sensation of somersaulting head over heels through the air. It was not a dream, however; it was very real. Gethyn had fallen from earth and entered into another dimension.

Within a few seconds, the vehicle disappeared into a dense fog cover hanging over the mountain. It was eerily quiet as the night held its breath, waiting for the greedy claws of gravity to reach up and pull the vehicle from the sky. The force of the landing caused a massive cloud of dirt and rocks to momentarily swallow the car before it was propelled forward, end over end. Then a fury of noise followed as the vehicle cut a destructive path through seedlings and high chaparral. Deer sleeping nearby were instantly alert and wide-eyed and went hightailing it into the underbrush in four different directions, while frightened blue jays took to the air, sounding a warning as they sought refuge in trees further down the mountain. Once the SUV came to its final resting place, the mountain fell silent again. Headlights cast an eerie glow as the vehicle lay motionless, waiting for the morning sun to reveal the grim scene. The radio was still softly playing…

I hear her voice—in the morning hour she calls me
The radio reminds me—of my home far away
And driving down the road—I get the feeling
That I should have been home—yesterday—yesterday

Gethyn's parents had a niggling feeling when they rose early to find their daughter wasn't home since it had always been their tradition to attend Easter sunrise services together as a family. Their son, Emmit, had arrived at around ten o'clock the night before from San Francisco and was eager to see his little sister and spend quality time with her. Mrs. Fields tried calling Gethyn's cell phone several times, but it just went to voice mail.

While Joe made coffee, Mary Ann picked up the phone to call Gethyn's fiancé, Dave West. Before she could dial the number, however, there was a knock on the door, setting the stage for the nightmare that was about to unfold. Life as the Fields knew it would never be the same, nor would they. Emmit answered the door to find Dave standing there. Mary Ann's heart sank as she realized her daughter was not with him, and Dave only had to look at the worried faces of Joe, Mary Ann, and Emmit to know that Gethyn had not made it home. Who knew silence could be so deafening?

Joe Fields was the first to speak. "Son, where is Gethyn?"

By now, Dave's face had grown ashen and his voice shaky. "We…we…totally lost track of time, and before we knew it, it was almost one o'clock," he stuttered. "I tried to get her to stay the night, but she was afraid of oversleeping and missing church. Against my better judgment, I let her go. I made her promise to call me when she got home, but she never called. I didn't know what else to do, so I got in my car and have been driving up and down the mountain for hours. The fog is so heavy though, I can't see anything."

Joe grabbed his keys from the kitchen counter and said, "Let's go. Mary Ann, call the sheriff's department." Dave and Emmit followed Joe to his car and were soon heading down the mountain in search of Gethyn.

It was several hours before the fog lifted and the SUV was discovered. The authorities couldn't say with any certainty how the accident happened, although it may have brought some measure of consolation to the Fields had they known their only daughter experienced no pain or terror in her last moments on Earth. She had simply grown tired and closed her eyes.

Like the baby bird in her dream, Gethyn had stood too close to the edge of her parents' carefully constructed nest. While initially stunned by the fall, she would soon come to realize that no matter how much she may long for the comfort and contour of her treetop home, she would never see it again.

Gethyn had been the only one traveling the mountain road in those early morning hours. However, there *was* a witness to the accident. It was God. Later when the shock wore off and anger stepped in to take its place, some of the young woman's family and friends would blame *Him* for standing by and doing nothing. Overcome by unimaginable pain that felt like jagged glass penetrating their hearts, they would look up towards the heavens, shake their fists, and demand to know "Why?"

In His own grief and sorrow, God knew all too well that the young woman's death was senseless and served no greater cause. As He watched Gethyn fall from Earth, He remembered the day He first imagined the person she would become and how He had knitted her in her mother's womb, endowing her with uncommon beauty and grace. It was *He* who had breathed life into her lungs when she was born and whispered words of hope and encouragement into her tiny ear. There was never a time when He hadn't wanted the best for her, and it grieved His heart to think anyone could think otherwise.

There was a fraction of a moment right before Gethyn's neck was broken that she was conscious, although dazed and confused. She cried out, "Sweet Jesus, help me!" The sad truth was she had fallen victim to gravity, an irreversible law of nature written in stone and set in motion back in the beginning of time. God couldn't reverse gravity or change the law. However, He could *suspend* time, or at least time as humans know it. During the fall, as Gethyn's life hung precariously between the shores of Earth and Eternity, a loving, merciful God stepped in. It was in that split second, right before she was irreparably broken, that He stretched out His arms and held the hungry hounds of death and darkness at bay to allow the young woman a conversation with Jesus in her most desperate hour of need.

When Gethyn's eyes opened, she saw the handsomest of men walking toward her with arms outstretched. She could tell the person was exalted as a brilliant light encircled the well-proportioned figure. As He approached, she saw a man who stood at least six feet tall with skin the color of wheat. Long chestnut-colored hair was parted naturally in the middle and fell over broad shoulders, framing a face that exuded wondrous grace yet at the same time inspired reverence. The man's nose was prominent although slightly curved, and His beard, which was the same color as His hair, was worn short. There were other things Gethyn noticed about the one whose countenance radiated love and light. His robe was made of pure white linen and worn draped over one shoulder, and the aura about Him was one of dignified nobility. Gethyn saw long slender fingers on hands she knew had the power to heal. However, once her gaze met His, she could not pull away from the deified man's penetrating blue eyes.

He didn't have to speak for Gethyn to know it was Jesus. She had fallen in love with Him at the tender age of three while learning the words to the song "Jesus Loves Me." In her little girl's voice, she had sung loud and confident as though proclaiming the news to the whole world:

> *Yes, Jesus loves me—Yes, Jesus loves me*
> *Yes, Jesus loves me—The Bible tells me so …*

Gethyn's parents had shared their knowledge of the Lord with her until she was old enough to study and discern the Word of God on her own. It was a happy day for all when, at the age of twelve, she became baptized into the family of God. She acknowledged Jesus as being the only begotten Son of God and having been crucified and buried, rose on the third day and ascended into Heaven. As a girl and then as a young woman, Gethyn was active not only in church but also participated in Bible study classes every Wednesday night. She prayed and fasted, and like all Christians, she went through intermittent periods of doubting her salvation. She was a sinner, although she didn't want to be, and failed as many times as she succeeded when attempting to resist temptation. Sometimes Satan bested her, and she'd wrestle with thoughts of unworthiness. However, when that happened Gethyn would seek and find reassurance in the promises of God.

Now here He was at her side. The man who was enveloped in brilliant light touched the girl's cheek with the back of His hand, instantly stilling her fears just as He had once stilled the turbulent waters on the Sea of Galilee.

"Thank you for coming, Jesus," she whispered in a voice barely audible. With great effort she reached out to Him, beseeching "Please don't leave me, Lord," even though she knew He wouldn't. Her eyes never left His as strong arms lifted her broken body from the car.

He sat with her, stroking her long, red-gold titian hair. "Gethyn, do not be afraid for I am with you now and for always," Jesus said, His voice exuding love and compassion. "I promise never to leave or forsake you." His presence allowed the young woman the dignity to accept the fate she knew was inevitable.

As she entered into the valley of the shadow of death, she simply stated, "I'm dying." Jesus nodded His head and said unto her, "As it is written in John 11:25, I am the resurrection and the life. He that believeth in me, though he were dead, yet shall he live: And whosoever liveth and believeth in me shall never die. Do you believe this?" The young woman's eyes fluttered and with her last breath replied, "Yes, my Lord."

Jesus looked down at the girl in His arms. He tenderly moved a tendril of red hair aside that had fallen over her brow and kissed Gethyn softly on the forehead. Then, with face raised to the heavens, He said a prayer to the Father on her behalf. Afterward, Jesus's gaze returned to the young woman and in a soft whisper said, "Rest now, my precious child, for today you shall be with me in Paradise." His words echoed and brought to mind another Easter some two thousand years ago when He had offered those very words of comfort to a dying man. Reassured, Gethyn went without a struggle. Jesus's face was the last she saw as she let go of life, and His words were the last she ever heard on Earth.

The exalted man rose with ease and turned towards a towering angel standing nearby. "Zendor," He called, motioning for the celestial being to come closer. The magnificent creature approached and knelt before its Master. With head bowed and eyes cast downward in subservient reverence, it answered "Yes, Lord. I am here."

The celestial being felt downcast at its ineffective attempts to protect Gethyn from harm as it was her guardian angel. For twenty-two years, it had watched over, cared for, and loved her. "How could things have gone so terribly wrong?" Zendor agonized inwardly. The angel had shouted several warnings of impending danger as they crept slowly up the mountain. "Turn back!" the being had exclaimed. "Wake up before it's too late!" But Gethyn did not hear the angel's voice, and once her vehicle went over the side of the mountain, her fate was sealed.

The Lord read the creature's tortured thoughts and knew His servant was not to blame. He felt sympathy for the burden Zendor was carrying and offered words of consolation to the large angel who knelt before Him weeping.

"Zendor, rise and look at me."

The celestial being stood and looked into Jesus's eyes, knowing they had the power to pierce as deep as a two-edged sword had He wanted to. There was no anger in the eyes that met Zendor's, only love and understanding.

"I know you are deeply saddened by Gethyn's death. However, do not blame yourself as nothing you could have done would have changed the outcome."

The Lord's kind words rather than the incrimination the guardian angel felt it deserved made the servant love its master even more.

"You have served Heavenly Father well. However, through no fault of your own, the purpose for which you were sent to Earth has been interrupted."

The towering angel bowed its head again, awaiting further instruction.

Then the Lord announced emphatically, "I must go on ahead to prepare a place for Gethyn. Meet me in the garden by the River of Life at sunrise and do not tarry, as humans grow very ill if they go too long without eating of the fruit that grows on the trees at the water's edge. Unlike you, who being a spirit have no need of sustenance, people are both human beings *and* spirit. However, Heavenly Father designed them to live in a physical environment. It is their nature. As such, once humans arrive in Paradise, they are given temporary bodies that require sustenance. Without a temporary body and special sustenance, they could not survive in the spiritual realm. Once Father declares, 'Thy Kingdom Come!' I will call their earthly bodies to arise from the grave where they slumber and again unite them with their spirits.

"Remember, there are many dangers lurking in the air around you, as the adversary will be watching and waiting, hoping to catch you off guard. I bid you a safe journey and God speed." Then Jesus vanished before the words "Yes, my Lord" ever left Zendor's mouth.

2

Once the Lord departed, Zendor approached Gethyn and gazed upon her in quiet reflection. Luxurious reddish-gold hair framed a heart-shaped face and spilled over delicate ivory shoulders.

Human life is so fragile, Zendor thought while gazing upon the girl who lay deathly still, the light in her Caribbean-blue eyes extinguished.

In quiet times, the guardian angel had often daydreamed about the day it would stretch its powerful wings to their full length again and ascend into the heavens. At night while Gethyn slumbered peacefully, Zendor would sometimes look out the window at the moon and the stars, reminiscing about the exhilarating sensation of wind ruffling through its feathers. The angel had imagined going home hundreds, if not thousands of times, and of the warm welcome it would receive from Heavenly Father for a job well done.

Ever since arriving on Earth, the winged creature had been aware that the day would eventually come when its mission would be over. However, never thought it would come so soon. Whatever pleasure and satisfaction it had previously anticipated when it envisioned taking Gethyn home after having lived a long, full life was now replaced by sadness and regret at her unexpected and premature demise.

A tear fell as Zendor stooped down and lifted Gethyn effortlessly with arms both strong and gentle, freeing her spirit from the wreckage of life. The celestial being drew the young woman protectively to its massive chest, stood to its full nine feet, and then extended wings spanning twenty feet. For the first time since arriving on Earth twenty-two years earlier, the angel took to the air.

Once high above the clouds, Zendor met up with a convoy of guardians numbering in the thousands and quickly fell into a *V* formation behind them. As people were both being born and dying every day, there was always a steady stream of guardian angels coming and going—one group heading towards Earth on new assignments and the other escorting spirits of God's children to either Paradise or Hades, depending on whether they were *believers* or *nonbelievers*.

They flew with a single purpose, chanting, *"Holy, holy, holy is the Lord God Almighty. All of creation is full of His glory."* Once through Earth's atmosphere, the procession of celestials paused for a moment in the black eerie silence of outer space to look back at the luminous blue and green orb from which they had just come. Had their mission not been so serious, they might have even felt giddy about leaving the doomed planet.

The angels had been with God when the foundation of Earth was laid, and Zendor remembered well how the sound of rejoicing had reverberated throughout the heavens. Earth had been wonderfully and perfectly made by a Creator omniscient, omnipotent, and omnipresent. However, once sin was introduced into the world, there came with it a downward spiral of decay and corruption. Over a time period of thousands of years, the original sin multiplied and mutated into a cauldron of lust, greed, sickness, and violence. While living on Earth, the guardian angels recognized signs of the end times and pitied those humans who were either unaware of or unconcerned about the fate in which they were headed. There were wars breaking out in countries everywhere, and plagues, earthquakes, and tsunamis seemed to be occurring on a daily basis worldwide. The angels knew these calamities were nothing in comparison to the destruction, devastation, and death that would befall them someday when Earth erupted into a fiery blaze of lawlessness and godlessness. All they could do was watch and fervently pray for each and every soul to surrender to Jesus while there was yet time so as to be saved from experiencing the terror of the Apocalypse, which loomed like a massive black storm cloud on the horizon.

They did not linger long before getting underway again. Their spiritual bodies were luminous, leaving a trail of light in their wake as they followed an invisible northerly route. They chanted and praised Almighty God while traveling at breathtaking speeds, all the while staying alert to danger. Keeping their movements deliberate and stealthy, they maneuvered through complex galaxies and past constellations. Zendor looked down at Gethyn. Her dark eyelashes did not move or flutter, nor did her chest rise and fall. She was very still.

After traveling hundreds of thousands of miles from Earth, the multitude of heavenly creatures passed in succession over the extremely cold nighttime side of the moon. They didn't stop. However, as they flew over its surface, they stole glances at its deep craters.

A telepathic consensus was reached among the group, and it was agreed that they should stop and rest on Mars for a while. Before accepting the assignment on Earth, Zendor had traveled to many places in the universe and beyond. The winged creature had seen the landscape of Mars numerous times, however never tired of exploring it. There was a giant canyon system nine times longer and four times deeper than the Grand Canyon. Its terrain was rugged. One of Zendor's favorite places to explore on Mars was a giant volcano one hundred times the size of Mauna Loa in Hawaii. It was a steep climb to the summit, and once there, Zendor would stand triumphantly on the ancient volcano's rock-solid shoulders and peer down into the dark abyss.

While the multitude of angels hovered overhead looking for a suitable place to land, they engaged in telepathic chatter. Zendor listened initially but tuned out the cacophony of noise when they began discussing how billions of years ago Mars had contained water and vast oceans. Whenever the topic came up, it seemed a loud debate always ensued with everyone offering their theories as to why the water and oceans had vanished. Zendor had heard it all too many times before over a time span of hundreds of thousands of years and felt it was a mystery known only to Almighty God; therefore, saw no point in idle speculation. The Creator of heaven and earth had no obligation to mankind or the angels to explain Himself. God was entitled to His secrets and was within His rights to reveal things in His own time, if and when He chose to do so. What right did anyone have to question His reasoning as only He is God.

Once rested, they continued on their way, passing through hundreds of billions of stars in the Milky Way and at one point even witnessed new ones being formed. Zendor counted sixty-one moons circling Jupiter, the largest covered by a thin layer of ice. Without breaking formation, the angels veered away from the planet so as not to get caught up in a giant storm that had been raging there for well over three hundred years. The high-pressure storm, similar to hurricanes on Earth, was very dangerous, and they couldn't risk getting caught up in the force of its gales.

Once past Jupiter, the convoy made their way past Saturn, Uranus, Neptune, and then Pluto. They entered an enormous star field located twenty-five trillion miles from Earth. It was there that Zendor counted 1,500 galaxies before losing count, each galaxy containing billions of stars. In the center of one dusty spiral, Zendor saw very old yellow and red stars and on the outer region were younger ones, blue in color, as well as dark areas of interstellar dust that pockmarked the galaxy.

The long procession paused for a few moments to study several of the oldest deep space objects in the universe, some being more than ten billion years old. Once everyone's curiosity was satisfied, the journey continued. Next they came upon a cloud, inside of which were stars known as red supergiants. The celestials stayed their distance as the red supergiants blasted material at speeds up to two hundred miles per second. The angel's eyes lit up and reflected all the wonder and awe of a child as they paused to watch God's fireworks.

The guardian angels flew three thousand, five thousand, and then eight thousand light-years away from Earth. Flying through the heavens was both fascinating and exhilarating to Zendor and the others. While carrying the precious spirits of God's children, they marveled at the creative genius of their Maker, all the while chanting *"Holy, holy, holy is the Lord God Almighty. All of creation is full of His glory."*

3

With the Book of Life tucked under His arm, the Son of God strode into the station at the border crossing in His immaculate white robe. His gait was not hurried, nor was His brow creased with concern or worry at the sight of the menacing guards posted there. As always, He was neither early nor late but right on time. The guards had once been mighty angels possessing great power and authority within the government of God as they patrolled the universe in their glittering jeweled robes. However, all that changed after Lucifer recruited them into His army with the intention of overtaking God's throne. As a result of their fall from grace, they were stripped of their garments, and their authority and stature was forever diminished. Now, instead of holding prominent positions helping to oversee the cosmos, they were relegated to languishing at the border crossing until the last of God's chosen people had passed through its gates.

Jesus came here routinely bringing passports for citizens of Heaven who arrived daily at the border on the way to their temporary shelter in Paradise. The spirits of God's children required a place to rest while waiting for the end of the world to unfold according to Revelation. However, it was only after all prophesies contained in the book had come to pass that they would be allowed to continue on to their final destination—home on the newly resurrected Earth. It would be called Heaven.

The Lord placed the large, heavy book on a nearby table and took a chair. He was a magnificent man to behold, perfect in every way. The shifty-eyed border guards watched every move Jesus made and were irresistibly drawn to yet simultaneously repelled by His radiance and beauty. Opening the book, the Lord silently perused its pages, blue eyes filling with both waves of joy and sorrow at what He saw printed there. One by one, He called out the names of the believers who would soon be arriving. The guards, afraid of incurring the wrath of God, did not interrupt Jesus as He spoke. However, once the names had been read, they vigorously protested. The Lord waited patiently as one by one they accused each believer of being guilty of multiple sins, even bolstering their claims by producing wanted posters listing each person and every crime or infraction of God's laws they had ever committed in their lifetime.

Once their arguments were spent, the room fell into an uneasy silence. Not knowing what was about to happen, the guards went into self-preservation mode. Like cornered animals, all attempted to make themselves appear as large as possible so as to intimidate their rival. Standing as tall as they could muster, they puffed out their chests and crossed their arms defiantly in front of them. The contempt they felt for the Lord was evidenced by the malevolent smirks on their faces.

Jesus was no more intimidated by the lot of them than He was by a pesky gnat. He closed the Book of Life and stood to face each of the accusers.

"Yes, what you say is true," the Lord admitted, nodding His head affirmatively. "Each believer has sinned, and a just God cannot allow their sins to go unpunished as He demands that only those holy and righteous can enter into His Kingdom."

The guards gloated as they shook their smug heads in agreement at having been proven undeniably right by the Son of God. However, their glee was short-lived as the radiant man continued.

"As it is written in Jeremiah 33:8, 'I will cleanse them from all the sin they have committed against me and will forgive all their sins of rebellion against me.' And in Isaiah is it not written 'Though your sins be like scarlet, they shall be as white as snow; though they be red like crimson, they shall be as wool.'"

The guards were rendered speechless as the Lord quoted one verse after another from God's Holy Bible. "In Micah 7:19, it says, 'He will turn again, he will have compassion upon us; He will subdue our iniquities; and Thou wilt cast all their sins into the depths of the sea.' and in Hebrews 8:12, it is written, 'For I will forgive their wickedness and will not remember their sins no more.' Isaiah 43:25 says, 'I, even I, am he that blotteth out thy transgressions, for my own sake, and will not remember thy sins.'"

They could only listen with their mouths agape as they were force-fed words they begrudgingly knew were true but did not want to hear.

Jesus bent down and picked up the wanted posters that had been strewn on the floor by the adversary's servants. As He tore each one up, He said, "For as the heavens are high above the earth, so great is His mercy toward those who fear Him; as far as the east is from the west, so far has He removed our transgressions from us." He looked at each of the guards, adding, "So is it written in Psalm 103:11–12."

The Son of God spread His arms out wide, the sleeves of His white robe falling away to reveal the scars of His crucifixion. "I have willingly paid for the sins of the world in advance with my blood and have granted eternal life to all those who have chosen to accept my free gift of salvation."

Jesus handed over the passports of God's spirit children, saying, "You will not in any way detain the believers whose names were called but will allow them to cross the border in the company of their guardian angels. Those whose names were not called are to be taken into custody immediately and transported to a holding cell in Hades to await sentencing at a date as yet to be determined. Do you understand?" At that point, all the deflated guards could do was nod their heads in agreement.

With travel arrangements for God's chosen taken care of, the Lord left the station in a cloud of glory, speeding toward Paradise.

4

Eventually, the convoy came to another enormous star field, in the center of which was a familiar landmark. The V-shaped formation veered to the right and then to the left, never losing sight of the still-distant star. They conversed telepathically while flying at lightning speed, knowing the border patrol station was just beyond the familiar landmark.

The stream of angels kept their steady course until at last they came to the giant superstar. They proceeded cautiously, knowing the adversary's armed henchmen would be patrolling the area. Approaching the border, thousands of guardians simultaneously fell away, tipping their wings as though to say good-bye. They were now divided into two groups, each according to the destination chosen prior to death by the spirits of those they ferried.

The convoy escorting the spirits of the believers slowed down but did not stop as the Lord had given explicit orders allowing them to pass through without incident. The others were not so lucky. They were ordered into the station and detained. It was with great sadness that their guardian angels relinquished the spirits of the nonbelievers to their jailers. Afterward, they flew away from the border station as fast as their enormous wings would carry them and did not look back. Upon their return home, they would have to give an accounting to God knowing that His heart would be broken at the loss of even one soul. It had never been His wish for anyone to perish but to have everlasting life. However, free will mandated that each be unrestricted in choosing his or her own fate.

While relieved Gethyn was a believer, Zendor did not envy those spirits taken into custody. They would not be going to an oasis of extravagant beauty like Paradise but to a rocky, barren place where the landscape over which they would tread was comprised of endless peaks of sorrow and bottomless valleys of regret. It was where humans with no hope resided, a place where vultures of death hungrily waited to feast on the spiritual carcasses of those who refused salvation.

Zendor had protected Gethyn while she lived on Earth. However, with their journey almost complete, the angel realized the young woman needed protection from peril even more now. Even though the border patrol had allowed the guardian angels carrying the spirits of God's children to continue on their way, Zendor was all too aware that the adversary with its legions of powerful angels would love nothing more than to prevent them from reaching their destination. The winged creature affirmed its resolve not to let its guard down until he had safely delivered Gethyn to the garden that lay like a lustrous white pearl in the center of Paradise.

After traveling a nearly impossible distance, Zendor took stock of the surroundings and knew they would reach home well before sunrise. Though beginning to feel a little weary from the long flight, he agreed with the others to push on. The procession flew through invisible corridors that had been traversed by millions of angels before them. Flying parallel to them was another convoy of angels flying south towards Earth, likewise in an orderly *V* formation.

The celestial being looked down at the young woman cradled in its massive arms whom it loved as though its own precious child. Once it reached the outer gates of Paradise, its purpose would enter a second phase, as its responsibility towards Gethyn did not end with her earthly demise. Zendor would always be her guardian, if only in the capacity of guide, mentor and friend, and would answer her plethora of questions, except those that only Jesus could answer. In general, the angel would help the young woman become acclimated and oriented to the afterlife. There was so much to teach Gethyn, but it would all come in good time.

One of the things Zendor looked forward to most was the moment when Gethyn regained the ability to see and converse with angels. Of course, at first she would be startled by their size, as most humans are when seeing a celestial being for the first time. Zendor thought it funny how people always expected angels to look like those depicted in art and literature, although in reality it was seldom the case. In a sense, guardian angels were a dichotomy—neither male nor female but rather a distinct and perfect embodiment of both genders. On one hand, they were supernatural specimens of extraordinary strength and courage more than capable of battling the adversary if need be yet simultaneously possessing a maternal instinct. Once a guardian took a charge under its wing, its only objective was to love and nurture. Although Gethyn's angel was a towering nine feet tall in stature, its natural countenance was that of kindness and gentility. The creature had eyes the color of amethyst that were both soulful and expressive with a wild mane of thick black hair cascading down its muscular shoulders and back, much like that of a Friesian horse. A crisp white robe and gold sandals were the only clothing the angel wore, and the exposed parts of its body were the color of burnished bronze.

Zendor was ready for the dynamics of their relationship to change, as for most of the young woman's twenty-two years, it had been one-sided. It knew there were stories of birth and childhood that could only be told from its perspective. Too, the guardian angel felt she would be interested in hearing of the challenges faced on those occasions when the need for intervention arose. Although Gethyn had been unaware of Zendor's existence, it was nevertheless the common memories they shared together on Earth that would forever bind them to one another.

There was one story, however, that the angel wished would never come up in conversation, and that was her death. Without invitation or warning, a torrent of teardrops fell upon the dry, parched landscape of Zendor's face. The creature knew it was inevitable that the young woman would eventually ask the dreaded question, which was why, if it had been appointed by God to protect her from harm, had she not been saved when divine intervention was needed the most?

Humans reacted differently upon learning of their deaths, and there was no way to predict how Gethyn was going to react. Knowing humans would be afraid to leave their bodies and earthly home behind, it was a loving God who instilled an image of the garden in the hearts of all His children. He knew that as people aged and their frail bodies increasingly failed them, their longing for Paradise would grow ever stronger until they not only accepted their transition from one life to the next but also welcomed it. By then, they would have grown anxious and impatient to join their parents, siblings, and friends who had already passed. God also knew babies and young children were more apt to accept their deaths as they hadn't lived long enough to become earthbound. They embraced the afterlife wholeheartedly without question, curious for all it had to offer. Teenagers and young adults were the ones who seemed to have the most difficulty accepting death, as they tended to struggle with the unfairness of their fate. Jesus felt particularly compassionate towards them and understood their feelings, for He had died in the prime of life as well. He held those who grieved in His loving arms until the tears of their sorrow subsided.

There were many things Gethyn would need to learn once she accepted her passing. However, for now, Zendor had the responsibility of carrying the young woman's spirit safely home. Once there, she would live in Paradise along with others who had come before her and those who would come after until the day God chose to destroy the heavens and Earth. Like a phoenix rising out of the ashes, He would then resurrect the new heavens and the new Earth.

What a glorious day that will be! Zendor thought. A new heaven and Earth free of sin, suffering, and death. It would be a place of unimaginable beauty and rich in culture and education, a place where people of all nations would coexist peacefully together and where the lion would lie down with the lamb. It was there that God would once again walk among men.

The guardians came to a place where no stars existed to illuminate the heavens, so they relied solely on their own luminous bodies to see them the rest of the way home. They never strayed from their tight *V* formation or from chanting *"Holy, holy, holy is the Lord God Almighty. All of creation is full of His glory."*

Zendor's mind wandered, and for a moment, seemed to be once again walking down the wide gold-paved street leading to the magnificent holy city of God known as the New Jerusalem. As foretold in Revelation 21, one day, God would cause the city to descend from the clouds, after which it would become known as the cultural mecca of the new Earth. Everyone in Paradise looked forward to the day when God would proclaim, "Thy Kingdom Come, Thy will be done, on Earth as it is in Heaven!" Christ would then be reunited with His bride, and the marriage supper of the Lamb would begin. As much as Zendor looked forward to all the future had to hold, the celestial being knew many events would need to transpire as foretold in Revelation before that day would come.

Zendor snapped out of the daydream. Although exhausted from the arduous journey, the thought of the sprawling gold city and all that lay ahead sent a jolt of renewed strength and vigor to the very tips of the angel's weary wings. Flying onward, the anticipation for what lay ahead mounted. Sounds of gaiety and rejoicing would erupt in a deafening roar at the massive outer gates upon their return as throngs of people lined the streets searching for loved ones they were told would be coming.

Up ahead, Zendor saw the golden stairway leading to Paradise. Again, the thought arose as to how Gethyn would take the news of her death. As the celestials neared the landing area designated for returning convoys, the guardian knew it wouldn't be long before the answer was known.

5

The flight had been long, and it felt good to finally be standing on solid terra firma. The convoy's wings ached from flying practically nonstop from Earth. After shaking the kinks from their feathers and adjusting their robes, they gave praise to God for their safe journey home.

Before them was a long golden stairway, its banister made of creamy white ivory. There were one thousand steps to ascend before reaching the outer gates of Paradise. The guardian angels quickly formed a single line, two abreast, and began the steep climb on foot.

Higher and higher they ascended. At the halfway point, Zendor heard excited voices coming from within the fortress walls and saw golden light spilling from the open gates. Shouts of exclamation rang out: "Look! There they are! They're coming!" Before long, welcoming faces peered down at them, and once they had reached the top of the stairs, Zendor and the other guardians stepped into a hero's welcome. People lined the gold-paved street for as far as could be seen. As the procession filed past, Zendor acknowledged friends, both angels and human, with a nod. Everyone's spirit was light; and however expressed, whether by singing, laughter, dancing, or prayer, each person or angel found a way to show relief and joy for the safe arrival of God's children.

Having been away for so many years, the sight, smell, and sounds of Paradise were intoxicating. It was as beautiful as the angel remembered, maybe even more so, and Zendor looked forward to seeing everything again through Gethyn's eyes. For now though, it was imperative to get her to the River of Life where Jesus waited.

Though the sky was veiled in darkness, there was plenty of visibility, for the spirits of the celestials as well as those of the resident humans cast a warm glow of light. There were many miles to walk before sunrise. Leaving the welcoming crowd behind, the long parade of guardian angels moved swiftly toward God's holy city. Like an eagle's nest, it was perched high on a mountaintop in the far distance, where only those possessing wings of faith could ever hope to reach.

They followed a wide boulevard made of pure gold. Shady trees and park benches were artfully and strategically placed along twin tributaries, which meandered down the length of the thoroughfare. In addition, other silvery paths of water forked from them, bringing life to distant areas of Paradise.

The road led to the inner walls of the holy city. The great wall surrounding the New Jerusalem was made of jasper—or diamond, as it is known. Its foundation consisted of twelve layers garnished with all manner of precious stones, each layer representing one of the twelve apostles. The first was made of jasper; the second, sapphire; the third, chalcedony; the fourth, emerald; the fifth, sardonyx; the sixth, sardius; the seventh, chrysolite; the eighth, beryl; the ninth, topaz; the tenth, chrysoprasus; the eleventh, jacinth; and the twelfth layer, amethyst. There were a total of twelve entrances in the wall, three for each direction of the compass, and angels armed with swords were posted at each of them. The gates were made of giant pearls, each inscribed with the name of one of the twelve tribes of the children of Israel.

In the center of the city was the Garden of Eden, as lush and beautiful as the day God removed it from Earth. There were no birds or wildlife, but someday, the sound of their voices would once again fill the peaceful sanctuary. For now, the only animals inhabiting Paradise were the King's horses and those of His army of angels.

In the garden were dozens of trees, each heavy-laden with twelve different kinds of fruit which grew along the banks of the River of Life, providing shade and sustenance. There were labyrinths to walk, paths to follow, and trees, foliage, and flowers of every description and variety to stop and admire. The garden served many purposes, but for now, it served as a breathtakingly beautiful place to rest after life's long journey.

Zendor walked with the multitude of other guardians along the gold-paved boulevard until they reached the inner wall of the New Jerusalem with its twelve glittering foundations. It was close to sunrise as they filed through the holy city's gate and made their way to the garden's entrance. From there, they walked down a well-worn path to the river.

As the angel stooped over, layers of long wavy black hair fell across one side of its face and swung freely. The towering creature gently set Gethyn down on a soft emerald blanket of grass with her back propped against a tree before taking a step back. Once the other guardian angels had done the same, Jesus appeared in His pristine white robe and commanded everyone's attention. With a voice of authority, He spoke, saying, "It is time now for the spirits of God's children to awake."

6

Day One

Sunrise

Jesus knelt at the river's edge and scooped crystal clear water into a silver chalice He held in His right hand. He appeared to each person simultaneously as only one with the ability to be omnipresent is capable of doing, and placed the goblet of life-giving water to their lips.

Gethyn's spiritual eyes opened immediately, and the first thing she saw were the comforting blue eyes of Jesus smiling back at her.

"Welcome home, beauty," He said in a voice as soft and tender as a lover's caress.

"Where am I?" the girl asked while trying to ascertain her surroundings. Though her spirit was now fully awake, her body felt severely fatigued, and she winced as crippling pain shot through her joints and muscles. Feeling dizzy and confused, her hands went to her head.

The Lord found a comfortable position on the grass in front of her before answering, "You are with me in Paradise, Gethyn."

A quizzical look crossed her face as she stammered, "Paradise? How did I get here?"

The Lord smiled. "You got here through your belief in me, God's only begotten son."

Although the young woman's mind was fuzzy, she leaned forward and asked, "Am I dead?"

Before the Lord could answer, she was overcome by a wave of vertigo and collapsed back against the tree for support. As Gethyn looked at her hands, arms, and legs, trying to make sense of what was happening, Jesus responded, "Only your human form is dead. However, I have given you the use of a temporary one for now. Your spirit is very much alive though, and in God's time, your original body will be resurrected so that your body, soul, and spirit will be reunited."

The girl pressed her fingers against both sides of her temples, struggling to comprehend all that was being said. "I don't remember dying," she mumbled, again looking confused and disoriented.

"Do you remember being born?" asked Jesus.

The young woman shook her head from side to side, answering, "No."

"That's right. It isn't meant for you to remember your birth or your death. However, the memories in between the bookmarks of your life will stay with you forever," Jesus explained in a calm and soothing manner.

The sky was just beginning to show signs of color overhead. The Lord rose gingerly and stood looking at the tree before Him. His long fingers reached for a piece of fruit high on a limb. While plucking it, His sleeve fell away, revealing the scar on His wrist where it had been pierced by a nail. The young woman winced although she said nothing.

Jesus handed her the fruit before resuming a position beside her. "Eat this fruit, Gethyn."

The girl took the fruit offered and turned it around in her hands and studied it, although she was unable to identify it as being anything she had ever seen before. It looked somewhat like a pear but was of a color she did not recognize.

Seeing her curiosity, Jesus said, "The fruit is special manna from God and is to sustain your temporary body. Without it, you would not be able to live in Paradise."

By now, the girl was feeling short of breath, and her ears had begun to ring. "Lord, I feel sick. What's wrong with me?"

Jesus put His arm around Gethyn while offering an explanation. "You feel ill due to the increased pressure of your rapid ascent. Like scuba divers who get the bends from coming to the surface of the water too fast, you are suffering from a form of decompression sickness. On Earth, you would undergo hyperbaric treatment. However, it is unnecessary here. All that is required is for you to eat the fruit of one of these trees daily. Otherwise, you will be unable to live at this altitude for long."

Gethyn obeyed Jesus's instructions and took a bite of the fruit. It was sugary sweet and delicious with no seeds or core, and her fingers didn't feel sticky afterward. What surprised the young woman most was that the joint and muscle aches were gone as was the vertigo, fatigue, the ringing in the ears, and other symptoms. Her mind was no longer cloudy, and in a way she couldn't describe, she not only felt like herself again but she felt better than her best day on Earth had ever been.

A question arose in her mind, and she asked, "Lord, why wouldn't I be able to live here?"

There was character in Jesus's face, and when He spoke, it was as a teacher of great knowledge. "When God created man, He did not create a spirit first and then put a body around him. Much to the contrary. As it is written in Genesis 2:7 of the Bible, He created man's body from the dust of the earth and then breathed into his nostrils the breath of life. That is when man's spirit entered his body, and he became a living soul. Unlike God and the angels, there was never a time when man was a spirit without a body. Man is just as much a physical being as he is a spiritual being, and one without the other is not fully human. That is why for now you must have a temporary physical body to house your spirit, as otherwise you would be unable to exist in the spiritual realm of Paradise. In order to sustain your health, you must eat the fruit that grows on these trees every day or you will grow weak and very ill. Do you understand, my precious Gethyn?"

The redheaded girl nodded her head and answered, "Yes, Lord."

Memories began to flood the young woman's mind Suddenly, without warning, she began to sob uncontrollably, thinking how her heartbroken family must be grieving her loss.

Jesus took the hem of His robe and wiped away her tears and then put a comforting arm around her waist and leaned his head against hers. "There, there, sweet Gethyn," He whispered. "I know it hurts to think of your family and friends. However, it is necessary for your memories to stay with you."

The young woman hung her head and between sobs blurted out, "Why, Lord? It would be easier if I didn't remember them at all."

"True," the beautiful man said. "It *would* be easier." There was a silent pause before the Lord spoke again. "Gethyn, it is important to remember the life you had on Earth as you will need to help those who will be coming."

The young woman, her face now puffy and tear-streaked, looked into the compassionate eyes of the man who sat beside her. "Help them how?" she asked.

Jesus kissed the top of her head. "They will need your prayers. You see, my beloved, there are many kinds of prayers. There are prayers humans send up to God, and there are prayers that God as well as angels and humans send down to Earth. And believe me, Earth desperately needs all our prayers."

The girl was now curious and asked, "Did God hear all of my prayers?"

In a matter-of-fact voice, Jesus responded, "Yes. Every one of them."

Gethyn thought for a moment before probing further. "If God hears all of our prayers, will those on earth also hear or be cognizant of prayers we send to them?"

The Lord answered, "The spirit dwelling within each person receives prayers filtering down from Paradise, which are then delivered to its host's subconscious."

Gethyn was still trying to grasp the meaning of the Lord's explanation when He offered an analogy.

"Imagine your mind as a mailbox and your spirit as the postman who delivers prayers meant just for you. Once a prayer has been delivered to your subconscious mailbox, you receive it in the form of a thought. Weren't there times when you were going about your business when all of a sudden your grandmother's face popped into your mind?" After she nodded yes, the Lord confirmed, "Well, that was your spirit's way of letting you know she had just said a prayer for you. There was a glimmer of a spark in Gethyn's eyes and a slight smile on her face as she thought of her beloved, long-deceased grandmother.

Jesus adjusted His sandal and then once again looked over at the young woman. "Did you know there are people here you've never heard of or met who prayed for you every day?"

"There are?" she answered, astonished. "Yes, child. Did you ever have a vivid dream about someone you'd never met or seen on Earth before? Well, that person does exist, and he or she was sending a general prayer to everyone in the world, including you."

Gethyn interjected, asking, "Kind of like back home when we received mail addressed to resident or occupant?"

The Lord laughed softly, and His blue eyes twinkled. "Exactly. Those in Paradise pray for everyone on Earth, whether they are believers or nonbelievers, as it is the Father's desire for all His children to be saved and return to Him. If you could not remember your loved ones, how would you be able to pray for them personally? And knowing the moral and spiritual decay that is destroying the world, how in God's name could you not want to pray for those left behind?"

There was a lull in the conversation. Jesus and Gethyn sat in silence for a few minutes, enjoying the peaceful, relaxing sound of the river flowing downstream. The slow, steady current wrapped itself around the girl's thoughts and carried them to another place and time.

In a faraway voice, she asked, "Lord? Why did I die?"

Jesus had anticipated the question. "Everyone dies, Gethyn. It is only a matter of when."

"But Lord, I was so young," Gethyn said wistfully, adding "and there was so much more I wanted to experience."

Jesus put His arm around her, and when he spoke, His words were like creamy butter melting on warm bread. "Gethyn, a fetus inside the womb of its mother grows and develops physically until ready to be born. Life in the womb is not one's real life but rather a gestational period designed to prepare him for the world to come. Then Earth becomes the womb for a time. It is where a person is shaped by his perception of himself and others, the world view he adopts, the environment in which he lives, reactions to life experiences, character adjustments made as a result of lessons learned, and his relationship with God. The life you thought was your life, the one you just left, was not your real life either but rather another gestational period of your development necessary to help prepare you for the next phase of your evolution.

"Some people are born prematurely, and some die prematurely. Death is a natural birth process everyone goes through to enter eternal life. You might even say death is the birth canal of Mother Earth. Could you imagine someone wanting to go back to being a fetus once they experienced life outside the womb?" Gethyn shook her head no. "Of course not," said the Lord. "And once immersed in the wonders of Paradise, you will not long to go back to Earth. My beautiful child, I want you to know that whatever you have lost will eventually be restored to you a thousand fold, whether it be opportunities, potential, or purpose. Your life has not ended. It is only beginning. You will see."

The young woman could have stayed in the exalted man's company forever, talking by the River of Life. However, after much time had passed, Jesus announced it was time to go. He rose with great ease and agility, long chestnut hair falling over shoulders that had carried the weight of all the world's sins, and then helped Gethyn to her feet. The young woman began to be filled with anxiety at the thought of being separated from Jesus's comforting presence, but the Lord read her thoughts and spoke reassuringly.

"I am with you always. You need only think of me and I'll be there. Until then, my servant Zendor will help you get settled and show you around."

Gethyn saw Jesus looking to a place behind her and turned to see an enormous nine-foot angel gazing down at her. She immediately fell to the ground, covered her head with her hands, and trembled and cowered in fear.

7

The gigantic angel leaned over and gently put tender, loving hands under the young woman's arms, lifting her up into the air until they were eye level with one another. She held her breath and dared not look into the pale amethyst eyes that were unlike any she had ever seen before.

In a soft, gentle voice, the creature tried to assure the obviously distressed girl. "Do not be afraid, Gethyn. I am Zendor, your guardian angel. I have been with you, cared for you, and loved you since the day you were born. I mean you no harm."

As the words slowly sunk in, the girl opened her eyes and looked into those of the celestial being who held her. Gethyn's heart melted somewhat when she saw that its countenance appeared to be one of love and compassion. Although aware that the Lord had left her in the being's care, she was nevertheless hesitant to let go of the fear that gripped her. Tentatively, she met the creature's gaze and, in a quivering voice, said, "Hi, Zendor." Not knowing what else to say, Gethyn added, "Are you really my guardian angel?"

Suddenly, silver bolts of lightning shot forth from the celestial being's eyes and pierced her heart. She recoiled involuntarily while at the same time reaching for the security blanket of fear she had hid behind earlier.

"Yes, I am, and I've been looking forward to this day ever since you were born."

Without being asked, Zendor set Gethyn down gently on the riverbank as though she were something very fragile that might break. She examined her body for burn marks after having been touched by lightning but found none. The girl watched in curious wonder as the dark-haired angel knelt in front of her and then casually sat back on its heels. With long legs tucked beneath it, its height was greatly reduced. Zendor casually pushed massive wings aside like a matador pushing a cape over broad shoulders, exposing bronzed muscular arms. Following the angel's lead, the young woman sat down as well.

When they were both settled, Gethyn was the first to speak. "How come I can see you now, but I could not see you on Earth?"

Without hesitation, the angelic creature answered, "Up until you were around three years old, you *could* see me. Your parents thought you had invented an imaginary friend, although that was not the case."

Gethyn's blue eyes grew wide as she searched the guardian's face for confirmation that what it said was indeed true. "You're kidding! How is that possible?" she asked incredulously, her voice clearly having gone up an octave.

The celestial's head tilted slightly, and its body pulsated with light. "People's spiritual eyes are open at birth but close once they are seduced and wooed by the persuasive powers of the world. Humans quickly develop insatiable appetites for carnal desires, and once that happens, they lose the ability to see spiritually. Most of the time, a child has spiritual consciousness until around the age of two. But sometimes, as was the case with you, they retain the ability to see and communicate with their guardian angel for up to three years. From that point on, children go on with their lives with no remembrance or recollection of their guardian. The day you could no longer see me was a dark day, Gethyn. It was as though the sun could no longer rise and put on its morning clothes. I could stand right in front of you, but you would look right through me, completely blind to my existence. It almost broke my heart. The only consolation was in knowing that someday Jesus would open your spiritual eyes again, allowing us to resume the friendship we started long ago."

The young woman looked within herself trying to remember the winged creature who sat before her. Had she folded up the memory like a piece of paper and put it away in a drawer in the back of her mind? She thought she felt a faint, tenuous connection, something familiar, but she decided to wait and see what developed before jumping to conclusions. While contemplating Zendor's words, she wound and unwound a strand of red hair around her forefinger, a habit she had acquired in childhood.

The guardian watched the girl sawing back and forth on its words and with one finger lifted her chin until their eyes met. "Because I'm a spiritual being, after you turned three, I could not be seen by you in the physical world. I was appointed to guide and protect you without interfering with your free will to make choices for yourself. Therefore, it was necessary to remain invisible."

The girl thought for a moment and then queried, "But how about the angel who came to the Virgin Mary and others the Bible says were seen by humans? Weren't they visible?"

The guardian realized that what it had said before must have sounded like a contradiction to the young woman. Forked lightning darted from Zendor's eyes and again coursed through Gethyn's being. Since nothing bad had befallen her before, rather than flinching, she decided to embrace the unusual phenomenon. To her surprise and delight, she recognized the sensation that time.

That's how the creature expresses happiness. It's how it smiles, she told herself. She was startled by the revelation and inwardly asked herself, *How do I know that?* When the answer came, it both surprised and comforted the young woman. In her heart of hearts, Gethyn knew without a doubt that she had known Zendor long ago. Although her memory of the guardian was still too hazy to bring into focus, she was certain of one thing. She remembered how the angel's smile had made her feel.

Zendor looked at the beautiful young woman and replied, "The answer is both yes and no. Those you speak of were and still are invisible spirits. However, being messengers of God, they were able to take on temporary physical bodies in order to carry out their earthly missions."

Gethyn chewed on the answer for a moment before coming up with a new question. "Since we are no longer on Earth and my free agency is no longer a factor, how is it I can see you now, since you are an invisible spirit?"

The angel carefully thought while forming its words of explanation. "Jesus opened your spiritual eyes when you first arrived by giving you water from the River of Life. While temporarily living in the spiritual realm, it is necessary for you to see me. Although you have no further need of a protector, I am still your guardian, and that will never change. However, my purpose now is to orient you to life in Paradise and be your friend, both of which would be impossible if you were unable to see me."

As they talked, Gethyn grew more comfortable in her guardian angel's presence. She studied the creature's face and saw that it was not as frightening as it had seemed at first. "Zendor, you don't look like what I always imagined an angel would look like," the young woman admitted with a hint of trepidation.

The celestial being pretended to be surprised. "Oh?" it said, feigning puzzlement, followed by a jagged streak of white light that burst forth from its extraordinary purple eyes. An hour earlier, the sight would have unnerved Gethyn. However, by now, she had managed to overcome her inhibitions, realizing the gigantic angel was as gentle as a lamb. "How did you picture us?" the angel asked, wavy black hair hanging over one side of its face.

The young woman's eyes were as turquoise and tranquil as the Caribbean waters off Mexico, and in a melodic voice that sounded like that of a dreamy schoolgirl describing her first crush, she answered, "I imagined them as being beautiful young women with long blonde tresses and halos, wearing flowing chiffon gowns and playing golden harps while floating on fluffy white cotton candy clouds."

After a short pause, the angel emitted a loud belly laugh that shook the ground. From its pale amethyst eyes came a volley of lightning bolts, one after another. In addition, there were blue and yellow sparks raining all around her, making Gethyn feel as though she'd been caught in a sudden spring shower without an umbrella. Before long, the young woman was soaked from head to toe in the angel's joyful laughter until, unable to resist, she succumbed to fits of laughter as well. It was several minutes before the two of them were able to speak without relapsing into contagious outbursts of the giggles.

It was Zendor who was the first to speak. "Oh! Gethyn! That was the best laugh I've had in a thousand years!" while wiping away tears of joy. "I suppose I shouldn't have been surprised by your description of angels as humans have so many misconceptions about us."

The girl leaned forward, drawing her knees up and clasping her hands around them. "Tell me about angels," she said, smiling and looking at Zendor with keen interest.

Growing serious again, the creature cleared its throat. "Well, one widespread belief of humans is that when a person dies, he goes to Heaven and becomes an angel. However, as you can see, this is a mistaken belief. A human can never become an angel just as an angel can never become human. The two are separate and distinct entities, each with their own unique characteristics and abilities. Another misconception is that some angels are cute cherub babies, which is untrue as well. There are no baby angels.

"Angelic beings are creations of God. Therefore, they have not existed from the beginning. We were created after the heavens but before Earth came into existence. While our number is in the millions, we were not created individually, but rather all at once. As such we are not a race nor did we descend from a common ancestor. Unlike humans, we are not subject to death or any form of extinction. Therefore, our numbers never change. We are adult, asexual spiritual beings. We are neither male nor female, and we never marry or reproduce. We were created by God for His purposes with each of us ranking differently in dignity and power.

"There are three hierarchies, with each being organized into three orders, or what is known as choirs. They make up the government of God. I will start with the three choirs of the first hierarchy. The first choir is the highest order of all God's servants. They are known as the *seraphim* and are the caretakers of God's throne. They constantly chant in order to keep negative energy from getting through to divinity and also provide guidance for humanitarian and planetary causes. The second choir is the *cherubim* and act as guardians of light. These angels of harmony and wisdom channel positive energy from the divine. The third choir is known as *thrones*. They are living symbols of God's justice and authority and are known as the lords of wisdom as they inhabit the world of the divine spirit. This choir is known to create, send, and collect positive energy.

"The second hierarchy is comprised of the *dominions*, the *virtues*, and the *powers*. The first choir is called the *dominions* and are heavenly governors, wielding orbs of light fastened to the heads of their scepters or on the pommels of their swords. As angels of intuition and wisdom, they provide guidance and divine wisdom for mediating and arbitrating, and in addition, they help carry out the law of cause and effect. Part of their responsibility is to regulate the duties of lower angels. This choir has dominion over all the nations on Earth and only rarely makes itself known physically to humans. The second choir of the second hierarchy is called the *virtues*. Their primary duty is to supervise the movements of the heavenly bodies in order to ensure that the cosmos remains in order. Sometimes they are referred to as the *miracle angels*, as they strive to help those who go above and beyond by helping them accomplish and achieve what others call impossible. In addition they guide loving, positive people who try to help, enlighten, and lead others to harmony, and they are known to heal through their elemental energies of earth, air, fire, and water. The *powers*, also called *authorities*, are the third choir of the second hierarchy and sometimes collaborate in power and authority with the *principalities* (*rulers*). They are the bearers of conscience and the keepers of history and world religions. One of their duties is to oversee the distribution of power among humankind and, when needed, dispense both justice and chaos. These angels are warriors created to be completely loyal to God.

The *principalities*, the *archangels*, and the *angels* make up the third hierarchy, which is the lowest sphere. The *principalities* work closely with the *powers*, carry out orders given them by the *dominions*, and also bequeath blessings to the material world. They oversee groups of people and inspire works of science or art. They guard continents, countries, and cities working toward global reform and are the protectors of politics and religion. In addition, they provide guidance for the extinction of animals, leadership problems, human rights, and discrimination. The second choir is the *archangels*, who are chief angels and warriors and who fight for the souls of mankind on Earth. They are the generals of all the angels. They are concerned with issues and events surrounding politics and military matters as well as commerce and trade. I belong to the third choir of the third hierarchy, the *angels*. Some of us are messengers involved in human affairs, delivering divine messages to people from God. Others, like me, are assigned to humans as guardians. We defend, protect, and serve as intermediaries between God and humans. Also, angels provide guidance during the transition between life and death."

Gethyn interrupted long enough to interject, "And all this time I thought heavenly choirs referred to singing."

Zendor nodded in agreement, stating, "Yes, that is another common misconception humans have of angels—that we all sing in heavenly choirs."

The celestial being picked up where it had left off. "Like man, angels have a soul. While we are superior to human beings in intelligence and power, we too are imperfect. Originally, we were all holy. At the time of our creation, we were given free agency to make decisions for ourselves, and some, like Lucifer, who later became known as Satan, chose *not* to resist temptation. Many humans don't realize that Lucifer was *created* by God as a spiritual being and, as such, was *never* nor will he *ever* be equal to God in intelligence, wisdom, strength, or power. Because Lucifer succumbed to the temptation of daring to overthrow the government of God, he was removed from the Almighty's holy presence along with others who followed him, and he will be sentenced at the time of judgment."

Zendor saw Gethyn soaking up the knowledge like a sponge, so continued speaking. "As you can see, angels are giants in stature and possess incredible strength. Each angel carries out specific missions designed to serve God. Some worship and praise God continuously while others serve as messengers to communicate God's will to men. Some guide, some provide, and some protect, while others deliver God's people from danger once they're in it. There are angels who strengthen and encourage and others who God uses as His means of answering the prayers of His people."

The young woman sat for a moment and digested Zendor's words before speaking. "I never thought of the universe as having a governing body before, but after listening to you, it makes sense. I find it so interesting that God has appointed three hierarchies of angels to assist in maintaining law and order with Him, the Creator, as the Godhead. It's very similar to how things are run on Earth, only we have the house, senate, and congress running the country with an elected president acting as the public figurehead. You know, on Earth, many people consider politicians corrupt."

The winged creature pulsed with light as it considered her words. "Lucifer was the first corrupt angel. He held a seat of high power until he became greedy and tried to usurp God's power. God has a strong disdain for chaos and disorder. That's why He created laws and boundaries and cause and effect for the heavens and earth. He thought out and designed the universe so that every living thing would have a time, a season, and a purpose for living within the confines of space and time. Your earthly government is not perfect, but nothing in heaven or earth is. Not since the fall of Adam. For the most part, it works and does what it is designed to do which is to serve, govern, and protect the people.

"I was created to serve as a guardian angel for all time and can never be anything other than what I was designed to be. Once I accepted my earthly assignment, my primary purpose was to protect and guide you for all your days and then, upon your death, to carry your spirit to Paradise. That being completed, I have now begun the second phase of my purpose."

Gethyn's thoughts shifted, and she grew pensive. "My parents told me God has a purpose for everyone. I thought I knew what mine was, but I died before ever getting a chance to pursue it. Will God punish me for not fulfilling what I was sent to Earth to do?"

Zendor could see the girl's heart was troubled by the thought of having displeased Heavenly Father and instinctively stretched a protective wing around her. "You have not let God down, Gethyn, if that is what you are thinking. He loves and cherishes you and has no desire to punish you. Please let me explain purpose to you. It is true that God gives everyone and everything, whether visible or invisible, at least one purpose. Even a rock has a purpose, if only to hold up a mountain. Not everyone discovers their purpose while on Earth or has the opportunity to fulfill what they believe they were sent to accomplish. As hard as it may be to believe, sometimes a person's true purpose isn't discovered until after he or she dies. You see, purpose, whether lost or never found, doesn't end with death, so don't let your past define you or your expectations of what lies in your future. There are endless possibilities ahead. You will discover many new purposes and become all God intends for you to be. The second aspect of purpose is not about looking for or finding what you were created to do, but rather living your life *with* purpose."

Standing up, the celestial being dusted its feathers off and said, "Why don't we go for a walk. I have something to show you."

Gethyn had enjoyed spending the morning sitting on the bank of the River of Life, first with Jesus and then with her guardian, but she perked up at the idea of seeing something new.

"That sounds like fun." She nodded in agreement. While getting to her feet, she asked the towering Zendor, "Where are we going?"

The winged creature grinned in its special way, unable to keep the surprise to itself. "Well, I thought you might like to see where you're going to live. Jesus Himself prepared it especially for you."

8

They turned around to walk up the embankment, and Gethyn was surprised to see a massive stone wall on the crest running parallel to the river. It was comprised of a series of grand arches that were spaced evenly along its length, with deep red and purple bougainvillea runners climbing its surface. The young woman marveled at the engineering feat of its construction, which brought to mind pictures of ancient Roman ruins she had seen in travel literature. She followed her guardian downstream and with each step was met with pervasive beauty and splendor, which were unlike anything she had ever seen.

After a while, the two followed a flagstone path leading farther into the garden's center until coming to a small kidney-shaped pond spanned by a white wooden bridge. They had walked halfway across when Gethyn stopped and leaned against the railing. She stood admiring the pink-and-yellow-blossomed water lilies growing there and delighted in the reflection made on the water's surface by the surrounding weeping willow trees. Time did not seem to exist nor even matter in this place of enchantment. Gethyn found herself wondering if this place was just part of an elaborate dream. If it was a dream, it was one she wasn't sure she wanted to wake up from.

Eventually, the two of them moved on. They came upon a large, well-kept formal English garden with neatly trimmed hedges, trees, and other foliage. Its lines were rectilinear, and within its borders were statues, flower-filled urns, and sculpted topiaries as well as meticulously arranged garden beds. The centerpiece of the garden was a continuously flowing multitiered fountain that was surrounded on all sides by a shaded arbor where one could sit and breathe in the fragrance of sweet honeysuckle.

They passed through a large field of ranunculus flowers that were planted in rows, and Gethyn's face lit up in a bright smile when she saw how each row depicted a different color of the rainbow. From there, the willowy girl and angel proceeded down the garden path that led to a fragrant garden where hundreds of varieties of roses grew. It was an immense area, and visiting each section took quite a long time. Once satisfied, they passed through a decorative gazebo with lightly scented wisteria woven through its latticework and continued to follow where the path led.

After a couple of hours, they had walked through every kind of garden imaginable. Gethyn was hesitant when Zendor turned onto a trail leading into a dense tropical rain forest, but having no other choice, she followed the winged creature into its depths. It was dark and quiet and sometimes seemed impenetrable. The young woman was struck with the feeling of being somewhere no eyes had ever seen, with the exception of God's. Giant trees and plants crowded out the sky, and the forest floor smelled otherworldly. They came to a cascading waterfall where a pool of water collected at its base. Exotic-smelling flowers grew in the area, and it would have seemed insulting to God to have continued on without stopping to enjoy what He had obviously provided for their enjoyment. The area was surrounded by high cliffs and large, flat boulders, and by tacit agreement, the two sat down to savor the beauty of the place. The angel took off its sandals, and Gethyn, her tennis shoes, and slipped their feet into the cold, refreshing water. For quite some time, they talked and laughed like two silly children, all the while splashing, wiggling their toes, and turning their faces up to let the cool wet spray of fine mist cover their faces.

While taking it all in, Gethyn felt something ancient stir and awaken within her soul. It was as though she had fallen into the deep recesses of the collective memory of mankind and had accidentally stumbled upon a place that had existed long ago—the place where humans first originated. It seemed somehow familiar and made her wonder if there was an overgrown moss-covered path in her subconscious mind, hidden and obstructed from view by the slow passage of time that led to this place. Like

Adam and Eve who came before her, she wondered, *Was there an inherent desire and longing in a person's soul to find a way back into the garden?*

After being rejuvenated by the water, Zendor and Gethyn put their shoes back on and climbed down from the smooth rocks. They found the trail that had led the two of them to this mysteriously wonderful place and continued to follow it through the rain forest until they saw light filtering through an opening ahead. Once they stepped through the portal, Gethyn realized they were no longer in the garden.

In front of them was a boulevard wide enough to accommodate hundreds of people at once, and although she wasn't aware of it at the time, one direction led to the massive outer wall of Paradise and the other to the holy city of God, known as the New Jerusalem. She did not notice the domed buildings or spires in the distance as her attention was riveted to the gold-paved boulevard she stood on. On each side of it were tributaries and shade trees and benches where people sat resting or visiting with others. It was a lovely picture of tranquility, the young woman thought to herself.

Gethyn was most curious about the way people were clothed and felt compelled to ask, "Zendor, why is everyone dressed in Halloween costumes?"

The angel let out another belly laugh, followed by an explosion of sparks and lightning bolts from the pale amethyst eyes that looked back at her. "What you see are not people dressed in Halloween costumes. Each person is dressed in the style of clothing they wore and were most comfortable in during the era in which they lived." The young woman's mouth formed an "Oh," and her eyes widened as she took a more earnest look at those she saw on the boulevard. There were people dressed in robes, rags, prairie dresses, and military uniforms as well as religious garments, Victorian finery, and firemen's coats. There were men she recognized as train conductors by their hats and bib overalls, and she saw doctors, astronauts, and Indians in tribal clothes. It was thoroughly fascinating, and Gethyn couldn't help but gawk.

The thought of ancient people walking among them was not something that had ever occurred to her when thinking of Heaven. She looked down at her own clothing and saw the faded blue jeans and T-shirt that had seen their better days. It suddenly dawned on her that she was going to be wearing them forever and wondered had she known it would be her last day on Earth, would she have chosen something more suitable to meet Jesus in. She dismissed the thought, knowing Jesus didn't care what she wore; he was a "come as you are" kind of God. Gethyn's eyes took in the complicated clothing of some of those who passed by and thought to herself, *Well, at least I'll be comfortable.*

After walking further, they came to an area where a large group of people were congregated and stopped to find out what was going on. Gethyn found a vantage point from which she could see and glimpsed an old rabbi standing in the center of the crowd. She strained to hear what was being said and recognized passages from the Old Testament being quoted. Suddenly it dawned on her that the religious man was speaking in Hebrew, a language she didn't know! The young woman tugged on Zendor's wing. The angel turned its gaze towards her and saw a look of confusion cross her pretty heart-shaped face. The guardian guided her away from the gathering and found an empty bench where they could sit and talk.

"Zendor, I don't understand," Gethyn began. "How is it I can recognize and understand a language I never studied or even heard before?"

The angel smiled in its odd way while meeting her gaze. "It is a gift from Heavenly Father, Gethyn—a door He has chosen to open so his children will not be strangers to one another. You see, those who live in Paradise have come from all over the world. Every continent, country, state, city, region, and tribe is represented here, all having brought with them their own unique language and customs. Because of time, finances, and other circumstances, many people never had the opportunity to travel or learn other dialects and cultures during their past life. However, in the garden, God has removed all obstacles. In his infinite wisdom and knowledge, He knows that failure to understand those who don't look, speak, or act like those they know can lead to misconceptions and distrust. Therefore, He has removed the language barrier that once separated and divided his children so all may coexist together in Paradise in peace, harmony, and unity."

The celestial being stood, and its black hair swayed. "Come," it said, motioning for the young woman to follow. While climbing the mountain, the young woman found she was not exhausted or even short-winded from making the steep ascent. Having never been particularly athletic, she silently wondered if her newfound stamina had anything to do with the fruit she had eaten.

When they finally came to the summit, she took a sudden intake of air, as before her was a sprawling, jeweled city with golden domed buildings. Gethyn stood by Zendor, transfixed by the glittering sight. Never before had she seen anything so opulent. The nine-foot angel stood tall and erect, legs slightly apart and bronzed arms at its sides.

"Who built this city?" the young woman asked.

Reverently, her guardian answered, "It is called the New Jerusalem, and was built by the hands of Almighty God."

Gethyn's heart swelled with pride for her Creator.

Zendor broke the silence, instructing the girl, "Come. You don't live too far from here."

The words seemed strange to Gethyn, as she hadn't gotten used to the idea that Earth was no longer her home or that she would never again see the house where she grew up. Memories of her parents and her old life came to the forefront of her mind, and she temporarily pushed them aside for fear of inviting a deluge of tears. With great resolve, she let her curiosity for what lay ahead take over her thoughts.

Gethyn happened to look up at her guardian as they walked down the boulevard with its golden sheen. The sight of the angel towering above her brought to mind how, as a child who had shot to five eleven practically overnight, it had always been her who had towered over her classmates. Having red hair and blue eyes didn't help either, and she was cruelly and incessantly teased until well into her teens.

Then something unexpected happened. Gethyn began to flower and blossom until her undeniable beauty took center stage. It was only then that her peers began to notice her for reasons other than her height. Even so, boys her age were still growing and few were taller than her.

Next to Zendor, I feel really short, thought Gethyn as she tried to readjust the perception she had always had of herself. *Well, I always wanted someone tall to come into my life, but this is ridiculous!* she thought, looking up at the nine-foot angel and laughing inwardly.

They passed through the glittering inner wall of the city and past several tall buildings, each one more grand than the one before. Lost in private thought, the young woman didn't seem to notice when Zendor stopped.

"We're here, Gethyn," the celestial being announced.

The young woman strained her neck in an attempt to see the top of the skyscraper. It was impossible. "I live here? In a high-rise?" the girl asked in disbelief.

"Yes," acknowledged the angel.

"Wow! Nothing is as I imagined it would be," she said, shaking her head and realizing for the first time that she hadn't really given the afterlife much thought before. However, who could have blamed her? After all, she was only twenty-two years old.

"Are you disappointed?" the girl's guardian angel asked in its soft-spoken manner.

"No, I'm just surprised, that's all. I had always heard that everyone lived in big mansions in Heaven."

A distinguished-looking man with salt-and-pepper hair stood in front of the building greeting people. Besides wearing a starched white shirt and a narrow silk tie, the gentleman wore a doorman's uniform consisting of a long black coat with shiny brass buttons over perfectly creased gray trousers. The cuffs and collar of his coat were gold-braided, and there were epaulets on each shoulder. To complete the outfit, he wore black wing tip shoes buffed and polished to a high gloss as well as a black military-style hat with the words "The Landry Hotel" embossed in gold across the front. He smiled and held open one of the heavy glass doors as they entered into a large lobby with a high vaulted ceiling.

The first thing Gethyn noticed was an atrium with several varieties of exotic plants. There were sitting areas in the spacious room as well as intimate built-in coves for people to gather and converse in private. Zendor, with Gethyn in tow, headed for the elevators around the corner.

As they waited, the angel began a commentary on its charge's previous statement. "Some people *will* live in mansions in Heaven according to their rewards, but not here. Just as people on Earth may have more than one home, in Heaven, they may have an apartment in the city, a country home, *and* a palatial residence."

Gethyn gasped involuntarily, feeling a sudden attack of anxiety. "If this isn't Heaven, then where am I?" she blurted a little louder than intended.

"You are in Paradise," answered Zendor. Judging by the look on the girl's face the angel could tell she was still baffled, so it continued to explain. "Paradise is where God's children go immediately after death, unless they have chosen to go to Hades instead. Anyway, while Paradise is certainly better than Earth, it is *not* Heaven. Let me put it in a way I heard described once that I think you'll understand. Imagine trying to purchase tickets for a straight flight to Heaven, only to learn there are none. You are told that in order to reach your destination you must stop for a layover in Paradise first. You are advised to expect a long delay, but you are told that everything possible will be done to ensure your temporary stay will be pleasant. You are informed there will be tours of the city and gardens, refreshments, and first-class accommodations provided free of charge, not to mention many interesting people to pass the time with, some of whom you may already know. Eventually, you will be able to board the plane again and resume your flight to Heaven without further delay."

Gethyn's mind was swirling, all the while trying to process everything she was being told.

The elevator doors opened and people dressed in assorted styles of clothing exited. The two entered the spacious car, and the young woman noticed at once the ceiling was high enough to accommodate the towering celestial being. The sides and back of the elevator were made of glass, and as they ascended, Gethyn looked out at the glittering gold city below, taken with its beauty. Turning to look at Zendor, she noticed there were no floor buttons and quickly spoke up.

"Zendor, there are no buttons!" she exclaimed, a question mark registering on her face. The angel looked upon the girl and replied, "There is no need. The elevator is powered by the energy of your spirit and will automatically take you to the level you live on."

Still confused, the girl asked, "But how does it know which level I live on?"

Zendor was happy to answer all Gethyn's questions and was enjoying this new role in her life. "Your energy will raise you to the level of your spiritual truth and understanding, but as you grow, where you live will change. Eventually, you will outgrow the place you live in, and then the energy of your spirit will automatically ascend to a higher level."

Once arriving on her floor, they stepped onto a hallway that was painted a pale blush. On its walls were beautiful paintings and large ornate, gilded mirrors. The ceilings were twelve feet high, and the carpet beneath their feet was soft, plush, and a deep royal blue in color. Zendor took the lead, and Gethyn followed until at last they came to a door with a placard affixed to it reading "Gethyn Fields" in gold script. Everything seemed surreal to the girl, and inwardly, she began wondering if she was experiencing some kind of hallucination.

"I'm going to leave you for a while," advised Zendor after handing the redheaded beauty a gold key. Before she could protest, the colossal angel explained "You need some time to enjoy your new home alone, and I must go see Heavenly Father. I will meet you tomorrow by the River of Life and each morning after that. With that, the angel turned and strode down the long corridor, its massive wings folded behind it, one on top of the other.

9

Gethyn hesitated for a moment before inserting the key. Then she turned the knob and slowly opened the door but was totally unprepared for what she saw. There was an audible gasp as the young woman's hands flew to cover her gaping mouth.

Before her was an exact replica of the cabin her parents used to have on Lake Lone Pine back home, a place where she had always felt the most comfortable. Because of financial difficulties, her parents had been forced to sell the property. The memory came back to Gethyn of how she had made a vow years earlier that someday when she grew up she was going to own the cabin and live in it forever.

This is impossible! Gethyn thought, wondering if maybe she'd lost her mind. The interior was exactly as she remembered—warm and earthy. It was a one-room cabin with a screened-in porch on the back, and she couldn't have loved it more had it been a palace. The walls were of rough-hewn logs, and the floor was of distressed, knotted pine. There was a weathered yet comfortable love seat with deep red, hunter green, black, and tan horizontal stripes placed in front of a gray stone fireplace and two extra wide chairs with plump pillows flanking each side. She walked over to one of the chairs, eager to run her hand over the faded fabric with its familiar yellow and red pattern. To the right of the fireplace stood a bookcase that held many treasured hardbacks and paperbacks, books like *The Adventures of Tom Sawyer*, *To Kill a Mockingbird*, and *Gone with the Wind*. She perused them eagerly with renewed interest, remembering how she used to love to curl up with a good book in the chair closest to the window on days when the weather was too stormy to go outside. There was also a spiral notebook and pen on one of the shelves. Gethyn had always kept it there for moments when she was filled with inspiration and felt compelled to write. Then the girl's eyes were drawn to a pretty heart-shaped red leaf she had discovered one sunny autumn afternoon many years earlier. She let her mind go to that place where memories lived and recalled the day vividly. The air was clean and crisp with big white fluffy clouds dotting a brilliant blue sky. Gethyn had been overjoyed upon discovering the heart-shaped leaf and rushed back into the cabin to show her parents and brother, Emmit. "Look!" she exclaimed, holding her hand out so everyone could see her treasure. "God gave me a Valentine in September!" Gethyn's parents smiled, telling her that God had purposely intended for her to find the Valentine so she would not forget that He loved her with all His heart. The thought had given the girl comfort, and from that day on, she looked for other signs of God's love and found them all around her.

Gethyn was soon adrift on an ocean of nostalgic reverie and willingly surrendered to its lure and seductions. She allowed herself to be carried by gentle, white-capped waves of emotion, to where memories lay like pretty seashells waiting to be found and collected on the distant shoreline of her heart.

The young woman could almost smell the pungent aroma of morning coffee brewing and see her mama standing in the kitchen in her striped pajamas and powder blue chenille robe. A memory of her mama frying up sizzling smokehouse cured bacon and flapjacks that were always slightly burnt around the edges came to mind, and Gethyn smiled. She looked at the round dining table and chairs where she and her family had sat and shared many meals, board games, and conversations together.

Then, like a fickle wind, her thoughts changed directions, and she smelled the woodsy scent of sugar pines and cedars. She remembered how she, Emmit, and their dad would wake up early on summer mornings and walk down the pine needle path to the lake where their boat waited. They would untie the rope secured to a metal cleat on the wooden mooring post and then quietly motor towards their favorite fishing hole. Once there, they would kill the engine and sit drinking coffee from thermoses while watching the sun rise gracefully over the lake. Gethyn smiled as she remembered being teased for liking a little coffee with her sugar and milk. Afterward, they would cast their lines into the water in hopes of catching a stringer of bass or trout for lunch. It seemed like a lifetime had passed since being enveloped by the cozy arms of the little cabin, but here it was welcoming her home again.

Gethyn's eyes shifted to the bed sitting diagonally in the corner where her parents had always slept. As for her and Emmit, they had slept in twin beds that sat on opposite sides of the screened-in patio. The young woman stepped onto the porch and at once remembered hearing crickets, katydids, cicadas, and bullfrogs while drifting off to sleep and how she never tired of hearing the nightly insect orchestra. Sometimes she would lie in bed looking out at the moon hanging suspended over the lake and fall asleep lulled by the mournful sound of a loon. In the winter, she and her brother slept in bedrolls in front of a crackling fire. Like a squirrel store-housing enough acorns to hold it for a long winter, Gethyn was thankful to have gathered so many wonderful memories of the life she had with her family. She didn't know how long it would be before she would see any of them again, but like the squirrel burrowed in its nest, she had no other choice than to wait out the season.

The young woman went back into the cabin, walked over to the full-sized bed that was covered by a heavy quilt, and sat down. She looked down at the quilt with a renewed sense of appreciation. She thought about the laborious amount of time and effort that had gone into making it as she studied each patch of material with its complex and unusual pattern of concentric circles. While it had no doubt once been bright and colorful, over the years, the dyes of the fabric had faded. However, that fact did not diminish its sentimental value. On a scorching hot summer day when she was around twelve, Gethyn's mother explained how rare and unique the quilt pattern was and how they must always handle it with kid gloves. She told of how it had been made by her great-great-great-grandmother, who in turn got the pattern from one of her greats, and so on. No one knew for sure where the pattern originated, and it was more than likely that no one ever would. As the young woman looked upon the quilt fondly, she recalled her mother telling her that she would inherit the prized heirloom someday. The redheaded beauty's eyes brimmed with tears, and her heart filled with pride as she looked at the antique quilt that had been made long before she was ever born.

Her eyes left the keepsake and moved to the pine headboard her daddy had made by hand. It was a simple design, but what made it special to Gethyn was the outline of a full moon over a lone pine tree he had carved in its center. She traced it with her finger and was reminded of the countless times she had done the very same thing as a child.

The tall beauty folded back the quilt and stretched her long frame out on the bed. With ankles crossed and hands clasped behind her head, she closed her eyes. Like a parade, images of her parents, grandparents, friends, teachers, and others she had known slowly passed by. She found it odd yet interesting how, in the short amount of time she had been in Paradise, her perspective on some things had changed. It was though she could see those she had known before with newfound clarity. She found herself discovering things about them she hadn't known before, such as their thoughts and intentions towards her. Sometimes it warmed her heart and at other times broke it.

Gethyn's thoughts turned to something Jesus had said down by the River of Life—something about how it was important to remember those left behind and to pray for them. He had said that when she did, a thought of her would pop into her loved ones' minds, like mail being delivered. Knowing what she needed to do, she rose quickly and knelt beside the bed. After much time had passed, she finally brought the prayer to a conclusion, feeling satisfied that everyone she knew had been included.

She stood and pulled the quilt up, smoothing out its wrinkles before turning around to survey the room. Everywhere she looked were reminders of her other life. Cozy rag rugs dotted the room, and acrylic paintings depicting country landscapes hung in gray barnwood frames on the walls. Everything was as Gethyn remembered, right down to the moose antlers over the fireplace. Strangely enough, being there didn't evoke feelings of sadness. On the contrary, she felt serene and at peace. If what Zendor had said was true, that Jesus had prepared this place especially for her, then she knew the Lord really *did* know the secret desires of her heart.

10

Once the celestial being left Gethyn at the luxury skyscraper, it paused on the sidewalk to pray and request an audience with God. The prayer was spontaneously answered, after which the towering angel found itself before the Creator of the Universe.

There was an emerald rainbow around the great throne of God and guarding each side were four angels called seraphim. Each seraph had a different face, with eyes all around and within them so that nothing escaped their attention. One seraph had the face of a lion, one an ox, another had the face of a man, and one of an eagle. Each had two wings that covered their faces, two covering their genitals, and two used for flying. A great light emanated from them that burned eternally from their love and zeal for God. So bright was their light they could not be looked upon, not even by other angels. Continuously, they sang, "Holy, holy, holy, Lord God Almighty, which was, and is, and is to come."

Angels named cherubim guarded one side of the throne and had four wings. One pair spread out from the middle of their backs while one pair covered the body. The cherubs had legs of a man with cloven feet that shone like polished brass and had human hands under each wing.

In addition, there were four living creatures around the throne. They were unusual-looking compared to the other celestial beings in that they were the color of beryl and appeared as a wheel within a wheel, their rims covered with hundreds of eyes.

A cloud of glory encircled God's head as He alone was holy and no one was worthy enough to see His face. The towering angel humbly knelt before the throne with head bowed.

"Father, I am home."

Lightning bolted from the cloud, and when the Almighty spoke, it was with a powerful booming voice like the sound of a thunderous waterfall. "Zendor, my beloved and faithful servant, I am pleased to see you. Let us talk for awhile."

They talked of things both great and small, and after much time had passed between them, Zendor left the magnificent throne room of God. Extending its wings to their full twenty feet, the creature effortlessly took flight and headed toward the city of Jerusalem. No longer earthbound, Zendor was free to come and go at will. For the time being though, the angel was right where it wanted to be—at home in Paradise, soaking up the glorious sights and heady smells of the place it loved most. Someday when Gethyn was ready to explore new worlds, it would take her to the far reaches of the universe, to places uncharted and unimaginable to mankind.

Zendor landed with ease at the inner gate of the New Jerusalem and began walking alone down the sidewalk. There were other angels flying to and fro above, some going for an audience with God and some on their way to other parts of Paradise.

The celestial being thought of Gethyn and how it had been with her every minute of every night and day for the past twenty-two years. It had given up its personal freedom upon accepting the assignment from God but, having the gift of free will, could have chosen not to go had it so desired. It was always an honor and privilege to be called to serve God and what better way to serve the Creator than for one to fulfill the purpose for which it was created. God made Zendor a guardian angel and had listened intently as Zendor gave a solemn oath to guide and protect Gethyn. The angel was aware it would serve in that capacity for the duration of Gethyn's life.

Gethyn's death was unexpected, through no fault of Zendor's. The guardian had tried to warn her, but in the end, its efforts had failed. The creature was sorry the mission on Earth had been cut short, but there was nothing left to do but go forward. What was done was done. Gethyn no longer needed protection as it was impossible for any harm to befall her in Paradise. Zendor would show the young woman around the city and garden, give her guidance, and answer any questions she might ask. Above all, it would be her devoted and loyal friend, although not her only friend. There was Jesus of course, and in time, Gethyn would meet other human beings and form lasting connections, some old and some new. The celestial being would introduce her to its own friends as well, and before long she would feel like part of Paradise's large, cohesive family, which indeed she was.

The angel heard someone shout "Zendor!" and snapped out of its thoughts. Looking up, it saw its old friend Sydon. "You're back! I haven't seen you in five thousand years, old friend!" the approaching angel exaggerated.

Sydon's long hair was the color of rich, dark coffee beans and was worn braided and wrapped around the head in an intricate pattern. The angel had a round, jovial face and a countenance that exuded warmth and friendliness. They both laughed, and a dazzling show of sparks and lightning shot from their eyes.

When they were abreast of each other, Zendor replied, "Well, that might be stretching it a bit, but it has been a long time. It seems like the last time I saw you, we were on Earth, possibly around the 1920s, give or take a few years. You had just accepted an assignment in England, if I'm not mistaken."

Sydon confirmed the assessment with a nod of the head, adding, "Yes, 1923, to be exact. I had a doozy of a time keeping up with my charge, William Davenport—or Willie, as he was called. My, he was a wild one and just about ran me ragged. You know, looking back, I'm convinced he took a hundred years off my life!"

The two guardians broke down into raucous laughter, after which Zendor said, "Why don't you walk awhile with me? I want to hear all about Willie."

After listening to the audacious exploits of the mischievous English lad, Zendor told Sydon about the redheaded beauty, Gethyn. The two had a marvelous time catching up on each other's lives, and once it was time to part, Zendor asked, "Did you bring Willie back with you to Paradise?"

A cloud suddenly came over Sydon's face. Quickly looking down, the angel looked down at its dusty sandals and shook its braided head no. "You know, I laugh when I talk about him, but it's mostly to keep from crying. Trying to protect someone who is reckless and who has no regard for the value of his own life is something I hope I'll never have to do again. He was a likeable enough fellow, but he refused to grow up. I kept trying to guide him towards the light, but he never matured spiritually. Willie's spirit was rebellious and unrepentant until the moment he drew his last breath. Leaving his spirit at the border station knowing that the adversary's guards would be transporting him to Hades was one of the hardest things I've ever had to do."

Zendor put a comforting arm around Sydon and asked, "Do you plan on accepting another assignment soon?"

The angel considered the question before answering, "Yes, I trust that God has another purpose for me and that it is only a matter of time until He calls me into service again. When He does, I will be ready, willing, and able to meet my destiny."

11

Day Two

Morning broke victoriously through the shroud of darkness that hung over the city. It was a glorious sunrise, and the sky was soon filled with a profusion of pink, lavender, and indigo colors. It was going to be another beautiful day in Paradise.

Gethyn's eyes fluttered open, and the first thing she saw was the rough-sawn beam overhead. She smiled inwardly before quickly burrowing back under the crisp white sheet, much like a prairie dog raising its head to take a peek at the outside world before disappearing again into the dark, earthen ground. She had always slept well at her parent's lakeside retreat. Maybe it was because of the fresh, clean mountain air or perhaps the coziness of the one-room cabin. Whatever it was, it nourished her soul.

After a few more minutes of luxurious decadence, the young woman sat up and leaned her back against the pine headboard, all the while trying to adjust her eyes to morning. It was still hard to believe she was dead, even though she knew it was true. What other explanation could there be for waking up in the place that had been her most favorite place in the whole world, the presence of Jesus and Zendor, and the resplendent, golden, and jeweled city outside her window called the New Jerusalem? Death wasn't unpleasant. Actually, Gethyn was finding this new realm fascinating. She had learned things the day before that had astonished her, things that would take a long time to sort out and sift through. And that was just on the first day!

The young woman rose, made the bed, and dressed quickly. As she opened the window curtains, the eavesdropping golden sunlight fell into the room. From her vantage point, Gethyn gazed down on the beautifully landscaped garden below and the magnificent city surrounding it. The New Jerusalem was much larger than she had at first imagined and seemed to cover every direction for as far as the eye could see. Directly below, people and their guardians scurried back and forth and here and there, like ants square-dancing at a hoedown. Gethyn wondered who they were and how long they had been in Paradise.

There were several angels flying in the distance, and the very sight of the winged celestial beings held the young woman's blue-eyed gaze for a long time. By now, she was aware that Zendor had carried her spirit all the way from Earth, although she had no personal recollection of it.

Having never seen angels in flight before, Gethyn followed them with her eyes, feeling privileged to witness the sight. Their movements were elegantly timed and reminded her of how on occasional vacations to the beach she would look up into the sky and watch seagulls gliding gracefully through the air, banking first one way and then another. It had always made her secretly wonder how the sensation of flying would feel. Gethyn watched the angels until they were no longer in her line of vision.

The titian-haired beauty's energy was beginning to feel depleted, so she decided to head for the garden for some fruit and meet Zendor as agreed.

What a difference a day makes, Gethyn thought to herself. Yesterday, the colossal angel's size and appearance had frightened her, but the guardian's gentle demeanor had quickly dissolved her fears and put her at ease.

I guess it just goes to show you can't judge a book by its cover, the young woman said to herself, all the while knowing her sentiments sounded trite, no matter how true.

She locked the apartment, dropped the golden key in her jeans pocket, and then took her time in the long pale pink corridor with its deep royal blue carpet. Gethyn felt as though she were in an art gallery as she stopped to admire one oil painting after another. There were ornate gold mirrors as well. While stopping to study her reflection, she found it strangely odd that she looked the same as when she was alive. *Hadn't Jesus told me I was in a temporary body?*

she thought to herself. Not understanding how the two could look the same, Gethyn made a mental note to ask the next time she saw Him.

Continuing down the hallway, Gethyn admired several multilayered chandeliers hanging from the tall ceiling, each adorned with hundreds of brilliant crystals. The light from them was soft, and the young woman wondered if, like the elevator, they were also powered by the energy of her spirit. She continued with that line of thought, imagining the illumination that would fill every crevice and corner of the corridor had Jesus been there with her.

Gethyn walked toward the glass elevator with its spectacular view and could almost imagine what it must have felt like to live in the penthouse of a swanky hotel in downtown New York City. Out of curiosity, she began reading the names on the placards of the apartments on her floor. Frank Thielen Jr., Gladys Foust, Philena McClary, Larry Tolly, Wm. Edwin Carrico, Clara Ellen Jenkins, Cecil Willett, Hazel Caraway, Allen Hughes, Margie Warren, and Anna Louisa Kathryn De La Rosa were just a few of the names written in gold script.

I wonder who they are—or were? Gethyn said to herself, not sure whether to think of people in Paradise in the past or present tense. Another thought came to her that piqued her curiosity. *I wonder what their apartments look like and if they're like mine—exact replicas of the place where they felt most comfortable and at home on Earth.*

While waiting at the elevator, Gethyn saw a girl who appeared to be a little younger than her exit an apartment and begin walking toward her. She wore a floor-length olive green dress with a short cloak draped over her shoulders that was similar in color but made from a heavier fabric. Her red hair was wound in a tight bun, and she wore a white cap tied loosely under her chin as well as a white apron. The clothing suggested that the pious-looking girl was a Quaker.

As she neared Gethyn, she raised her voice so as to be heard. "Wilt ye please hold thy elevator?"

"You have time," Gethyn called out, assuring the girl. "The car isn't here yet."

During the less than twenty seconds it took for the young Quaker to make her way down the long hallway, Gethyn wondered about all the technological advances the younger girl had never seen in her lifetime and what she would have thought of cars, computers, and cell phones. The girl in the plain clothing smiled demurely at Gethyn, all the while trying to suppress a curious look at the young woman's blue jeans, T-shirt, and tennis shoes.

"What a good morning it is, friend. My name is Philena McClary. Hath ye a name?"

There was something about the girl Gethyn instantly liked, but she wasn't sure if it was her timid smile or green eyes, which reminded her of tender, new spring leaves.

"Hi," Gethyn responded politely. "I'm Gethyn Fields. I believe we are neighbors."

Philena's smile widened and revealed glistening white teeth. She touched the young woman's arm, remarking, "Oh how wonderful! 'Tis always delightful when one meets new friends. Wilt ye stop and visit with me sometime soon?"

"I will" was all Gethyn had time to say before the elevator arrived.

The car was occupied by fifteen to twenty other people, although Gethyn surmised it could have easily held one hundred or more without feeling crowded. Nervously glancing at the others in various styles of dress, the young woman felt underdressed in her casual attire. One of the older women met Gethyn's glance and smiled pleasantly as though to say hello. The woman was dressed fashionably in a business suit consisting of a gray tailored jacket, pencil skirt, and high heels. Her hair was short and crimped, and her full lips were made even more so with red lipstick. There was a black beauty mark on her cheek, and Gethyn wondered if it was real. The most interesting aspect of the outfit was a hat that sat just so. It was adored with a long pheasant feather a foot long and a veil that partially covered the woman's face. Gethyn guessed the period clothing dated from the 1930s.

The elevator descended much faster than the ascension had been the day before, which made Gethyn wonder if it was because there was more spiritual energy present to power the elevator. She didn't have time to pursue the thought too long as they were suddenly at the ground floor. Everyone, including Philena, dispersed quickly and either headed outdoors or milled around the lobby to visit with others. The uniformed doorman opened the heavy glass door for the building's patrons, and as Gethyn passed through, she smiled and nodded. The gentleman greeted her cordially as well. She walked a couple of steps, fully intending to keep going, but something made her stop.

She tossed her long, red-gold hair behind her shoulders, turned, and walked back to where the man stood. Extending her hand, she introduced herself. "Hello, I'm Gethyn Fields. I just arrived yesterday and remember you holding the door open for me and my guardian, Zendor. Do you work here?"

The distinguished gentleman shook her hand, and though his posture was formal, his manner was pleasant. "It's a pleasure to meet you, Miss Fields. My name is Clarence Townsend, and to answer your question, no, I am not employed here. However, I do offer my services as a volunteer. On Earth, work was a term generally used to describe duties one had to perform. It was common for people to work at jobs they didn't enjoy or weren't suited for just in order to make a living and support their families. My daddy always told me, 'Son, make a living doing something you really love or have a passion for, and you'll never work a day in your life.' And it was true. In my former life, I was a doorman at the Landry Hotel in Pittsburgh, Pennsylvania, and I loved going to work every day. My duties allowed me to meet thousands of interesting people such as you. And whether I held open doors, assisted with luggage, hailed cabs, gave directions, or simply offered friendly greetings as people came in or went out, I performed to the best of my ability. I worked there not because I *had* to but because I *loved* doing what I was doing. I always felt that a purpose greater than my own was being served. Upon arriving in Paradise, I was given the opportunity to continue serving others as I had done on Earth and I must tell you, it has given my life here meaning and purpose from which I derive immense pleasure and joy."

Talking with Clarence was uplifting and reinforced Gethyn's desire to discover her own purpose. Although thoroughly enjoying their conversation, the young woman knew she needed to go look for Zendor in the garden. She was relieved when the friendly doorman pointed out the main entrance of the garden, which happened to be directly across the street from the high-rise. She hadn't been altogether confident of being able to retrace the backdoor route she and Zendor had taken the day before.

Gethyn entered the quiet sanctuary, making a point to stop and smell the roses, so to speak. She didn't want to rush this intoxicating new adventure she had suddenly found herself a party to. Rather, she wanted to take it all in slowly and savor each new thing she discovered or learned. The young woman walked through a forest of trees that was as diverse as the people living in Paradise. She counted great oaks, elm, pine, cottonwood, and eucalyptus as trees she recognized, although there were many more she had never seen before. Flowers in full bloom were everywhere and displayed in beds of varying shapes and sizes, each immaculately kept.

Up ahead, Gethyn saw an elderly, barefoot black woman working in one of the garden beds. Her thin, long-sleeved white cotton dress was dirty and torn, and she wore a red scarf tied around her head. The bent woman was on her knees humming an old spiritual hymn as her hands efficiently worked the soil. Oblivious to Gethyn's presence, she continued tending to the business at hand. There were orange poppies, hollyhock, day lilies, jasmine, blue star columbine, tea roses, hydrangeas, and English lavender as well as varieties of flowers unfamiliar to Gethyn. It was a vibrant profusion of eye-popping color, and the scents married and intertwined, creating a sweet, fragrant perfume.

Pausing in admiration, the girl extended a hello to the woman, who was gently patting the soil around some newly planted Shasta daisies. "Hello there! I'm Gethyn. Do you work here or are you a volunteer?" she queried.

The old black woman looked up to see the young woman, red hair ablaze in the sun. She stood, put her hands on her hips, and with a disarming smile said, "Honey-chile', I'm Lottie, and I knows you must be new 'round here 'cause folks who done been here a while knows we ain't axed to labor in Paradise. 'Course, while we be here waiting fo' Kingdom Come, it fills the time to find some-um' a body can do, that's fo' sure. Befo' God delivered me from my toils and troubles on Earth, all these here hands ever knew was backbreakin' cotton pickin' back home in Alabamy. We's no choice but to do what Mas'ta said or we gets a-beatin', so day in and day out we all picked cotton 'til our fingers was plum raw an' bleedin'. But all that's changed now, honey-chile'. Praise and glory be to God! My new Mas'ta is good and lets Lottie use these old hands to make some-um' purdy grow. You'd a-thought I's never wants to work with the soil again, buts it's not true! While growin' these here flowers and tendin' them, I thinks I's done grow'd too. I do think these here flowers have soothed and healed the hurt in my soul."

Gethyn's heart went out to Lottie, and she felt love for the old woman as though she'd known her all her life. While listening, she had a revelation and decided to share it with the older woman. "Lottie, flowers are part of nature's beauty, and beauty has always been known to have healing properties. While your hands were once made to serve a cruel slave owner, you've discovered a new purpose for your hands, which reaps joy too great to be measured. You have put your heart and soul into growing something beautiful and have healed not only yourself but others who have looked upon your flowers. I believe whenever beauty is planted in the fertile soil of our souls, healing takes root and allows inner peace to flower and grow."

The old woman folded her arms over her ample bosom and shook her head in agreement. "Um-hum. You's be right. I love workin' with these ol' hands now 'cause I can see some-um good comin' from it. Why, tendin' the flowers don't even feel like work. The Lawd told me I's can do anything I want to do, and workin' in the soil makes ol' Lottie feel good, honey-chile'."

As with Clarence, Gethyn was having such a wonderful time visiting with her new friend that she almost forgot Zendor was waiting by the River of Life.

"Lottie, I've got to go meet my guardian, but I hope to see you again soon." The young woman began walking down the garden path but after a few steps turned and waved at the old black woman. Lottie looked up from her planting, pulled out a threadbare handkerchief that had been tucked inside her dress, and waved back at the young woman.

The River of Life was ahead, and the young woman made her way towards its green velvety banks. Not seeing Zendor, she plucked one of the unusual pieces of fruit from a low-hanging limb and took a bite of it. It was as sweet and as ripe as she remembered, and once she finished it, she felt satisfied. Just like yesterday, her mind seemed clearer after eating the fruit; and in a way she couldn't describe, she felt like a better version of herself.

As Gethyn sat waiting for Zendor, she saw the Lord walking with a matronly woman on a path further down the river. The woman was petite and wore a long blue dress with a white collar that started above her breast and went to her neck before rounding off. Over the dress, she wore a blue mantle with a hood that had wide sleeves and fell open in front. The two sat down on a wooden bench inside a pergola and continued talking. Their conversation appeared intimate, and Gethyn averted her eyes so as not to intrude on their privacy.

The redhead waited for a few minutes more and was beginning to feel anxious when she saw Zendor on the garden path walking toward her in a hurry.

"I hope you haven't been waiting long," he offered apologetically. "I guess I lost all track of time."

12

Gethyn had watched in amazement as her guardian flew into the garden and touched down with gentle ease on the garden path a few feet from her. She stood mesmerized by the beauty, grace, and elegance of the angel in flight and for a moment got caught up in wondering what the sensation would feel like to fly.

The young woman smiled her beautiful smile and replied. "No worries. I've been enjoying the view and have been people-watching. I even saw Jesus a few minutes ago walking with an older woman. They went into one of the pergolas down by the river's edge to sit and talk."

Zendor pulsated with light and then asked, "Was she wearing a blue cloak?"

Gethyn nodded her head before answering, "Yes."

The angel looked in the direction of the pergola and then said, "That's His mother, Mary. You can see them every morning taking a stroll through the garden."

The redhead's jaw dropped. "Mother Mary? You mean the Virgin Mary?!" she exclaimed, looking towards the pergola and hoping to get a better look.

"One of these days, I'll introduce you to her," Zendor offered.

Gethyn went somewhere in her mind, imagining what it would be like to sit and talk with Jesus's mother.

She snapped back to the present when she heard Zendor ask, "How did you like the home Jesus prepared for you?"

Warm memories flooded Gethyn's heart as she thought of what the cabin meant to her. She looked up at the dark-haired angel looming above her and with wistfulness in her voice replied, "It was like being transported back to the happiest time of my life. I can't wait to thank Jesus in person. By the way, where can I find Him later on?"

Noticing that the young woman was straining her neck to see into his face, the angel sat down as it had the day before and tucked its bronzed legs underneath its enormous body. "Just summon Him with your thoughts. He likes to meet people where they live, but if you call on Him, He will meet you wherever you are. It works the same way as when you were on Earth and called out to Him, whether out loud or in your thoughts. Although you couldn't visually see Him then, He was there."

Gethyn realized Zendor was right as she remembered feeling Jesus's presence many times in her life. She decided to summon Him later that evening once she had returned to her cabin in the sky.

The young woman looked around and saw others sitting, reclining, and walking along the banks of the River of Life with their guardian angels. She glimpsed expressions of shock, awe, and confusion on some of the people's faces and acknowledged they probably mirrored those of her own the day before. Gethyn was reminded of her first day of high school and how she and her fellow freshmen had felt awkward and out of place until learning the ropes. Being the new kid on the block was as overwhelming then as it was now, but she wasn't alone. There were countless others going through the same adjustments and orientation as she. Yesterday, Gethyn had felt like a stranger in Paradise; but today, she felt a little less apprehensive and unsure. Still, she was struck by the feeling that there was something unseen keeping her from accepting her new surroundings wholeheartedly. What it was the young woman didn't know. She didn't have time to think about it right now, so she pushed the intrusive thought to the far reaches of her mind.

"Would you like to do some sightseeing in the city today?" asked Zendor.

Gethyn scrunched up her nose and shook her head no, not ready to be totally immersed in Paradise yet. "I would really just like to walk through the garden and talk, if that's okay."

The guardian could tell something was on her mind but decided to wait for her to broach the subject. The two stood, and the angel shook and groomed its wings, dislodging any loose blades of grass that might have clung to them.

The two passed several flower beds, each one more beautiful than the last, until at last they came to a large labyrinth. Side by side, they walked the wide circular pattern toward its center.

After a while, the girl spoke. "Zendor, tell me about our life together on Earth."

The enormous angel's pale amethyst eyes perked up, and blue curlicue sparks came from them as it smiled its unusual smile. The guardian's luminous spirit pulsated with light, which Gethyn had come to conclude meant it was thinking. Zendor's mind was an expansive library of knowledge, and in a moment's time, the celestial being had perused its shelves until locating the volume where memories of its mission on Earth was recorded.

"What would you like to know?" Zendor asked, poised and ready to answer any question.

"Tell me about my birth," asked the young woman.

The towering angel thought for a moment before answering, and when it finally spoke, its voice was as gentle and warm as soft summer rain. "I'll never forget Heavenly Father presenting me with the opportunity to be your guardian angel. It was the day I had been dreaming about for my whole existence. After accepting the mission, I immediately joined a convoy of others headed for Earth, each of us eager to begin the fulfillment of the purpose for which we were created.

"I arrived several hours before you were born and watched in silent wonder as your mother labored to bring you into the world. Not since Earth came into existence had I been present to watch the birth of a new creation, and I was filled with wondrous anticipation of what was to come.

"Even as the contractions grew more frequent, I saw intermittent expressions of joy on your mother's face. I listened as your parents told the nurse how they'd been counting down the days, practically from the first day they discovered you were on the way. I could sense you were very much wanted and how much your parents looked forward to bringing you home. It was then I learned you had a big brother named Emmit. Your mother and daddy explained to the nurse how excited he was over the prospect of finally having a sibling and how his being ten years older didn't seem to matter in the least. He was an exceptional boy.

"Your father was a comforting presence, managing to remain calm and collected throughout the whole experience. If your mother needed ice chips, he had a nurse bring them, and when beads of perspiration formed on her brow, he tenderly wiped them away with a cool, damp washcloth. He held her little hand throughout the whole ordeal and never once left her bedside. As she dilated, the contractions accelerated. He whispered reassuring words, saying how everything would be all right, how beautiful she was, and how much he loved her. There were many touching and poignant moments shared between the two of them, and the love in the room was palpable.

"Finally, the moment we were all waiting for came. A heightened sense of excitement and urgency swept over the room as the doctor arrived and everyone took their places. I stood beside your father and could almost hear his heart beating. Your mother began to inhale deep breaths and bear down as directed by the obstetrician, all the while squeezing your father's hand tightly. First your tiny head crowned, and then with a final push, your shoulders cleared, followed in quick succession by the rest of your body. Standing side by side with your dad I temporary lost my breath, as did he while witnessing the miracle of your birth.

"There was another presence in the room, but no one noticed. It was God, as it is only He who can give the breath of life. With tender, loving care, He blew into your tiny nostrils, and at once your spirit quickened. You gave a loud and healthy cry as though proclaiming your new existence to the world. Your parents gave many thanks to God for your safe arrival, and although I didn't see Him smile, I'm sure He was pleased to have been remembered. Other than myself, you were the only one aware of God's presence in the room. You strained your eyes in an attempt to see the One who had formed you in your mother's womb, but you could not as your vision was unfocused and blurry. God spoke to you, telling you of His love and even writing the words on your heart so you would always remember. When He was gone and you could no longer feel His presence, you cried inconsolably. A nurse wrapped you in a swaddling blanket and placed you in your mother's arms. It was only after hearing the familiar sound of her heartbeat against your ear and the soothing sound of her voice that your cries began to subside, and you fell fast asleep.

When your parents took you home from the hospital, I went with them. I stayed up with you when you had the colic, prayed for you when you were going through the pangs of adolescence, guided you toward your career path as you grew older, and was with you at your d——" The angel hadn't meant to bring up her death and stopped abruptly before saying the word.

Gethyn had no way of knowing how sensitive Zendor was regarding the subject or how the angel had dreaded the very thought of this moment ever since the accident had occurred. Would she hold the guardian responsible somehow when she learned the truth? Zendor wanted her love and friendship, and the possibility of her rejection was almost more than the angel could bear.

They came to the center of the labyrinth and had just turned around to walk back in the direction from which they had come when the words the angel dreaded hearing came.

"Zendor, how did I die?"

The angel could sense the girl looking up but deliberately chose not to meet her gaze. Long, wavy black hair fell over one side of the creature's face, which it hoped would conceal the tears beginning to well up. Instead of answering, Zendor diverted the conversation by suggesting they head back to the River of Life.

Walking along in silence, Gethyn was unaware of Zendor's inner anguish. The guardian's mind was reeling, as it wasn't at all sure what it should tell the young woman about that day. Zendor said a silent prayer, asking God for wisdom. After reaching the river, they reclined on its green grassy slope under the shade of one of the twelve varieties of fruit trees planted there. The celestial being made small talk in hopes that Gethyn had forgotten the question it could not forget.

The girl hadn't forgotten, however, and when Zendor finally ran out of idle chatter, she again asked, "Zendor, how did I die?"

Knowing there was no escaping the question this time, her guardian looked for a way to soften or diffuse the impact. "Gethyn, it's as Jesus told you, how you died is not important. It's how you lived. It is the choices made, the love shared, the kindness offered, and the hope given that matter. Those are the moments that will live on."

The young woman could sense Zendor's discomfort, which made her even more curious. "Why are you avoiding my question? What happened that you can't seem to bring yourself to tell me?" she asked, her brow now furrowed.

The angel seemed to shrink inside itself, and though it tried to speak, no words came. Gethyn resigned herself to the obvious. "You aren't going to tell me, are you?" She let out a deep sigh.

Zendor's eyes implored her to leave the subject alone. "It's not that I don't *want* to tell you. It's more a case of feeling you aren't ready to know yet. This is only your second day in Paradise, and I feel there are more important things you need to concern yourself with first."

Zendor's amethyst eyes seemed even paler than usual as they pleaded with hers, and it was only then that the young woman saw the depth and scope of the pain in them. Suddenly, her compassion for the angel overrode her desire to know the details of her death. Gethyn's hand reached out to console her guardian. "It's okay. It really is," she said gently, spreading her words as though applying a soothing balm over the angel's troubled soul.

By then, Gethyn wanted some time alone and sensed Zendor did as well. They stood and walked in silence toward the entrance of the garden, each lost in their own private thoughts. They came to the wide, gold-paved boulevard that ran through the city and were just about to cross over to the other side when the celestial being stopped the young woman.

"Gethyn, I *will* tell you someday. I promise."

She acknowledged the angel's answer with a polite nod and then hurriedly dashed across the street. Clarence the doorman from Pittsburgh saw her coming and opened the heavy glass door. Though he smiled and said hello, Gethyn appeared not to have heard him as she strode briskly towards the elevator. Zendor watched as the young woman disappeared inside the building before heading away from the city.

13

The elevator doors opened, and the young woman stepped out. She walked down the hallway with its fine oil paintings and gilded mirrors, but she was too busy replaying in her head the conversation she had just had with her guardian to notice or appreciate them. Gethyn couldn't help but wonder and be puzzled as to why the mention of her death seemed to upset Zendor to the point of not being able to speak. What was the angel hiding? She tried in vain to remember that fateful day, but no matter how hard she tried, she couldn't.

Gethyn didn't notice her neighbor Philena McClary standing in the corridor admiring the framed pieces of art and passed by without acknowledging her presence.

"Goodness, friend, where art ye manners?"

The young woman quickly snapped out of her thoughts and turned around to face the young Quaker girl.

"Oh, Philena, I'm so sorry. I didn't mean to be rude. I was thinking about something else and didn't even see you. Please forgive me," Gethyn apologized sincerely.

The girl smiled demurely. "Thee art forgiven only on condition that ye shalt come sit with me for a spell and talk of things."

Gethyn's only desire had been to go to her own cabin and mull over her conversation with Zendor. However, her mood changed to one of curiosity as she looked at the Quaker dressed simply and plainly.

"I'd love to hang out for a while," she responded to the girl's invitation and then quickly altered her words to "I mean, I'd love to sit with thee. Or is it thou?"

Philena saw the confusion in the young woman's face. Fingertips sprang to her lips, and she laughed softly. Then, she put her hands together as though praying and countered, "Thee doth not need change ye way of speaking for me. I understood ye perfectly when at first ye spoke."

Gethyn laughed too and followed her neighbor to the door with the placard reading "Philena McClary."

The girl's hand went to a pocket hidden deep in the folds of her plain olive green dress and pulled out a golden key identical to Gethyn's.

Gethyn saw it and wondered out loud, "I wonder why we need keys? You wouldn't think Paradise would have a high crime rate."

As the young girl put the key in the lock, she giggled. "Oh, 'tis nary because of anything to fear, friend. 'Tis that God desireth all His children to feel this art our home. He hath given everyone golden keys to the holy city as a way of saying we belong."

Gethyn smiled and piped in with "Kind of like getting a membership to the country club," although she wasn't quite sure if the joke was lost on Philena. She followed the Quaker girl inside, and as she looked around the home, she couldn't help but notice that it was very different from her own in that it was modestly furnished with little adornment. There were two rocking chairs facing a stone fireplace large enough to walk into. One of the chairs had a high back with four flat panels and straight arms, which she instantly recognized as being a ladder-back rocker. However, the other was short and had no armrests, and its bottom was woven in a two-colored checkerboard pattern. There were two baskets beside the smaller chair. One was rather large and made of sea grass with an inner lining of silk. Inside were various lengths of material and yarn. The smaller of the two was a bitty basket that held small snippets of material, scissors, a thread winder, and other notions. Upon seeing them, it became apparent to the young woman that Philena used the armless rocker to sit in while sewing. On the other side of the rocker was a small table where an oil lamp sat in the center of a hand-crocheted doily. In Gethyn's mind, she pictured the Quaker girl sitting in the rocker on long, endless winter nights sewing by the light of the oil lamp. They were so close in age, yet their lives had been profoundly different.

Gethyn's eyes swept the room and saw a settee, a table with a basin and pitcher, a rectangular dining table with four chairs, and a bucket-bench cupboard. Each piece of furniture was made of solid maple, dovetailed in their construction, and lightly varnished—the designs simple, functional, and without ornamentation.

The only decorations in the room were needlepoint samplers hanging in plain wooden frames on the walls. Gethyn walked over to look at them, and the floor creaked just as one would expect of an old house. She stood admiring the workmanship and minute details of the framed pieces, thinking to herself how lovely and quaint they were. One was of the upper and lower case letters of the alphabet, one was of a garden with flowers sewn in vibrant silk colors, and yet another depicted birds roosting on the limbs of a large tree. While all three samplers were charming, there was one that particularly held Gethyn's interest. It was of two women clad in Quaker attire standing face to face with hands clasped. There was a homily with Philena's name stitched underneath that read:

> How prized and esteemed 'tis a friend
> On whom thee may ever depend

"Oh, Philena, these samplers are exquisite! I can't even begin to imagine how many hours went into making each one. I wish I had had the time and patience to create something as beautiful," Gethyn gushed.

The young Quaker girl put a delicate hand to her face and in her shy way of speaking said, "Ahh, well, friend, if truth be told, time was something I had a lot of, and learning to decipher the Inner Light's will for my life from a wee age taught me patience. If ye hast a desire to sew, I would be happy to teach thee."

Gethyn's face lit up, and she quickly accepted the offer.

"Oh, dear! Now 'tis I who hath lost my manners. Ye wilt please come and sit down!"

Philena led her guest to the rockers by the fireplace. While crossing the room, the floor creaked again, but the only footfall heard was the sound of Philena's hard-soled shoes as Gethyn wore tennis shoes. Gethyn took a seat in the ladder-back rocker and was surprised at how comfortable it was. The Quaker girl untied the bonnet she wore, but did not remove it. She sat in the sewing rocker and reached down into the sea grass basket for a piece of material she had been working on. Her fingers worked nimbly as she and Gethyn conversed. She looked up from her embroidering and smiled demurely at her guest.

In a sweet, refined voice, Philena said, "It's splendid to have someone who art close in age living nearby, and I do hope to become fast friends. In my other life, I would have offered refreshments—a biscuit with jam and fresh apple cider, perhaps. Alas, there art no need of such here as the fruit that grows by the River of Life 'tis succulent and truly satisfies my hunger."

Gethyn was enjoying Philena's company and genuinely wanted to know more about her. "Philena, tell me about this place."

The Quaker girl's fingers stopped what they were doing, and her face looked just past Gethyn as though being transported back in time.

"This was my father's, Joseph McCullough's, cottage, and the happiest years of my life were spent here. When I was just a wee lass, my mother died of scarlet fever, so my father and this home became everything to me. My father was a gregarious sort of fellow. He could whistle like a bird, and in private, would always sing some silly song or tell me some long, drawn-out yarn that he made up just to please me. Oh, how I loved those stories." The girl stopped for a moment in remembrance of happier days but then added, "He played the violin too, although 'twas not allowed by the Society of Friends."

Puzzled, Gethyn asked, "Why?"

"'Twas felt that singing and playing instruments raised emotions not conducive to worship and that it stood in the way of God speakin' to thy heart."

Philena dropped her embroidery work into the sea basket, stood up, and quickly sashayed over to the settee against the wall. Stooping over, she reached down and pulled out a violin case from beneath it.

"Father loved music, as did I, but he could only sing and play the violin inside our home. 'Twas our secret, 'twas. Depending on the tune he played, I would either be compelled to dance a jig or cry my eyes out from the sad, haunting melodies he would play."

Gethyn stood up and, extending both hands out, asked, "May I?"

Philena answered "Aye," although she wasn't quite sure what her guest had in mind. Gethyn carried the case over to the dining table where she unclasped the latch and opened the lid. Looking down at the very old instrument, she remarked, "It's in remarkable shape."

Gethyn asked, "Do you mind?" Philena shook her head no.

Gethyn lifted the antique violin with the care given to something rare and delicate that might break. She rosined the bow, tucked the violin under her chin, and began playing. Unbeknownst to Philena, Gethyn had played classical violin in her school orchestra and was very gifted.

The Quaker girl's eyes brimmed with tears of joy as the sound of music once again filled the unadorned cottage. Once the piece ended, Philena threw her arms around Gethyn.

"Thank you, dearest friend! 'Tis been such a long spell since I hath heard the sound of my father's violin! Ye will have to visit me often and play the violin. Aye?" she asked.

As Gethyn returned the instrument to its case and put it back under the settee, she made a promise to return.

The two women, both close in age, returned to the rockers by the fireplace where Philena resumed her embroidering.

After a moment of silence, Gethyn asked, "What was your life like? Did you get married and have children?"

The young Quaker answered, "Aye," but didn't look up as she busied herself with her handiwork. "I met and married a handsome young lad from our meeting place named George Caleb McClary."

Puzzled, Gethyn asked, "What do you mean by 'meeting place'?"

Philena quickly responded, "'Twas usually a place where members of the Society of Friends would go to worship God and to wait upon the spirit in silence. The meeting place would change from time to time, but it was usually always at someone's home. Anyway, George McClary was well thought of in our circle. He and I had eyes each for the other, and my father let me know that he felt George would make a fine husband for me. I loved George but at the same time didn't want to leave my father for fear he would be lonely and sad. Alas, it was settled, and George and I married. I was sixteen, and George was twenty-one. We only had one son. His name was Samuel."

Gethyn interrupted to ask, "Where are George and Samuel?" The young woman looked around as if expecting the two to appear out of the back room or come walking through the front door.

Philena went to the window and pulled back the lace curtain. "Most likely, my husband and son art exploring God's garden. George filled Samuel's heart with a love for

God first and a love of nature second. The two feel most at home and closer to God when exploring the woods, and I suppose that knowing they are doing what they love most gives me great pleasure."

Gethyn asked if Philena ever saw them and for a moment thought she saw a hint of loneliness on the young girl's face. "Aye, occasionally I run into one or the other accidentally and there is always a joyous reunion. On occasion, when one of us gets lonely for the other, George, Samuel, and I know how to find one another. Before Samuel came along, George would sometimes disappear for days, so I would lose myself in chores. Afterward, if I found my hands idle, I would busy them doing things I loved, such as needlepoint, fancy embroidering, and piecing together quilts."

The young Quaker went back to her sewing and then opened up a new line of conversation. "There art so many things to look forward to when thee all go to Heaven. One of the things thee art looking forward to most is the sit-down feast on the day God proclaims 'Thy Kingdom Come.' Can ye imagine, friend? The whole lot of us being invited to dine with the King!"

Gethyn hadn't thought of it, but now that the thought was introduced, she tried to form a picture of it in her mind. She imagined a long banquet table farther than the eye could see and covered with a fine white linen tablecloth. In front of each chair were plates resting on gold chargers, golden utensils, fresh linen napkins, and goblets of ripe red wine. Once everyone was seated, Jesus would give a toast, after which mouthwatering succulent cuisine representing every country would be brought to the dining table on silver platters and placed before them.

"Just thinking about it makes my mouth water," said Gethyn. She thought about her favorite foods and could almost smell the savory aroma of freshly baked bread, roast beef, apple pie, and other favorite culinary dishes.

"What other things do you miss besides food, Philena?"

The Quaker girl rocked back and forth, and the sound the chair made was like that of a metronome clicking time. "Oh, I mostly be a-missing thy wee cat, Kip. She was orange with a fluffy tail resembling thy feather duster and had eyes the color of ripe green apples. Thee loved the wee cat, thee did. Thee remembers quite fondly how Kip would curl up at thy feet and sleep for hours while thee stitched something or other. In the wee mornings, she'd follow thee out to the barn and watch while I delivered thy Holstein cow Lucinda of her milk. That orange cat would stand off to the side while thee milked, all the while a-meowing. She was a-looking for favor and thee always knew there would be no rest 'til she got what she be a-wanting. Finally thee would squirt some warm milk in her direction and watch in amusement as thy Kip cleaned her mittens and licked her whiskers. Thy wee cat was something else she was, and thee loved the little mite with all thy heart."

Philena stopped rocking and sat with ankles crossed, back straight, and hands folded in her lap. "There art many other things I enjoyed on Earth, 'tis true. However, there art no time to be a-mourning them. Today is another gift from God, and I am content. The sky is blue, the air is fragrant and sweet, and there is much to see and be a-learning. What's more, I hath found a lovely new friend to share the day's wonders with, and that gives me such joy."

"I suppose you're right," agreed Gethyn and then added, "I wish I hadn't died so young though. I was engaged to be married. My fiancé, Dave, was going to be a missionary, and we were going to travel to other countries and make a difference in the world. My dream had always been to be a writer. I saw myself writing about our experiences in the mission fields and hopefully publishing a book. It would have been a perfect combination of both of our dreams." Gethyn sighed. Looking over at the younger girl, she said, "My life was just beginning, Philena. I never even had the experience of living on my own."

Philena looked into Gethyn's turquoise blue eyes and could tell by the troubled look on her new friend's face that she was still earthbound. "That may be true, my friend. However, ye liveth alone now, dost thee not? And I am confident ye art finding pleasure in the home the Lord hath provided," to which the young woman shook her head yes. "Look around thee, friend. There art plenty of opportunities to do meaningful work for the Lord. Hast thou not seen the city and the gardens around ye and people steadily coming every day?" Gethyn nodded yes. "Well," continued Philena, "there art much to be done in preparation of God's kingdom on Earth. We art all teachers and all pupils here, each being of equal value. Learn all ye can from those who hath walked down paths ye never knew existed and teach others what thou hast learned on thy journey. If ye had a dream to become a writer, then write. What is stopping thee from fulfilling ye dream? All ye desires will come, I promise. One of these mornings soon there is something I wish to show ye."

Curious, Gethyn asked, "What is it?"

"Ahh, ye shall have to wait," said Philena, smiling.

The hours passed quickly as they talked, and all too soon, it had grown late. Gethyn stood up first, followed by Philena.

"I could sit here all night talking with you, but I really must be going," the young woman said.

"Must ye goest so soon?" asked Philena, sounding disappointed. "There is much I would like to know about ye and thy past life, but alas, another day."

As Philena walked her guest to the front door, Gethyn turned and asked, "Would you like to visit me at my place next time?"

Philena touched the young woman's arm and excitedly answered, "Oh yes! That would be ever so lovely! I hath plans for the morrow, although perhaps I will call on ye the day after."

Gethyn smiled and gave the Quaker girl a hug. "I would like that," she said.

The red-haired young woman walked the few steps to her cabin, took the golden key from her pocket, and opened the door. Once inside, she realized that not only was Zendor withholding something from her but her new friend was withholding something as well. She shrugged absentmindedly, knowing she could do nothing until they chose to divulge their secrets.

Gethyn looked around the room, thinking how different her apartment was from Philena's. She had to admit her neighbor's home, though very plain, was more comfortable than it had first appeared. And at the same time, she couldn't help but wonder what the young Quaker girl would think of her cozy cabin.

14

Darkness fell over the New Jerusalem as Gethyn stood at the window gazing at its twinkling lights. There was no electricity in Paradise. The illumination that glowed in the windows of the high-rise buildings dotting the skyline came from the light of the spirits residing there. Just like her, someone was standing at their window looking at the light their spirit cast as well. While hers was but a flickering candle in the wind, she was reassured that in time it would become as strong and radiant as those she now looked upon. Gethyn gave herself over to the breathtaking beauty of the city and projected as much light as she could for all to see.

Overall, her second day in Paradise had been good. She had enjoyed walking in the exotic garden with Zendor and hearing the story of her birth, although she couldn't understand why her guardian was being evasive when it came to sharing details of her passing.

For goodness' sake, I'm dead, so what could be worse than that? she thought to herself, quickly adding, *Not that death is so bad.*

So far, the transition was proving to be quite different than her previous perception of it. As a child, Gethyn had sometimes had dreams of flying. In them, she saw herself soaring above rooftops and cornfields and over tall mountains and across the sea. The sensation was one of euphoria—the freedom to fly as high and as far as she wanted to go. The young woman imagined that's how her spirit should feel, but for her, it didn't. She felt like a caged bird that when presented with the opportunity to fly away didn't. Something unseen kept her tethered to the cage, and until she found a way to break the binds that held her back, her spirit would never truly be free.

Her thoughts moved past the heaviness tugging on her heart. The night was too beautiful for such things, and she let it go. She had made a new friend, Philena McClary, and was elated at the prospect of having someone to talk to and share new experiences with. Their lives had been worlds apart so to speak, yet Gethyn felt drawn to know more about the girl and her life as a Quaker. Too, Philena had mentioned there was something she wanted to show her, and the young woman was curious as to what it could possibly be.

Gethyn enjoyed the quiet solitude for a while longer and wrestled with the thought of tearing herself away from the view. She finally turned away from the window and looked at her home away from home. Suddenly she remembered wanting to personally thank Jesus. However, just as she was about to summon Him, she noticed a narrow closet no more than two feet wide by the front door. In the original cabin, its purpose had been for hanging clothes. However, seeing as her family never brought anything to wear other than shorts, jeans, and their bathing suits, the closet ended up being used to store miscellaneous gear of one sort or another. The young woman had overlooked the closet at first as it was wood-stained and it blended in with the walls of the log cabin.

For some reason, Gethyn felt drawn to the door, and she walked over to it. Upon opening it, she found a white robe hanging inside much like the one Jesus had been wearing at the river. The young woman took the garment off the hanger and held it to her nose, smelling its fresh, clean scent. Something compelled her to try it on. She laid the robe across the bed while removing her jeans and T-shirt, and once she slipped into it, she was surprised to find that it fit perfectly.

The sensation of the robe against Gethyn's skin felt familiar, and she was instantly reminded of a robe she had been given years before. It was on the day she had first confessed her sins and surrendered her life to the Lord. The young woman closed her eyes and recalled immersing herself in the warm spiritual bath of forgiveness and letting the loving hands of Jesus wash away all the sin, shame, and guilt that had soiled her. In addition, He had wiped away all her tears of sorrow and regret. After the spiritual cleansing, Gethyn had felt rejuvenated, refreshed, and clean. Figuratively speaking, Jesus had given her a clean white robe to wear then as well, and like this one, it had a lining of inner peace.

The young woman knew instinctively that Jesus had left the robe for her to wear during their visits. *That is so like the Lord*, thought Gethyn. *Going out of His way to make sure I feel clean and comfortable while in His presence.* She thought of the beautiful man/God she had loved since the age of three. She pictured the contour of His handsome face and how His deep blue eyes were the only ones who could see into the secret places of her heart.

The young woman summoned Jesus; and instantly, He was there, filling the cabin with His warm, radiant light.

"Jesus, I'm so glad you're here," Gethyn gushed like a young schoolgirl.

"Good evening, my beauty," He responded, smiling at the red-haired girl before kissing each of her cheeks.

Motioning to the overstuffed chairs, Gethyn asked, "Do you have time to sit and talk for a while?"

Jesus smiled at the girl who stood before him, answering, "I have all the time in the world, child."

Before taking a seat, the exalted man stopped in front of the stone fireplace where there were logs stacked and a box containing small pieces of tender. The Lord took some of the firewood and kindling and placed it on the iron grate. He did not strike a match or create a spark with a piece of flint; His eyes sent forth a flame. Soon the sound of a small crackling fire added to the warmth and ambiance of the room. The young woman was astonished and rendered speechless by what she had just seen. When Jesus stood up, His robe fell neatly into place and, although made of fine linen, appeared not to wrinkle. Taking a seat in the unoccupied chair across from Gethyn, He looked upon the girl who had summoned Him, waiting for her to direct the conversation.

Once she had sufficiently recovered and collected her thoughts, she spoke, her voice taking on a serious tone. "Lord, I've been thinking about the conversation we had yesterday down by the River of Life, and there is something I don't quite understand. You explained how it was necessary for my spirit and soul to be housed in a temporary body in order that I may live in the spiritual realm. What I don't understand though is if I'm in a temporary body, how come when I look in the mirror, I still look like me?"

Jesus's smile indicated He understood her confusion and was ready with the answer she sought. Without blinking an eye, He explained, "You look like you because what you are seeing is your soul." He could see Gethyn was still puzzled, so He expounded further, trying to throw light on His explanation. "While your original body is buried back on Earth, your spirit and soul are here in Paradise. Your spirit is the immaterial part of you. Everyone has a spirit. It is the source of power and control for both your body and soul. It can choose light over darkness, good over evil, holy or unholy, clean or unclean, of God or of Satan. But what makes you *you* is your soul. Your soul is comprised of your personality, thoughts, and emotions. It is your individuality, your 'I AM.' No matter what kind of body you are housed in, you will always look like *you* to you. In addition, you are going to meet people in Paradise you once knew or were acquainted with on Earth, and though they never met or knew you in your temporary body, they will instantly recognize and be drawn to your soul essence, just as you will recognize and be drawn to theirs. In other words, when you look at yourself through the eyes of your soul, you will appear just as you looked on Earth when looking at your reflection through your physical eyes."

Gethyn smiled and was comforted knowing the Lord had the answers to all her questions and she need only ask to receive them. She curled up in the chair with its familiar red-and-yellow pattern, covering her legs and feet with the long robe. They talked of things great and small until the fire died down and nothing other than red embers remained. The handsome man stood and walked over to the stone hearth. He bent down to add more wood, and Gethyn watched as a soft glow of firelight circled the exalted man's head in a golden halo. Once the flame caught hold, Jesus resumed his place in the overstuffed chair. They talked for a while longer until it seemed all conversation had been exhausted, and it was only then that the young woman brought up the matter that had been bothering her for most of the day.

"Lord Jesus, I have a confession. I know you said it wasn't important to remember my birth or death. However, I asked Zendor to share some memories of my life. It didn't seem unreasonable to ask Zendor to tell me about our life on Earth, seeing as we were there together." Jesus listened attentively as Gethyn continued. "I was awed by the miracle of my birth, and through Zendor's telling of it, I could almost feel my parent's anticipation and joy upon my arrival. The most surprising and incredible thing I learned was that Heavenly Father was there at the very moment I came into the world! I never knew that nor did it ever even occur to me. When Zendor described how God breathed life into my nostrils and whispered words of hope and encouragement in my ear, I was stunned! I mean, I had read in Genesis how God breathed life into the first man, Adam, although I assumed the scripture was speaking figuratively rather than factually."

Jesus looked within Gethyn and saw her burning desire to learn and acquire knowledge, and He was greatly pleased. "The scripture as it is written was meant to be interpreted both ways, but one does not contradict the other. There are many classes offering Bible interpretation being taught throughout the city by both me and the twelve apostles. You should come. You might enjoy and benefit from these teachings provided you are interested in learning more," suggested Jesus.

"Oh yes, Lord! I would be very interested!" Gethyn exclaimed.

From out of nowhere, a wrinkle creased the young woman's forehead, and although the radiant man already knew the cause of her distress, He inquired, "What troubles you, Gethyn?"

The words were slow to come, like catsup at the bottom of a near-empty bottle. When she finally spoke, the Lord detected guilt and shame in her voice. "Jesus, there *is* something else. I have another confession to make. I also asked Zendor about the details of my death."

The exalted man looked into her troubled eyes, not with condemnation but with compassion. "And did your guardian tell you?" asked the Lord.

"No," answered the young woman. "Zendor wouldn't tell me, or more accurately, evaded the question. If death is a forbidden topic, then I'm sorry for my transgression, Lord. Zendor acted so strange when I asked though that I couldn't help feel there was something the creature was hiding. Did something terrible happen to me, Jesus?"

Never taking His eyes away from Gethyn's, the deified man leaned forward in His chair and clasped the long, slender fingers of His hands together. "Yes, child. Something terrible happened. You fell asleep at the wheel while on your way home, and your vehicle went over the side of the mountain."

Tears welled up in Gethyn's eyes at the thought of how senseless the tragedy was. With sudden insight and clarity, she admitted, "I remember now. Dave and I were having such a good time that I ended up staying later than I should have. He asked me to stay the night, but I was equally adamant about getting home. It was Easter, and my family's tradition was to attend sunrise services together. I've traveled that mountain road thousands of times. I knew it would be foggy, but I just wanted to get home. I don't remember the fall itself, although I do remember waking up at some point and finding you there with me."

Jesus said, "I always come when my name is called upon."

Gethyn thought about her death, yet one thing still puzzled her. "Lord, why won't Zendor tell me about my death?"

When Jesus spoke, His voice was kind and gentle. "In all fairness, it is Zendor's right to answer and tell you what you want to know. I will tell you this though. Sometimes there is more than one answer to a question. I have told you truthfully how you died, but your guardian angel has its own reason for not wanting to discuss the matter. Until Zendor chooses to share the reason with you, there is nothing you can do other than be patient." Gethyn averted her eyes from His, twirled a strand of hair around her finger, and absentmindedly bit her lower lip.

The Lord leaned forward in His chair and in a calm and even voice advised, "Of course, you already know the answer."

The young woman looked back at Jesus, startled by the revelation. Dumbfounded, she countered with "I do?"

Jesus smiled and, in a voice that sounded almost as soft as a whisper, said, "Yes, child. And if you search deep within yourself, you will find it."

15

Day Three

Earth

Gethyn's eyes opened in Paradise long before the lid on her casket closed.

The young woman's funeral was attended by close to five hundred people, most of whom were close friends and relatives of the family. However, some were merely curiosity seekers attracted by the high volume of news coverage the tragic accident had received. They were the same kind of people who raced to the scene of a fire to see the faces of horrified homeowners as their home and possessions burned to the ground or to a sensational murder trial, showing up every day in order to hear all the gory details of the crime.

A collage of photographs sat on an easel on the right in the chapel, depicting happier moments of Gethyn's life.

Permeating the room was the sweet, cloying smell of white chrysanthemums as well as other floral tributes consisting of trumpet-shaped lilies, carnations, stock, pink roses, and other varieties of flowers and plants. Unobtrusive pipe organ music played softly in the background—songs like "The Old Rugged Cross," "Nearer My God to Thee," and "I Come to the Garden Alone." Gethyn Fields's head lay on a white satin pillow, her red-gold titian hair neatly in place. She was clothed in a cobalt-blue silk dress and an Easter lily was placed in her hands. Though her body lay inside a cream-colored casket, Gethyn was blissfully unaware of the send-off being held in her honor.

Her parents wept quietly on the front row, their broken hearts evident and on display for all to see. They went to their daughter's side many times before the service began, looking down at her in disbelief. Many thoughts flooded their tortured minds. They wished they could turn back the hands of time or that their precious Gethyn would arise so they could whisk her away from this place of death and sorrow. The thought of saying good-bye to their only daughter and leaving her in a cold, dark grave was unbearable.

Sitting next to the Fields was Dave West, who had been Gethyn's fiancé. He was dark and uncommonly handsome, and though usually exuding charm and charisma, he was now reduced to a heap of raw emotions and tears by the loss of the woman he loved. Distraught and crying uncontrollably throughout the service, he could not be consoled no matter how many tried. He was tortured with feelings of blame and regret for not insisting that Gethyn stay put on that fateful morning. The beautiful redhead had been the love of his life and had come so close to being his wife. Like all young couples, they had plans and dreams for their future. They were planning to marry in the summer and then take off halfway around the world to work as missionaries in a third world country. They wanted to make a difference and were ready to dig wells, build hospitals and orphanages for displaced children, or do whatever was needed. Gethyn and Dave were young, full of zeal, and idealistic passion. With God's guidance, they hoped to be the answer to the prayers of many. Now Gethyn was gone, taking their dreams as well as their future with her.

Afraid they would be unable to speak without breaking down, Joe and Mary Ann Fields had asked their son, Emmit, to give the eulogy. The thirty-two-year-old was ten years older than his sister, although theirs had been a close bond. He stood and buttoned the jacket of his somber black suit jacket before walking slowly and solemnly to the podium. Once there, he paused to look out at the sea of faces before him. Emmit had not prepared a speech. Rather, he had decided to speak from his heart. From the moment he opened his mouth, the room fell into a reverent silence.

"Thank you for coming to pay your last respects to Gethyn. She would have been humbled to know so many people loved and cared about her, although how could one not? She represented the good in all of us, and I believe each of us looked up to her, striving to be a better human being because of her example." Emmit paused a moment to wipe a tear that had fallen down his cheek with the handkerchief he clutched tightly in his hand. When composed, he began again. "She was twenty-two years old, vibrant, and in the springtime of her life, yet she never seemed cognizant of how gorgeous she was, for it seemed her main focus was in exposing the beauty of all those around her. Gethyn motivated and encouraged us. She inspired us and saw in us what we didn't see in ourselves.

"My sister had her whole life ahead of her. She was above the norm in that, unlike many others her age, she didn't need to try on different identities searching for the best fit nor did she need someone else to tell her who she was or what was right for her. Gethyn had a world view and belief system from an early age, and she felt secure in the knowledge of who she was at her core.

"One of the things I loved and respected about her most was her deep-rooted desire to be her brother's keeper. Whether it was naïve or not, I don't know, but she seemed to believe most of the world's problems could be solved if everyone loved and cared for each other as much as they loved themselves. If Gethyn had any ambition, it was to do something good for the sake of others. She was firm in her resolve to use the God-given talents and abilities given her to make the world a better place for those less fortunate, and she had many.

"Gethyn was so happy to have finally finished college, and it was just a matter of time before she and Dave were to embark on their life journey together. Gethyn was the type of person who wanted to do something that required jumping in and getting her hands dirty. She loved people more than anything, especially children, and she wanted to join the Peace Corps or an outreach ministry or anything that would have fulfilled her desire to make a difference. My sister was a talented writer. Whether it was songs, poems, books, greeting cards, or letters, she had a way with words that touched people on a soul level. She was also a composer of music and a gifted violinist. She loved inspiring and encouraging people and always seemed to know the right thing to say at just the right time.

"I'm sure those of you who knew Gethyn really well know that she impacted the lives of many people for the better who were fortunate enough to cross her path during the short amount of time she walked the Earth. Had she lived, she would no doubt have gone on to do many selfless acts of charity and goodwill. The world was a better place for her having been in it, and our grief and sorrow at her passing will not soon be forgotten. As a Christian, however, it gives me comfort in remembering her light has not been extinguished but lives on."

By the time Emmit left the podium and took a seat beside his grief-stricken mother, there was not a dry eye in the congregation. But the service did not end on a sad note. For over an hour and a half, one person after another stood up to share favorite memories of Gethyn. After everyone had paid their respects, the minister offered a few more words of comfort and a closing prayer, and then people began trickling out of the chapel. Once everyone was in their cars and had formed a line, two motorcycle policemen escorted the funeral procession to the cemetery, one in the front and the other bringing up the rear.

The casket, covered by a spray of pink and white roses, was carried from the shiny black hearse and set upon elevator straps that would soon lower Gethyn's body into her final resting place. Family members walked beneath the gravesite canopy, taking front-row seats in green folding metal chairs, while a wide circle of mourners who had come to say their last good-byes stood wherever they could find a place. The grave was sanctified with holy water, Bible passages were read, and a prayer beseeching God to receive Gethyn's spirit was offered. The minister then took a handful of dirt and sprinkled it over the casket, saying, "Dust to dust, ashes to ashes. From out of the earth was thou taken. For dust thou art, and unto dust shalt thou return, and the spirit goes back to God who gave it." At the close, Gethyn's brother rose and began singing "God Be With You" a cappella, his tenor voice poignant and sweet.

God be with you till we meet again
Neath His wings protecting hide you
Daily manna still provide you
God be with you still we meet again

(Refrain)
Till we meet, till we meet,
Till we meet at Jesus feet
Till we meet, till we meet
God be with you till we meet again

By the time the last note was sung and white doves were released, Gethyn had already been in the presence of the Lord for three days.

Gradually people left the cemetery in groups of twos and threes. Hushed whispers were overheard as to what purpose could have possibly been served by the young woman's death, as it seemed surreal for someone so young and beautiful to have been taken from them, especially someone who had as much to offer as Gethyn.

16

Clarence was standing outside the high-rise in his immaculately pressed uniform and glossy shoes, looking ever the part of the consummate professional that he was. Seeing Gethyn approach from the elevator, he held open the heavy glass door and waited to bid her good morning.

As she passed through the door, she flashed a smile that would have made the stars in heaven look dim by comparison, graciously extending a courteous "Thank you." Once outside the building, she stopped to talk and exchange friendly banter with the older gentleman. He basked in the young woman's attention, and it was quite obvious that she adored him as well. Clarence thought Gethyn was more than beautiful. The tall, willowy girl's reddish-gold hair looked like a wildfire out of control, and he could have easily lost himself in her captivating turquoise eyes. They reminded him of an ocean he had seen once on a tropical vacation. After a few minutes of good-natured chatter, their spirits were energized, and Gethyn went on her way.

After crossing the wide, gold-paved thoroughfare, the girl made her way down the garden pathway leading to the River of Life. Up ahead, she saw the old black woman named Lottie and sped up a little in order to fall into step with her.

"Good morning, Lottie," Gethyn chirped, happy and carefree as a meadowlark.

"Good mornin' to you too, honey-chile'. Ain't the Lawd done made another glorious day fo' His chillun. Um-hum."

The young woman looked around at the beauty that permeated everything in Paradise, answering, "He sure has. You know, I've only been here three days, but each day I wake up looking forward to finding something new to discover. In a way, I feel like a kid on a grand adventure. Everything seems new and exciting."

The old woman agreed, saying, "Um-hum, that's right. With the Lawd, you never know what the day is goin' to bring, but the one thing you do know is that whatever it is, you is gonna like it." Lottie laughed and slapped her thigh with her hand, then added, "You knows, I wakes up ever' mornin' and thank the good Lawd fo' what He done fo' me on that cross. Has you seen the scars on His wrists and feet? Why, the whippin's I got from Mas'ta when I's a slave was nuttin' compared to what the Lawd suffered. It just breaks my heart, honey-chile'! And if He ain't done enough already, He's still doin' fo' us ever day, not to mention ever thing He's promised to do when we all gets to Heaven. Just makes me want to sing His praises all the day long."

They walked through the arched stone retainer wall with its deep red and purple bougainvillea and then followed the path down the embankment to the River of Life. Gethyn saw Zendor was already there. The colossal angel was busy talking with someone, so she reclined on the bank, choosing to wait and eat her morning sustenance later with him.

Lottie snagged a piece of fruit for herself and took a big, juicy bite. "Ummm ummmm," she said. "Well, chile', got to go. The Lawd and me is plantin' flowers on the east side of the garden today." Lottie looked off into the distance as though she could see all the way back to Alabama and then in a soft, tender voice said, "Reminds me of when I's just a young-un pickin' cotton in the fields back home. The work was hard, chile'. You just can't even imagine. But my kind, we had no choice. We had to do what Mas'ta said. We toiled from sunup to sundown with that ol' sun beatin' down on our heads. We'd all be a-prayin' while we was pickin'. We would ask the Lawd to help us, and you know what, chile'? The Lawd showed up ever' day and worked side by side with us, helping us to carry our heavy load. I just don't know what we'd a-done without Him. Anyway, the Lawd and I is gonna be plantin' flowers today. No mo' cotton, tobaccy, or sugar cane. No mo' backbreakin' work, whippin's, or hot sun. We's in Paradise now, and we does things now just for the pure joy of it. I's tell you a secret, chile'. I've seen the Lawd stick His finger in da soil and watched as sumpin' purdy sprouted out of the ground. Halleluiah! Oh, chile', I's gots to be getting down the road. Bye now!"

Gethyn smiled as she watched Lottie disappear down the garden path and wondered about the special relationship her new friend had with the Lord. When she thought about it, she found it amazing that He had enough love in His heart to love everyone who had ever lived and who would live in the future, not to mention the personal one-on-one relationships He had with each of those who believed and gave their heart to Him.

Gethyn turned her attention to her guardian angel, observing its interaction with others. Seeing how patient and tender the creature was with the little children, she was reminded of her dog, Sergeant, and how he would good-naturedly allow her to pull his tail, bite his ear, and roll all over him when she was a toddler. While she was reminiscing, she saw Zendor give a pretty buttercup bouquet to an elderly woman who was out for a morning stroll, and it melted her heart.

The angel's soul essence was warm, friendly, open, kind, and compassionate, yet at odds with that was the fact it was withholding something from her. Gethyn thought of what Jesus had said the night before, how there were sometimes more than one answer to a question. Since Jesus had already answered how she died, that obviously wasn't the reason for Zendor not being forthcoming.

What other answer could there be? the young woman thought to herself as she approached the colossal angel.

"Good morning, Gethyn." The voice sounded cheerful, but no sparks or ribbons of silver lightning flashed from Zendor's pale purple eyes. The young woman was still getting to know her guardian, but she took the angel's body language to mean it was blue or troubled about something. While not sure, she felt as though she had a good idea what was wrong and quickly decided the morning was much too beautiful for there to be tension between them.

Before Gethyn could speak, Zendor interrupted her thoughts by blurting out, "Would you like to do some sightseeing today?"

Attempting to lift the angel's spirit, the girl replied enthusiastically, "Yes, I'd like that very much!" She saw a hint of a spark in the celestial's eyes and hoped it could see she wasn't angry about their conversation the day before. "First I need to eat some fruit so I'll have enough energy to keep up with you," Gethyn said, laughing.

The sun highlighted golden strands in her hair as she walked toward one of the fruit trees growing by the water's edge. After making her choice, she walked back up the slope. "Zendor, let's sit over there for a while," she said, pointing at an ancient oak tree with heavy boughs. Some of its limbs touched the ground, and without waiting for an answer, the young woman ran over. She found a limb that was just a little higher than a bench and sat down as though it were made especially for her. The celestial being took a seat beside the girl, its long legs turned out and the heels of its gold sandals digging into the ground. Zendor said nothing and was as quiet as a church mouse while Gethyn ate.

"Zendor, tell me stories of when I was a little girl."

The enormous angel sighed deeply, and Gethyn saw its shoulders relax. The light within the creature began to pulsate. Following its gaze to the river, the young woman sensed that the slow, steady current of the water was taking the angel to another time and place. She liked the warm resonance of Zendor's voice and listened as the winged creature recounted their lives together on Earth. "As I have explained, angels neither marry nor do they have children, so in a sense you were like my very own child," the angel said. "Just as no one can tell people how to be good parents, no one can tell an angel how to be a good guardian. It's something that is learned through trial and error along the way. While it is true God created me with the aptitude for being a guardian angel, it was up to me whether I excelled at my calling or not.

"From the moment you were born, I loved you, and it became my mission to be there for you in every way and never let you down." The guardian angel's throat constricted at the thought of its failure to protect Gethyn. It fought back tears, sure that they would expose the truth, and diverted the conversation to safer ground.

"You were a beautiful baby, very good and so easy to love. Even when you were teething and fussy, I could always coax a chuckle out of you by singing some silly spur-of-the-moment song I made up. We played many games too. There was one in particular I designed to help develop your hand-eye coordination. I would sit on the floor in front of your crib and let my hair swing back and forth like a pendulum. You would get all excited and, while standing there on your tiptoes, reach out for my hair in an attempt to grab it as it swung by. When you were successful, you would squeal and jump up and down."

Listening to Zendor, Gethyn didn't know if it was the stories themselves she was enjoying or Zendor's telling of them. Her guardian had a whole bag of tales to tell, and one by one he pulled them out. By now, the angel was standing in front of Gethyn, and the story had in essence become a full-length animated movie, with Zendor acting out all the parts. Before long they were both laughing hysterically. The creature's eyes were a hailstorm of sparks and light, and as the young woman was being pelted with the joy of Zendor's spirit, she put an arm around the tree trunk in order to keep from falling off the limb.

Once they had both exhausted themselves from laughter, the celestial being resumed its place beside the girl on the sturdy bough. Light pulsed within the angel as it sat regaining its composure.

"Bedtime was our favorite time together. I would plump up your pillow, tuck the covers in around you, then kneel down and stroke your tiny face with my finger. I would watch your eyes grow as bright as a hundred-watt lightbulb as I told you how someday you would live in the Kingdom of God and that Jesus, your Prince, waited for you there. When you would wake from a bad dream, I was always there to comfort you. I whispered how I would one day take you to Paradise and that we would walk together in the Garden of Eden and down the gold-paved streets of the New Jerusalem. I tried to give you an idea of what Heaven would be like, although I had to admit that no one, including me, knows what wondrous things the Almighty has prepared there for His children. While watching over you each night, I lulled you to sleep by recounting each promise of God.

"When you turned four, you could no longer see or hear me. It was a lonely time. I watched you turn six and go off to school and trailed behind. Adolescence was a hard time for both of us, as you were constantly getting teased because of your red hair and blue eyes. I found resisting temptation extremely hard as there were a few kids I wanted to strike down like bowling pins, but I had taken an oath stating I wouldn't interfere with man's free will. Too, I knew I would have to give an accounting to God at the end of my mission, and it is the hope of all guardian angels to hear Him say, 'Well done, my good and faithful servant.'"

Tears began falling down Gethyn's cheeks, and Zendor turned toward the girl, tenderly wiping them away.

"I'm sorry. I didn't mean to upset you," the angel offered apologetically.

"Oh no, Zendor! I'm not upset. I'm crying because I just realized for the first time how much you really love me." The young woman stood up and threw her arms as far around the angel as was possible then brought her guardian to tears by saying, "And there is nothing you could say or do that could ever change the love I feel for you right this moment." As the two of them cried in each other's arms, the angel was torn. On one hand, he wanted to believe Gethyn, sure that in her mind every word she said was true. Zendor knew the heart was a different matter though and could be fickle. Would the love she felt change when she inevitably learned the truth about her death?

Gethyn pulled herself away from Zendor and in an attempt to lighten the mood threw her head back and laughed. "Here we are wasting a perfectly glorious morning. Instead of standing here boohooing like a couple of ninnies, we ought to seize the day" said the young woman, blotting the last remaining tears off her face with the back of her hands.

"You're right," chimed her guardian. "There is something in the city I think you'll enjoy. Let's head that way.

They exited the garden and headed down the gold-paved boulevard. They passed many skyscrapers, official-looking government buildings, and city parks before finally turning off on a side street. Up ahead was a large amphitheater where many people were gathered. Seeing it, Gethyn wondered what was going on. The guardian angel found a bench where they could sit, and she followed, thinking they were about to see a play.

In a few minutes, an elderly gentleman wearing spectacles, dress slacks, and a smoking jacket approached the podium. She listened attentively as he began telling the story of his life.

"My name is Harry Davis Wainwright, and I was born on September 12, 1869, in upstate New York. My parents were wealthy, having made their fortune raising tobacco, but they did not fall into the same self-centered trap as others with money often do. They stayed humble and unpretentious and taught me the value of helping others. After I was grown and had amassed a fortune of my own, I continued practicing the lessons I learned as a boy. I learned that whenever God has blessed you with more financial wealth than you can ever spend in a lifetime, you should take what you need with a humble and grateful heart and use the rest to bless those who have little or nothing. In my lifetime, I helped build low-income housing and recreational facilities and parks, and I volunteered to work at soup kitchens in the poorest areas of town. Each year, I gave a college scholarship for a deserving albeit underprivileged boy who would never have been able to afford a proper education on his own. I gave to those who asked and to those who didn't, but it seemed no matter how much money I gave away, my wealth never seemed to decrease. In 1912, my wife and I sailed to Southampton, England, on business. Once there, we decided to stay a few extra days to enjoy the highlights of the city. On our return, we were fortunate enough to secure passage on a new ocean liner said to be the best ever built. It was a beautiful vessel with fine, first-class accommodations. Five days into the voyage, the ship hit an iceberg, and all the money in the world couldn't have saved the hundreds of lives lost that day. At that point, there was only one thing of value I had to give: my seat on the lifeboat. I knew the seat being held for me was a blessing that was not meant for me to keep, and as I slipped into the frigid, icy waters, I was relieved to know a young wife would not lose her husband nor her two little girls, their father. It was a loving God who allowed me to bestow the gift of life at the end of mine."

Next, an adolescent male stepped onto the platform. He was very dark-skinned and wore next to no clothing. Gethyn instantly recognized the ancient tribal dialect he spoke and listened intently to every word. The boy gave his name as Nabu and told of life within his tribe that had existed three thousand years earlier. "One day...out hunting... me had vision," he said in his guttural way of speaking. "In vision...me run...chased by black leopard. Me threw spear...missed. Black leopard jump on Nabu...me die. Me

145

frightened by vision…me not want to die. Then…Nabu saw cloud of light. Me rubbed eyes…but cloud still there. Then voice came out of cloud and say…'Leopard hungry… will consume Nabu…but I give life back.' Me ask how? Cloud say, 'Believe I am who I say I am.' Nabu ask, who is cloud? Cloud say, 'I Am…who made earth and sky and everything Nabu sees.' Just then…Nabu feel pain. Black leopard jump on Nabu's back. I look up at cloud…talking cloud say 'Believe?' Nabu say…'Yes! Believe!'"

Gethyn sat spellbound for the rest of the day as one person after another told his or her life story. After each person spoke, the audience had a chance to ask questions. What better way to learn about world history and the unique customs of diverse people who had lived than from the people themselves. As she listened, Gethyn came to the realization that regardless of how long she sat there on the bench, she would never hear all the life stories and testimonies there was to tell. Zendor took the opportunity to inform Gethyn that she would eventually get the chance to hear some of the greatest people who ever lived give a testimony of their time on Earth. The thought of hearing firsthand from those she had looked up to was thrilling to the young woman, and she looked forward to coming here often in the future.

Gethyn discovered all people are basically the same no matter where they were born or what time period they lived in. Regardless of their ethnicity, gender, politics, occupation, or religious affiliation, they all had had hopes and dreams, loves and losses. The young woman was beginning to see whether on Earth or in Paradise, we are all brothers and sisters—one big family in God's circle of life.

17

It had been a long day, yet Gethyn was not tired. After saying good-bye to Zendor, she returned to the cabin that represented home and curled up in one of the red-and-yellow overstuffed chairs to think about all she had heard and learned. Being overly sensitive to others, she felt an outpouring of compassion tug at her heart while listening to the trials and tribulations some of the people had shared at the amphitheater. *Such pain and suffering*, she thought.

When Gethyn thought of her own life, she could remember only happiness and joy. She was blessed to have been born into a kind and loving family who had nourished and protected her in every way. When she was ready, they had sent her into the world at large, much like an archer takes an arrow from his quiver, sets it against a bow, then takes steady aim and releases it, confident it will hit its intended mark.

While she was alive and had it been possible, she would have put her arms around all of God's children in an attempt to shelter them from the injustices and inequities of the world. There was so much Gethyn would like to have done, and although now dead, she found she still had a burning desire to make a difference somehow. She prayed every morning when she woke up and every night before going to sleep, but felt surely there was more she could do beyond praying.

Gethyn retrieved the robe from the narrow clothes closet and changed out of her jeans and T-shirt. Something about the robe made her feel clean and presentable to the Lord. She curled back up in the chair and then summoned Jesus with her thoughts, inviting Him to come into her heart and home.

Jesus was there immediately, looking as handsome as she remembered. "No need to get up, child. How wonderful to see you," He said with genuine affection, leaning over to kiss each of her cheeks.

"It's wonderful to see you too, Lord," Gethyn responded.

The tall, graceful man went to the chair opposite her and surprised the young woman by curling up in it, just as she was in hers. His casual demeanor instantly put the girl at ease, making her feel as though they were just two old friends talking, which was actually true.

"First of all, I want to thank you for this robe. In a way I can't explain, every time I put it on, I'm overcome with a desire to wear it continuously and never take it off."

The Lord smiled and offered an explanation. "When a person begins to desire the clothes of the righteous, it is a sign of budding maturity. I suspect you are beginning to feel dirty and unclean in your earthly rags, and rightly so, as you are the daughter of a King and will one day wear a crown of precious jewels."

Hearing Jesus's words made the young woman's spirit soar. "Oh! There is something else, Lord. Forgive me for not telling you last night how much I love the home you prepared for me. It's perfect and exactly what I would have chosen for myself. I still can't believe I'm living in my parents' cabin at Lake Lone Pine, even if it isn't on Earth. It is just as I remember, so warm, cozy, and unpretentious. Thank you, Lord. Thank you."

A gentle smile crossed the man's wondrous face and lingered. He responded to her gratitude. "It is only a small portion of the blessings and favors I have stored up for you in Heaven."

"Lord, what will Heaven be like?" asked Gethyn, burrowing into her chair a little deeper.

Jesus seemed to go somewhere else in His mind, but after a few moments of inner reflection, He began to speak. "Thy Kingdom Come is all that God has promised. It is a place where pain, sorrow, sin, sickness, disease, and death will not exist. A day will be as a thousand years, and without the fear of time running out, life will be fully enjoyed at a leisurely pace as was originally intended. Eternal life is a gift from God that allows all of one's hopes, dreams, and potential to be fulfilled. Although time will exist in the kingdom, you will not be consciously aware of it.

"When Thy Kingdom Comes, there will be no sun or moon, yet brilliant light will illuminate everything within its borders. The source of light will be God's glory as He once again walks among men. His love will be the air that is breathed and will give everyone's essence a warm glow. The absence of darkness will assure God's children there is no terror of the night to be found, no dark places for evil to lie in wait. Once God resurrects the new heaven and new earth, all of creation will be free of the curse that was placed on it after the fall of the first Adam. Love and goodwill will abound, and there will be no self-serving agendas. Emotions such as resentment, bitterness, jealousy, lust, greed, and hatred will not exist. Life in the kingdom will be as it was originally intended—perfect.

"People will live in their new, improved resurrection bodies and be able to explore endless possibilities of growth. Whatever was lost, broken, or taken from them during their lifetime on Earth will be restored, whether it is family, health, opportunities, potential, or purpose. Many who once lived died friendless or were unable to have children, and some who lived never knew love of any kind, not even from a parent. In Heaven, however, every need and desire will be fulfilled, and love everlasting will abound.

"Much of what you enjoyed on Earth will be replicated, and those things that aren't will not be missed as they will be replaced by something far better than anything your mind could ever perceive or imagine. There will be culture, art, travel, work, play, rest, and worship. Your life will be rich and full, and you'll never tire of learning and expanding your knowledge of God and all He has created."

As she listened, Gethyn's countenance conveyed her amazement and wonder. In a sense, she was once again the little girl who had stood mesmerized by the Christmas display in the window of Quincy's downtown department store. She hadn't known what Santa Claus was going to bring, although she was sure that he knew her heart and that she would not be disappointed Christmas morning when she discovered the beautifully wrapped presents he left for her under the tree.

Without being told, Gethyn understood how just as Earth is dim in comparison to Paradise, Paradise will be dim in comparison to the Heaven that is to come.

The young woman rearranged her position in the oversized chair. Putting her elbow on the armrest, chin in the palm of her hand, she said, "Heaven sounds so…well… heavenly. How could anyone not want to go there, Jesus?"

A cloud of sadness came over the Lord's face, and then He spoke. "Have you ever kicked over a rock and seen worms or insects hiding beneath?"

Gethyn said quickly, "Yes. When I was a child playing in the woods around the lake, I did that many times."

Jesus nodded his head in agreement. "Did you notice how once their dark hiding place was exposed, they began scurrying around in a panic, desperately seeking another refuge away from the glaring sunlight?"

Again, Gethyn said yes.

The deified man explained, "That is how people without God are. They prefer the darkness and are squeamish and uncomfortable when God kicks over the rock they have crawled under. When given a choice between Heaven and Hell, they choose Hell, as they don't want to stand in the light of God's truth. Sin is the rock they hide under, and they would rather stay in darkness than give it up."

The part of Gethyn's nature that wanted to save the world was deeply affected by what the Lord had said. The girl sniffled and wiped away a salty tear that suddenly slid down her cheek and rested somewhere near her chin.

"That is the saddest thing I've ever heard. Isn't there a way to make them see that they're making a mistake?" she cried, tears now gliding down her cheek one after another, like children on a playground slide.

Jesus was touched by Gethyn's compassion for the lost, though He knew nothing could be done. "My dear, Gethyn, God is a just god. He exposes His light to everyone as He doesn't wish anyone to perish. However, He can't make anyone do anything, not even love Him. Were He to force His children to love Him, then it wouldn't be love, as love surrenders itself willingly. God gives everyone free will to make their own choices, which includes the right to choose good or evil, light over darkness, love over hate, and life over death."

A thought came to Gethyn—one she was almost afraid to ask. "Lord, will there be family or friends I had in life who won't go to Heaven?"

"I'm afraid so, child," He answered as gently as possible.

The young woman's hands covered her face, and she wept harder.

Jesus spoke a single word: "Gethyn."

She looked up at once. There was something in the way He said her name that commanded her attention and made her want to obey. Across from her was the most handsome man she had ever seen, whose penetrating blue eyes seemed to look into the deepest part of her soul. If she had been standing, she would have staggered as she could scarcely believe what He said next.

"Child, you won't miss them."

Like a toddler who has been deprived of its security blanket, the young woman wailed in anguish, "How could I not miss my family and friends?"

Jesus got up and sat on the side of her chair. He put an arm around her heaving shoulders while offering words of consolation. "Gethyn, in Heaven you will only want what God wants. His friends will be your friends, and His enemies will be your enemies. Those who have not chosen to stand in the light of God's truth will be cast into the

Lake of Fire. Although it's painful for you to hear right now, when the time comes, you will rejoice with the rest of God's children."

Gethyn was shaken by the Lord's words and knew what she must do. With great resolve in her voice, she said, "I must pray for them, Lord."

"Yes, pray for them, child," he whispered, stroking her red-gold titian hair.

When the young woman was again composed, she commented, "Lord, it seems I cry more now than I ever did on Earth. What is wrong with me?"

With His arm still around Gethyn, Jesus answered, "Do you remember having growing pains when you were an adolescent?" to which the girl answered yes. The Lord gave her shoulder a little squeeze and explained, "Well, you're having growing pains. You are maturing spiritually in leaps and bounds and are finding it hard to keep up with all you are learning. What you're going through is a normal reaction, child. I am here with you to dry your tears and reassure you everything will be okay and to remind you how someday when Thy Kingdom Comes there will be no more tears or sorrow."

Gethyn looked up into the Lord's eyes and asked, "When will Thy Kingdom Come?"

"Only the Father knows," He replied.

18

Day Four

When Gethyn reached the meeting place, she saw that
Zendor was engaged in conversation with another angel.
Not wanting to intrude, she killed time by inspecting
the trees that grew all along the water's edge until finally
selecting a piece of fruit that was midnight blue in color.
Biting into it, she was delighted to see it was baby blue
on the inside and tasted like nothing she had ever eaten
before. The young woman took one bite after another of the
delicious food until all that was left was the memory of its
mouth-watering flavor.

A couple of minutes later, Gethyn glanced over and
saw that Zendor was still talking with the stranger. She
took a lesson in patience and found a comfortable position
on the manicured green grass by the River of Life to wait.
Watching the steady current of the river, Gethyn thought

of its many tributaries that branched out to nourish other parts of Paradise.

The young woman couldn't help but be curious about the celestial being with Zendor and stole a couple of glances in their direction. The two looked similar as far as being about the same height; however, the girth of the other creature was considerably larger, and it had a full, moon-shaped face. Gethyn silently studied the contrast between the two. Zendor's mane of thick black hair was like that of a Friesian horse, while the other angel's hair was dark brown and worn braided intricately around its head. She also compared their eyes—Zendor's being pale amethyst in color, while the other creature's looked like sparkling green emerald jewels.

It was the first time Gethyn had really looked at another angel since arriving. Since arriving, her brain had been on sensory overload, trying to take in all that was visually beautiful and interesting in her new environment, not to mention making mental notes and filing information of all she was learning as well.

While studying the faces of the two guardians, the young woman had a revelation that made her feel a little ashamed. She had assumed every angel looked the same due in part to Zendor explaining how God had made all the angels at the same time. Erroneously, she took that to mean they all looked alike as well, although now she saw how ridiculous it sounded. Of course each angel was individually different, not only in appearance but in personality and soul essence as well. *If God created each person as well as each snowflake that fell from the sky unique, then why wouldn't He make each angel unique too?* she chided herself.

Zendor turned towards Gethyn, and a succession of lightning bolts shot from its pale amethyst eyes. The beautiful young woman had come to understand the phenomenon as being a joyful expression and that it meant the angel was smiling.

The two guardians approached, and upon seeing her make a move to get up, Zendor bent down to help Gethyn to her feet.

"Gethyn, I'd like you to meet Sydon, an old friend of mine. We go way back...well, practically to the beginning of time."

Both celestials broke out in a fit of hysterical laughter that lasted two or three minutes. Blue, red, and yellow sparks flew from their eyes in every direction followed by one silver ribbon of light after another. As the young woman watched the spectacle in amazement and awe, she was reminded of the many July 4 celebrations she had witnessed as a child. Just as they once had, Gethyn's eyes reflected her delight as she watched the fireworks explode overhead in a brilliant profusion of color.

As the three of them talked, the young woman learned Sydon had come to share good news with Zendor. Heavenly Father had given the guardian a choice of accepting another assignment on Earth. Without hesitation, the jovial angel had gratefully agreed to the mission offered, elated at having been given another opportunity to fulfill the purpose for which it was created. Like all guardian angels, Sydon's deepest desire had always been to serve God. Although the celestial being would miss Paradise, it looked forward to meeting the child it was being sent to love and protect and hoped this time around would have a better ending.

Once good-byes were said, Sydon walked out of the garden to begin the long walk to the outer gates of Paradise where the next convoy was preparing to leave for Earth.

Turning its thoughts to Gethyn, Zendor asked, "Did you have a nice evening?"

An image of Jesus curled up in the oversized chair opposite her came to the forefront of Gethyn's mind. She thought back on His words and how He had said that some of her loved ones would not be in Heaven. Internally, she was still trying to process the information.

"The Lord stopped by" was all she was willing to share.

Even as Gethyn said it, the towering nine-foot angel could tell she was holding something back. Concerned, the angel lifted Gethyn off the ground with one hand and held her up so as to look in her eyes. "Do you want to talk about it?"

There was a glazed faraway look in her blue eyes as she looked past her guardian to the River of Life. "No, not really. It's just something I've got to work out for myself."

The angel respected her wishes and gently lowered her to the ground until she was once again standing on her feet.

All night she had struggled with the ecstasy and agony of what Jesus had told her about Heaven. On one hand, she was ecstatic about all that awaited her, but she was brokenhearted to think some of her loved ones wouldn't be there to share it with her. *How could anyone willingly choose to live apart from God?* she wondered, and it was the agony of not knowing who was in danger that preyed upon her mind.

Gethyn's first thoughts were of her parents. She knew they were grieved by her death, but at least they knew she had a personal relationship with Jesus. They knew she was with Him, and that alone would have given them some measure of comfort. The girl flipped her long, red hair over ivory shoulders, thinking of all the people who had ever lived and died and those whose families didn't have that same kind of assurance. She was relieved her loved ones wouldn't have to suffer with the uncertainty of wondering where she was. A warm feeling came over the troubled young woman, and all of a sudden, she knew down in the deepest part of her soul she would see her parents and her brother Emmit again. Just as they knew where she was, she knew with all certainty where they would be eventually. Each of them had given their hearts to Jesus years ago and had been saved! She began thinking of others she cared about, those she knew who walked with the Lord and those who were a question mark. At least now she had a good idea who to pray for.

Zendor could tell something had changed in Gethyn as her countenance had gone from resembling someone sinking in a quagmire to one of a person who had just won a mega lottery. The guardian didn't pry, although was happy the girl had worked out whatever was troubling her.

"It's another beautiful day in Paradise. Are you ready to go exploring?" asked Zendor.

With a ready smile, Gethyn answered, "Yes!" She never bothered to ask where they were going, although it wouldn't have mattered. Zendor could have said they were going to take inner tubes and float down a bayou infested with mosquitoes and alligators, and she would have said, "That sounds like fun!"

19

The guardian pointed out many places of interest, explaining how each building would play a significant role in the New Jerusalem once Heavenly Father proclaimed "Thy Kingdom Come!"

"Now this will be a grand library," pointed out Zendor, "where people interested in reading works by authors of world renown will congregate, and what's more, the authors themselves will make appearances every day and provide workshops."

Gethyn thought of all the authors she had admired and respected on Earth and looked forward to the opportunity to meet and get to know them. Zendor's voice became background noise as the titian-haired beauty's mind traveled to that place where her secret desires resided. She had been writing all of her life, whether in the form of poems, songs, short stories, or letters. It was who she was. Thoughts, like Post-It notes, were stuck on every wall of the young woman's mind where she could gaze upon them—things she had to say and wanted to write about. All of

Gethyn's writings thus far had been practice. She knew it took a lot of time to sharpen and hone the skills it took to craft great literary works both profound and inspirational. Gethyn looked at the library before her and sighed, sad in her belief that the words stored in her heart and born of her soul would never be on one of its shelves for others to read.

The young woman found herself following a deep river of thought. She realized that as human beings, most seek validity and want confirmation that what they think and who they are matters. They seem to need affirmation that their life has made a difference to society in some notable and significant way. Gethyn considered some of the great people who walked the earth—Jesus, for sure, and Moses, Noah, Lincoln, and Einstein. There were also artists, sculptors, actors, and inventors who fit into that category and still others who found medical cures, walked on the moon, or were known for heroic acts of great courage while faced with extreme hardship and adversity. There is no doubt that these people existed, for society has immortalized them. They will live on eternally because memories of them have been passed down from generation to generation. *Maybe eternity starts on Earth*, Gethyn thought, *and merely requires that you live your life in such a manner that when you are gone, you will have mattered and your memory kept alive.* But what of those not remembered? When no one remembers your name, it's as though you never existed. Gethyn wondered, *In a generation or two, no one will even know I lived and breathed or that I had hopes and dreams. Maybe I would have accomplished something wonderful had I lived long enough. Of course, we'll never know.* She sighed in resignation.

All of a sudden, the young woman realized Zendor was speaking and snapped out of her private thoughts. Gethyn followed the angel up the wide marble steps of the magnificent gold building, marveling at the stately pillars standing at precise intervals as though they were sentries posted to guard the entrance.

After admiring the architectural details of the future library, the two resumed their walk down the city sidewalk. The angel was talking a mile a minute while at the same time pointing out the significance of each building they saw. A voice behind them called out, "Zendor!" Turning around, they saw a celestial being waving from the other side of the boulevard. Gethyn watched as the large angel hurried across the street, accompanied by a young man. She glanced past the winged creature to the tall stranger wearing boots and straw cowboy hat, totally caught off guard by the man's ruggedly handsome good looks. As they approached, she discreetly sized him up, surmising he was probably not much older than herself.

Zendor recognized the celestial being as Tanniz, a good friend. Tanniz slapped Zendor on the back, and a volley of questions and comments immediately ensued between them.

"Zendor, my friend, how are you? When did you get home? I want to hear all about your journey! I'm getting ahead of myself though. I want you to meet my charge, Jace Covington."

Zendor countered by introducing Gethyn. The dashing cowboy removed his straw hat, revealing dark auburn hair, and held it to his heart as though he was about to say the Pledge of Allegiance.

"Pleased to meet cha, ma'am," he said with a drawl.

Eyes the color of dark molasses met hers, and she found herself drawn to them, much like a wave is drawn to the shore. The young woman found it difficult to pull her gaze away and wasn't even sure if she wanted to. Suddenly, a picture of Dave flashed in Gethyn's mind. The thought of being disloyal to her fiancé was deeply disturbing, and she silently admonished herself. Once she had cordially said "Hello" to Jace, she quickly averted her eyes.

Realistically, Gethyn knew the life she and Dave had planned together was gone and that he would probably grieve her loss for a few seasons until eventually life's current forced him to move on. Could *she* move on though? she wondered. Thoughts of the future she had looked forward to floated to the surface of her mind like ethereal apparitions. How long would she walk down the dusty, desolate road leading to the lonely graveyard in her mind, the place where "what might have beens" were buried? Would their ghosts haunt her forever?

Tanniz and Zendor were still engrossed in small talk when Gethyn snapped out of her thoughts. She turned her attention back to the conversation that had continued despite her heart's and soul's absence.

"We arrived in Paradise four days ago," Zendor said, looking first at Tanniz and then at the polite cowboy.

Tanniz countered, "Give or take a couple of months, we've been here about two years."

The young woman noticed that like Zendor, Tanniz had black hair but wore his slicked back in a long ponytail. The angel's eyes were interesting and unusual, and she discreetly tried studying them without appearing rude. They were like that of a tiger eye gemstone, brownish gold in color, and seemed to grow darker or lighter depending on the angle of the sun.

Zendor explained to Tanniz and Jace that they were on a tour of the city and asked if the pair would like to join them for an afternoon of sightseeing. Tanniz and Jace readily said yes. With one hand, Jace set the weathered straw hat back on his head, and the four set off to see the city highlights, the guardians taking the lead with the young couple falling in behind.

"You might find this interesting," volunteered Tanniz while pointing to a building with a high steeple.

"There are churches in Paradise?" asked Gethyn, voicing her surprise.

"Of course. There are churches, temples, and mosques all over the city," commented Zendor's friend.

Gethyn's guardian took up where Tanniz left off, advising, "Just because people are in Paradise doesn't mean they don't need to worship God anymore. Fellowship, worship, songs of praise, and Bible classes are all an integral part of life here. And just you wait! You've never heard a more wonderful orator until you've heard Jesus deliver a sermon!" Zendor told the young woman excitedly.

The tall, strapping cowboy standing beside Gethyn nodded his head in agreement before jumping into the conversation. "He's right, ma'am. Tanniz took me to church not too long after we got here. Once everyone had congregated, a choir made up of both humans and angels alike began singing from the balcony. My soul wept from the sheer beauty of it. The glorious light of God's presence was felt throughout the sanctuary, and my spirit rose like fine particles of dust floating towards the sun. Then there was the Word, and the Word was with God. When He spoke, I immediately fell to my knees."

Gethyn could tell from the way Jace spoke that he loved the Lord as much as she did. Looking at his soul essence, she saw someone who was worthy of being admired and respected, and yet he frightened her. Fighting to keep her misgivings at bay, she dared to look into his face and was immediately overcome by the sensation of falling from a high precipice. The feeling was so strong that she stumbled and almost fell. Ever the gentleman, Jace quickly steadied her by taking hold of her elbow; and at the touch of his hand, the young woman's face flushed.

"Whoa, missy," he said. "Are you all right?"

Though embarrassed, Gethyn tried not to show it. "I'm okay. Just clumsy, that's all. Maybe you could take me to church sometime," she blurted then bit the inside of her lip fearing she had sounded forward.

Jace smiled, revealing deep dimples and straight, even white teeth. "Why, ma'am, I'd be happy to escort you to the house of the Lord anytime you get a hankering to go," he said in a rich baritone voice.

The young woman felt torn between feeling unfaithful to her fiancé and this new unwanted feeling that had suddenly come over her. She decided the best thing to do was discuss the matter with Jesus later, as He always knew the right thing to do.

They saw many wondrous sights that afternoon. One was the space and discovery expedition center, where one day people would not only learn but also travel to planets and galaxies not accessible to them during their lifetime on Earth. It was built for those who had pioneer spirits and hearts full of courage and curiosity. In Heaven, those who longed for adventure would never run out of new trails to blaze or worlds to chart, as God was continuously creating new ones.

As they passed by small groups congregated all over the city, Gethyn heard excited chatter. People were discussing plans for the new Earth and how, with the exception of the New Jerusalem, everything would need to be rebuilt—roads, bridges, towns, and so forth. Everyone's talents, skills, and abilities would be utilized with the fruits of their work bringing glory and honor to God. Gethyn and Jace exchanged glances and saw hope for the future reflected in each other's eyes.

The young couple talked about their lives while following their guardians around the city. The tall, good-looking cowboy revealed he was born in Oklahoma and had been a successful rodeo star traveling a wide circuit and competing for prize money.

"When I finally had my fill of broken bones and being laid up for months, I decided to heck with that and left the bright lights and applause of the crowd," he said with a disarming grin. He had had the foresight to know there would come a day when he could no longer ride ornery old bulls and bucking broncos, so he had diligently set aside most of his earnings. With the money he'd saved, he'd started his own business training horses.

"Growing up on a working ranch, I know horses like the back of my hand," he said, a sound of pride in his voice. With a chuckle, he added, "And ma'am, working with horses is a sight bit easier than tangling with a thousand-pound bull." They both laughed. The tone in his voice changed and at once became soft and humble. "However, that was before I became acquainted with Ringo."

Jace explained how Ringo was a black roan he had agreed to train as a favor for a friend. The first time he'd seen the crazy, feral look in the horse's eyes, he'd almost backed out of the deal. However, he'd already shook his friend's hand, and where he was from, a handshake was as good as a man's word.

After working with the horse for two or three days, he had managed to get a saddle on him and a couple of days after that was finally able to sit the horse. Jace's face grew solemn, as he continued. "I remember being dog-tired from working Ringo for the better part of the afternoon and decided to wash up and head to the house for some supper. When I went to dismount, my boot caught in the stirrup, causing me to stumble and fall to the ground. It was as though that crazy horse had been waiting for me to make a mistake, and then everything happened so fast there was nothing I could do. He reared up on his hind legs, and before I could crawl out of the way, he started pummeling me with his hoofs. The last thing I remember was the murderous look in Ringo's eyes as he was stomping me in a blind fury."

Visualizing the horror of the scene, Gethyn's heart went out to the cowboy. Jace changed the subject and asked about her. The young woman told him of her life and her dreams of becoming a writer but left out any mention of Dave. She feared that if she shared the memories closest to her heart, they would blow away like dandelions in the wind.

Jace asked about her death. Gethyn told him she'd fallen asleep at the wheel and how she had sustained a broken neck when the vehicle went over the side of a mountain. With a wistful faraway look in her eyes, the young woman told him how she had been less than half a mile away from home when the accident occurred. "It was all such a senseless tragedy," she said, fighting back tears of regret.

Gethyn raised her head in surprise when the cowboy said "No, ma'am" with conviction.

"Forgive me for saying it, as I don't mean to offend you, but your death was *not* a tragedy. I reckon a tragedy would have been dying without ever knowing the love of Jesus or not having the hope of His promises to hold onto. Losing your earthly life was unfortunate, untimely maybe, but not a tragedy from a Christian point of view. Your life is not over. You will live on forever in the presence of God. The tragedy lies with those who will be unnecessarily living in eternal hell when it could have been avoided. Those are the lives that should be mourned."

Gethyn hadn't thought of it in that way before and realized he was right. She stole another glance at Jace Covington, this time seeing a man who was not only charming and handsome but also wise beyond his years. She was inspired by him, for in his gentle, unassuming way, he had helped her to see that there were still dreams left to dream.

Gethyn found herself telling Jace how she had always seen herself as an author and of her disappointment in knowing none of her works would be in the magnificent library she had seen in the city.

Jace turned to face the beautiful redhead and took both her hands in his. "Missy, don't you know? All your dreams will be realized in Heaven. Finish what you started on Earth. Write! Your books *will* grace the shelves of the library, right alongside some of the most valued literary works of all time. Sometimes on Earth, people dream and craft masterpieces in their hearts and minds that don't come into realization until after their passing. Follow your passion, for there's every reason to believe that someday your books will be cherished and loved by others."

The foursome toured buildings that would one day house museums, galleries, theaters, restaurants, and various learning centers—each designed specifically to house art, cultural interests, continued education, and much more. The golden city would be unlike anything the world had ever known. Gethyn surveyed all that lay before her and felt something stir within her spirit. She recognized it as being a seed of anticipation. Though she hadn't been in Paradise long enough for it to firmly take hold and grow, she instinctively knew in time she would join the others who anxiously looked forward to the day when God in all His power and glory would finally say the words everyone longed to hear: "Thy Kingdom Come!"

20

The young woman returned home after a full day of sightseeing, her spirit buoyed by all she had seen and done that day. Too, she had enjoyed meeting Zendor's friend Tanniz as well as his charge, Jace Covington. Gethyn was both guarded and intrigued by the good-looking young man and replayed over in her mind all she had learned about him.

Without being consciously aware of it, she went to the window and stood looking out upon the magnificent city. She thought about her family and how much she longed to tell them she loved them, and then she remembered the spiral notebook and pen. Gethyn sat down at the kitchen table and began writing.

> You will always be a part of my heart
> For the memory of your smile makes me warm
> And there is nothing that could ever change
> The way I feel for you
> For in my eyes, you do no wrong

When I'm alone and my thoughts return home to you
My heart aches knowing all you did for me
And what I've put you through
And for all the times I never told you
Just how much you mean to me
And that my pot of gold has always been
The treasure of your company
I know that these words could not possibly be enough
For what you've given me, words could never repay
Just know my love is woven through each and every line
And my heart wrote every verse
I only wish I'd thought to tell you yesterday…

Gethyn put down the pen and closed the notebook. She stretched out on the couch and her mind involuntarily went to all the things that would never be—marrying Dave, traveling to exotic locales, being an ambassador of goodwill, children she had hoped to have someday, and books she wanted to write. Never having been the type of person to wallow in discontent for long, she thought of what Jace had said earlier in the day about her death not being a tragedy and about how some dreams weren't realized until after a person's passing.

Gethyn sighed deeply, turning her mind to the pleasures and privileges that were a part of her life in Paradise. God still provided for her daily needs just as He had always done and had given her a comfortable home, sustenance, friends, a beautiful garden for peaceful contemplation, and a golden city to explore. Her guardian angel was with her and, of course, Jesus. All she had to do was call on the name of the Lord and He was there. When the young woman thought of all her blessings, she knew she had no cause to feel discontent. She hoped that she would eventually discover her purpose, something to give her new life meaning.

Gethyn went to the clothes closet for her robe, but before she had time to take it off the hanger, there was a faint tapping on the door. She opened it and was delighted to see Philena standing in front of her wearing the plain olive green dress and cloak with the crisp white apron tied around her impossibly tiny waistline. Though her hair was pinned into a severe bun, the prim bonnet she wore could not entirely conceal red wisps of hair that were determined to peek out from underneath.

"Philena, please come in!" said Gethyn, hurriedly ushering the young girl inside as though there was a blizzard outside.

The Quaker looked around the room and seemed taken by the cozy comfort of the one-room cabin. "So this is where ye spent ye favorite times on Earth?" asked Philena.

Gethyn put her hands in the back pockets of her jeans. "Yeah. It was a cabin retreat my parents had on Lake Lone Pine. We spent many summers there as well as some winter weekends. It was always my dream to live in the cabin, but finances got tight and my folks had no choice but to sell it."

Gethyn's guest glided gracefully into the room, the hem of her long dress sweeping the floor, until she was standing by the large overstuffed chairs. Philena inspected the red-and-yellow fabric, feeling the texture of the material with her fingers as well as that of the faded horizontally striped love seat. Although the girl tested the plumpness of the cushions, she did not make a move to sit down. Without speaking, the young Quaker walked around the room. She walked over to the round table and rested her hand on the back of one of the chairs sitting around it. Gethyn could sense her picturing the family sitting together for a meal in her mind. Next, Philena peeked out onto the screened-in back porch with its twin beds and then came back inside. The girl casually yet methodically scrutinized each acrylic painting hanging on the walls as well as their weathered frames. It seemed as though she was keenly interested in determining the location of the area depicted in each landscape and looked upon each one for the longest time.

Gethyn was just about to ask Philena if she'd like to sit down and make herself comfortable when she noticed the girl's attention had turned to the bed positioned diagonally in the far corner. Philena walked over to it, followed by Gethyn.

Philena bent over and touched the quilt. "'Tis quite beautiful. May I ask how ye came to acquire it?"

Gethyn explained the quilt had belonged to her fourth great-grandmother and had been carefully preserved and passed down from one generation to the next. "I've always loved this quilt and would have most likely inherited it someday from my mother had I not died first. It seems funny how many things that I thought were lost to me have been restored, such as this cabin and the quilt. In time, my family will be restored as well," Gethyn said, feeling a sudden yearning in her heart.

Philena picked up on the young woman's feelings and reached out to touch her shoulder. "What is ailing ye?"

Fighting back tears, Gethyn managed a halfhearted smile. "I guess I'm just missing my family. I never even got to tell them good-bye." She reined in the runaway tears. "I know through God all things are possible and how, in His time, I will see them again. You know, I always had the impression that when someone died, relatives and friends who passed on before were there waiting at the gate to welcome them, but no one was there for me. Either I assumed wrong or, God forbid, none of my ancestors were believers. I would have at least thought my grandparents would be there. I know they lived good Christian lives," stated Gethyn with conviction before her trickle of tears became a downpour.

Taking the young woman in her arms, Philena comforted her. "There, there, Gethyn. Ye hath nary cause to be a-fretting thyself. 'Tis not as bad as all that. Ye shalt see."

Although 341 Earth years separated the two young women in life, there were some things that transcended time, such as love and compassion.

When the crying spell ended, Philena looked into Gethyn's blue eyes, smiling demurely. "I hath something which shall make ye feel better. Will ye come with me?"

Before Gethyn had time to answer, the younger girl already had her by the hand and was pulling her toward the door. They went out into the hallway and then walked the few steps to Philena's apartment. The girl, both proper and modest, reached into the deep pocket of her dress and pulled out her key. Looking at it reminded Gethyn of what the girl had said a couple days before—that God had given each of His children golden keys to the holy city. She smiled inwardly, thinking how God had considered everything pertaining to the happiness of His children right down to the smallest detail, such as a key. In all His wisdom, He knew people could live in houses, but it was not until they took possession of the keys to the house that they truly felt it was their home. That was how God wanted His children to feel—at home.

Once inside, Philena removed her cloak and hung it on a peg. Gethyn was surprised when the girl then led her into an adjoining room. The young woman had noticed it before and had been curious but thought it would appear rude to venture into it uninvited. Before her sat a chest of drawers, a bed, and a deep, lift-top chest similar to the hope chest Gethyn had in her own bedroom on Earth. Philena went to the heavy chest, opened it, and began rummaging around as though searching for something in particular.

"Close thy peepers and do not dare to look," the girl instructed playfully. Gethyn obeyed until at last Philena said, "Thou mayest look now."

The young woman was not prepared for what she saw. In the girl's hands was a quilt, and though its colors were different, the pattern consisted of the same identical concentric circles as was used in the heirloom quilt passed down from her fourth great-grandmother.

"How can this be possible? This pattern has always been a well-kept secret only divulged in private to members of my family!" blurted the young woman, looking disbelievingly from the quilt to Philena and then back at the quilt.

"Bring the quilt and ye self and let us sit for a spell. I hath much to tell ye, dear Gethyn," said the young Quaker.

Philena sat in the sewing rocker looking pious, her delicate hands folded properly in her lap. She looked at the young woman who was not much older than herself, holding the antique quilt that connected the two of them.

"Would it surprise thee to know ye art related to me by blood?"

Gethyn, her mouth agape, looked incredulously at the girl in the simple clothing, unable to believe what she had just heard. It took a few moments for her to process the information, but finally, she ventured to ask, "We are *family*?"

Philena nodded her head affirmatively. "'Tis true, and I wouldn't wish ye to go on believing nary a single soul was a-waiting to welcome thee when ye arrived at the gate, for all ye family, including ye dear grandparents, was there. Ye wast unable to see them, however, as ye hath not had thy spiritual peepers opened yet by Jesus. The Lord says 'tis always a mite bit better to wait before springing too much on a soul when first they be arriving, so 'twas decided upon betwixt thy family for me to tell ye when the time was right, seeing as I lived so close to ye."

"It is my hope I hath not made ye faint of heart," said Philena, her voice taking on a concerned tone.

Gethyn reassured the girl she was all right, actually more than all right, really. Her spirit felt light and joyous upon learning she had family in Paradise, and now that she knew they were there, she could hardly wait to see them.

"Philena," the young woman asked tentatively, "how are we related? Are you one of my great-great-great-cousins or aunts?"

The Quaker girl straightened her back and quite proudly replied, "I am thy fifteenth great-grandmother."

Gethyn gasped audibly. She leaned forward and with hands clenching the arms of the ladder back rocker exclaimed, "But how can that be? Why, you're younger than I am!"

The girl in the white bonnet rocked, punctuating the moment further with a silent pause. After considering how strange it all must seem to Gethyn, she picked up the thread of conversation and continued embroidering the story she had begun.

"'Tis true. I died at the tender age of nineteen, although not before giving birth to a wee lad named Samuel who grew up to be thy fourteenth great-grandfather."

Gethyn looked at the girl, her eyes wide with wonder, trying to wrap her mind around these new revelations. The only thing she could think to ask was "Where did you live on Earth?"

Philena smiled, and her bright green eyes sparkled and danced around the room. They reminded Gethyn of how, as a child riding in the car with her mother, she would watch prisms of rainbow-colored light skip and twirl on the ceiling when the sunlight glanced off her mother's diamond wedding ring.

"My mother country was Ireland," Philena answered.

Gethyn quickly said, "So that's where I get my red hair!"

"Aye," responded the Quaker girl.

"When I was just a girl of eighteen, my husband, George, and I had to flee Ireland to escape religious persecution. At the urging of William Penn, we traveled by way of an immigrant ship to the Americas in 1686. Soon after setting sail, I learned I was with child. Oh, 'twas a treacherous journey and I was dreadfully sick. There were many times I thought my family would surely perish. However, God was with us, and we were spared. I can't tell ye how good 'twas to stand on land again after having been months out at sea. After arriving, my family traveled down the Delaware River and settled near Brandywine Creek in Pennsylvania. I didn't get to enjoy our new life long though, for alas, I died three months later on my nineteenth birthday while giving birth to Samuel," Philena said, looking down at her lap.

"Philena, I'm so sorry," Gethyn said.

The young girl said, "Oh, I didn't mean to let on like thee was pining away. Heavens, no! Samuel is here and getting to know the lad hath given me much joy and happiness."

Gethyn decided to change the subject. She looked at the girl who in actuality was her elder and with due respect asked, "Since you are my fifteenth great-grandmother, what should I call you?"

Covering her mouth slightly with her fingertips, the girl giggled and replied, "Thou mayest call me by my name, or Philly, as some of my dearest friends do, as I hope ye will think of me as a friend rather than a stuffy old distant relative."

Gethyn was relieved as she had already begun to think of the two of them as close friends.

Feeling the time was right, the Quaker approached the next subject without hesitation. "Now, would I be correct in assuming ye would be desiring of a get-together with all thy family who came before ye so as to get acquainted or reacquainted, whichever be the case?"

Gethyn, who was still holding the precious quilt, responded, "Yes, I would like that very much, and I will not be able to sleep a wink until I see my grandparents and whoever else is here."

"Then 'tis settled," stated Philena in a matter-of-fact tone. "Thy family will expect thee at Homecoming Park first thing in the morrow for a grand reunion."

Puzzled, Gethyn asked, "Where is Homecoming Park?"

The girl smiled. "'Tis in the garden. Follow the River of Life downstream and look for signs to point thy way."

A thought suddenly occurred to Gethyn. "Would it be all right if my guardian angel, Zendor, comes too?"

Delighted, the young Quaker girl clasped her hands together in front of her. "Indeed! I meant to invite thy angel too as ye guardian is part of thy family as well. Most bring thy guardians to the reunions, so Zendor shan't feel out of place."

It was getting late as Philena followed Gethyn to the front door. They hugged and gave each other a kiss on the cheek, saying their goodnights as any close friends would do. The young woman walked down the corridor to her cabin, her mind reeling with all she had learned.

Though her parents and brother, Emmit, weren't there yet, she would soon see her beloved grandparents and hopefully aunts, uncles, and cousins. The young woman knew there would be family members at the reunion that she never knew existed and looked forward to meeting them as well.

A memory from the past floated to the forefront of Gethyn's mind, and she reached out and took hold of it. It was a poem she had written as a teen in an attempt to sound mysterious, but in context to all that was happening, it seemed curiously apropos.

> Although I have never seen your face
> Your smile is one familiar
> And though I've never looked into your eyes
> Their warmth I have known forever…

While in quiet reflection, Gethyn realized there was one common thread tying her and her distant relatives together. Like them, she had followed Jesus's footsteps all the way to Paradise.

Once inside the apartment, the young woman knelt beside the bed to offer a sincere prayer of gratitude to God. She spent a long time on her knees thanking Him for all His many blessings and favors and even for the ones she wasn't aware of yet. At the prayer's conclusion, she said a personal prayer for her immediate family, followed by another on behalf of mankind in general, just as Jesus had taught her to do. Gethyn remembered the conversation with the Lord down by the River of Life when she first arrived. He had told her how the spirit of each person on Earth received prayers from Paradise and how they were delivered to the mind of a person in the form of a thought. The young woman hoped her prayers were received in the spirits of her parents and brother, causing them to think of her.

Gethyn folded back the delicate quilt and then crawled into bed. She reached above her head and traced the carving of the pine tree and moon on the headboard with her finger as she had done countless times before. She fell asleep trying to imagine the faces of those she would meet the next day.

21

Day Five

As excited as Gethyn was about the reunion, it was surprising she had been able to sleep at all. As soon as her eyes opened, she jumped up, quickly made the bed, and fluffed the pillow. Then she pulled the treasured quilt up, smoothing it carefully. The young woman looked at its concentric circles, wondering what her mother's reaction would have been had she known her daughter had met the one who most likely originated the pattern over three hundred years earlier, her fifteenth great-grandmother, Philena McClary. As she headed for the door, sun was filtering through the window, giving a preview of the glorious day to come.

The young woman stopped in the corridor briefly to look at her reflection. It was a momentous day, and she was sorry not to have something other than the faded jeans and T-shirt to wear. Of course, there was the white robe, but she wanted to keep it clean and pristine for her visits with the Lord. She shrugged her shoulders and went merrily down the corridor to the elevator.

If walking could be compared to a song, Gethyn's gait was a happy tune. Just as music and lyrics are meant to touch hearts in profound ways, so does the spirit and soul long to touch others with harmonious melodies of joy and love.

Exiting through the heavy glass doors, she greeted the doorman with a cheery "Good morning, Clarence," and when asked why she was so chipper, replied, "I'm on the way to my family reunion!"

The man's smile was like a rubber band stretched to its limits, and as Gethyn jogged across the wide, gold-paved boulevard toward the garden entrance, he called out after her, "Have a great time!"

The young woman saw Zendor up ahead on the garden path leading towards the River of Life and hurriedly raced to catch up with the nine-foot angel. When the creature was within earshot, she excitedly called out, "Zendor! Wait up!"

Her guardian stopped and, while patiently waiting for the young woman, groomed the feathers on one of its wings and adjusted its white robe. When they were abreast of each other, Zendor inquired, "How are you feeling today, Gethyn?"

As the girl strained her neck to look him in the face, she retorted, "I feel fourteen feet tall, although at moments such as this, I wish I really were."

Zendor let loose with a loud belly laugh, sending sparks and fingers of lightning bolts from the unusual pale amethyst eyes. Lifting Gethyn off the ground, the angel held her up until they were eye to eye. "Does this help?" it asked, smiling playfully.

"Yes, as a matter of fact, it does. Guess what, Zendor? We've been invited to a family reunion!"

The guardian already knew but, not wanting to steal the girl's thunder, pretended not to know. "Whose?" Zendor asked innocently.

Radiantly happy, Gethyn announced, "Mine! Okay, you can put me down now. You're wrinkling my T-shirt." Never pausing to give her guardian a chance to speak, the young woman continued. "It's hard to believe, but one of my neighbors, Philena McClary, is my fifteenth great-grandmother, and she's only nineteen years old!"

The colossal angel looked down at the girl with her long hair aglow in streaks of red-gold fiery flames. "Life is just full of mysteries and aha moments, isn't it?" the angel said, his black mane covering one side of his face.

"You're telling me!" Gethyn answered.

"Well, we'd better get going then," Zendor said, heading downstream.

Following the river, the young woman began to think of herself as being on a treasure hunt, with her family being the treasure she sought, which in a very real sense was true. She saw Lottie up ahead working diligently in a flower bed and called out to her. "Hi, Lottie!"

The old black woman looked up and then rested back on her heels. "Good mornin', honey-chile'! Who's that handsome angel you got with you?"

Gethyn looked at Zendor then back at her friend. "This is my guardian angel, Zendor. Zendor, this is Lottie. We're on our way to my family reunion at Homecoming Park!"

Lottie stood up, brushed the dirt off her hands, and then, careful not to crush any flowers, joined the two on the path. "I remember my first reunion, I do. We was singin', dancin', laughin', cryin', and down on our knees praisin' the Lawd for that happy day. I seen my mammy who I hadn't laid eyes on since she was taken away and sold. I was just a tadpole when that happened, but I never forgot the look in her eyes when we was pulled apart. But all that's history now. Thanks to the Lawd, I've got my mammy and other kinfolk back, and we's now free. Praise be to God for ever and amen!" Lottie gave Gethyn a hug, saying, "I sure hope you have a great time. I want to hear all 'bout it next time I see you, honey-chile'."

Gethyn and Zendor got on their way again. The two came to another of the many pathways that led deep into the garden. As though unsure, the celestial being hesitated for a brief moment before turning onto it. The young woman didn't worry as she knew her angel would get them where they needed to be. Gethyn rambled on while following Zendor blindly through the trees and foliage. As they walked, she told him of her Irish roots and how Philena had said she and her husband, George, had immigrated to America because of religious persecution. The guardian hadn't seen its charge look so happy since she arrived and smiled and listened attentively while she spoke. Her anticipation was contagious, and soon the angel found it was looking forward to meeting her extended family as well.

Once she had talked herself out, Gethyn began admiring the flowers, plants, and trees, taken by the beauty and serenity that enveloped her. They came to a sunny area and saw a flower bed island where a black knight butterfly bush, fragrant lavender, black-eyed Susans, and pink coneflowers had been planted. The lovely fragrance of lavender wafted through the air, and Gethyn breathed its scent deep into her lungs. Zendor began pointing out other flowers to the young woman, the names of which she was unaware of, as they walked past one beautifully landscaped bed after another. Ahead was a shady area where hostas, astilbe, columbine, sweet woodruff, violas, pansies, coral bells, ferns, pulmonaria, crocus, and grape hyacinth were displayed for all to see and enjoy. Foxglove and ferns bordered trees, and hanging from their limbs were baskets of impatiens. The two walked through a canopy of mimosa trees, their lacy fronds waving shyly like young senoritas with fans. As Zendor and Gethyn followed the pathway in search of the reunion, it seemed the colors and sensual fragrances of the garden changed from moment to moment.

Hearing the sound of excited voices ahead, the two picked up their step. Unconsciously, Gethyn flipped her red-gold hair behind her shoulders and then looked down at the jeans and T-shirt she wore. It wasn't the first time the young woman had felt self-conscious about her clothing since arriving, but she derived some measure of comfort knowing no one in Paradise was going to judge her. There was no "normal" here, and superficial things like money, clothing, and status was of no concern.

They came to an enormous clearing surrounded by oak, elm, and sycamore trees, and Gethyn was astonished to see a gathering consisting of several thousand people as well as angels who accompanied them. It reminded her of an international music festival. There was diverse music, and everywhere Gethyn looked, people were laughing, singing, and dancing. Although she saw tears, they were tears of joy, not sorrow.

"Surely I'm not related to *all* these people!" the girl cried out, wondering how she would ever find her grandparents. Her eyes darted here and there, searching. She was reminded of the times she had gone to the state fair and how she hadn't known where to go or where to look first.

This is like looking for a needle in the proverbial haystack! she thought to herself while trying to see through the crowd. Zendor must have sensed the girl's concerns as all of a sudden she was whisked high into the air. He stood

Gethyn on his shoulders, holding onto her ankles to steady her.

"Thanks, Zendor! You're an angel...literally," she exclaimed while scanning the area. "I'm afraid it's going to take a miracle though to find Grammy or Grandpa," the young woman said, sounding more than a little discouraged.

Way off in the distance, a group of people began waving frantically. Gethyn's eyes squinted against the sun in an attempt to discern who they were and was finally able to make out the shape of her grandparents, her Aunt Bell, and a little boy she had known from her early childhood. The young woman hadn't thought of the boy, Stephen Bowers, in years, and she suddenly remembered he had died of leukemia while they were both in the first grade. It had been her first experience with death, and the finality of his passing had deeply affected her. Finally, her mother was able to bring her out of the profound sadness she felt by assuring Gethyn she would see her friend again someday in Heaven.

Philena was standing with the others in her white bonnet, apron, and plain Quaker attire, trying to get her attention.

Gethyn acknowledged the group by waving back vigorously and in a voice shrill with excitement shouted "I see them, Zendor!" Pointing straight ahead, she shouted, "It's them! There they are!"

After the two bulldozed a path through the large crowd to where Gethyn's family was, Zendor set the young woman down. "Grammy!" she cried, falling into the familiar and comforting folds of her grandmother's arms. After a couple of moments, she threw her arms around her grandfather's neck, crying, "Grandpa!"

The white-haired old man gave her a tight squeeze and then held her away from him so he could look into her eyes. "We're so happy to see you, honey!" he said with a wide smile.

Gethyn's face was tear-streaked by now as was everyone else's. "You look just as I remember," the young woman said, looking the elder couple over.

"So do you," replied her grandmother in a soft voice.

Gethyn wondered if they saw her as she was before they died, a little child. The young woman then remembered Jesus telling her a person was recognized by their soul essence, not their appearance. Her grandmother was petite, with salt-and-pepper gray hair, and what few wrinkles she had could not hide the fact she had once been a beauty. Gethyn saw a twinkle in her Grandpa's blue eyes and remembered how he used to tease her playfully.

"Why, the last time I saw you," he began, "you were knee high to a grasshopper's belly," then tickled her as though she were still ten years old. "We were delighted when we heard you were coming, although we weren't expecting you so soon," he said. Trying to keep a straight face, the old man continued. "But that's life for you. Just when you think everything is going fine, *splat*, you end up squished like a bug on the windshield."

As Grandpa laughed, his belly jiggled, and Gethyn couldn't help getting caught up in his silly sense of humor. The young woman had almost forgotten that Philena, her Aunt Bell and childhood friend, Stephen, were standing there waiting to be acknowledged and quickly lavished hugs on each of them. She embraced her fifteenth great-grandmother warmly, kissing her cheek.

"Am I really related to all these people, Grammy?" asked Gethyn incredulously while looking around her.

Before her grandmother could answer, Grandpa cut in and, with eyes twinkling, said, "Yes, honey, and they are all dying to meet you."

In her demure, unobtrusive way, Philena said, "The truth 'tis ye art related to everyone who hath ever lived or ever will live, if only by a thin silver thread, as thee, thine, and everyone else art the seed of the same Heavenly Father. However, while some are here as dear relatives of ye, others are here to reconnect because of a friendship bond ye shared on Earth or because ye influenced, inspired, or motivated them by a kind word or deed. They hath come to honor and thank ye for your contribution to their lives and to add their joy along with all the others who hath come to ye homecoming celebration.

"Feel free to mingle and meet with thee kin as well as those with other connections to ye, Gethyn. Everyone is most eager to discuss family history and how ye art related however 'tis obvious ye won't be able to meet everyone in one day. Fortunately for ye, 'tis a reunion held in Homecoming Park every 'morn, so rest comfortable a-knowing there shall be many 'morrows for introductions. Ye hath all eternity to learn all ye have a desire to know. Now, I am off to find my husband, George, and son, Samuel. Carry on and I shall return after a spell." With that Philena disappeared into the thick of the gathering.

Gethyn was more than a little relieved knowing she could come every day if she wanted to as she had begun to feel a little overwhelmed. She turned her attention back to her beloved grandparents, aunt, and then little Stevie, who looked up at her with adoration. The young woman glanced over at Zendor and saw her angel congregated not too far away with a large group of other guardians who she assumed were friends. They looked happy and excited to see each other, some of them having been away on Earth missions for years.

The young woman feasted on the abundant joy of her loved ones before kneeling down in front of the little boy.

"I missed you, Stevie," Gethyn said, a salty tear falling from her eye.

The child was dressed in shorts and a T-shirt, and a baseball cap covered his bald head. "Jesus told me you was coming today, an' I runned here as fast as I could," he said. "I was hoping you'd 'member me but was scared you wouldn't after all this time."

Gethyn took the little boy in her arms, hugging him as though she never wanted to let him go. "Oh, Stevie, how could you think I'd ever be able to forget you? We were best friends."

He allowed her to hold him for a few seconds before wiggling out of her arms. "Back then, you was my *only* friend," he said matter-of-factly. "After I got sick an' couldn't run or play no more, the kids in the neighborhood quit coming around…all 'cept you. I 'member toward the end, Mama brought you to my room hoping it would cheer me up. The medicine I took made me feel like I was floating on a cloud, but I knew you was sitting on the side of the bed singing to me. Do you 'member? You sang:

> You are my sunshine, my only sunshine
> You make me happy when skies are blue
> You'll never know, Steve, how much I love you
> Please don't take my sunshine away

"I was so tired by then, Gethie. I wish I coulda told you how much being friends meant to me. I could tell you didn't want me to leave, but by then, my body was too weak and tired to stay."

A smile came to the little boy's face, revealing a missing front tooth. He extended both arms out as wide as he could and flexed his muscles. "I feel really strong now though and can do all the things I couldn't do before."

The young woman wiped away her tears and then laughed. "Okay, let's see," she declared. "Last one to the sycamore tree and back is a rotten egg. Ready, get set, go!" With that, Gethyn took off running with little Stevie right behind her.

Gethyn met many people that day. Grammy introduced her to her own parents and grandparents, and they in turn brought their parents and grandparents over to meet the red-haired girl. She met people who came to thank her for inspiring or encouraging them on their life journey, and their praise settled on her soul like sunshine on the first day of summer. Gethyn was thoroughly fascinated by all the life stories she heard as well as the colorful people in her lineage. Bell, her favorite aunt, doted on her and shared treasured memories. The young woman floated in the love and well-wishes of those around her, and the sensation was one of being immersed in liquid mercury. Later when she was alone with her thoughts, she would reflect back on those she had met that day and would come to realize that everyone you ever met or came into contact with on Earth, whether they became your best friend or worst enemy or was only a stranger you barely acknowledged while passing on the street, left an impression on your soul. The impression made may have had tremendous impact, its significance forever altering your life direction. Or it could have been so subtle that the memory of its existence had disappeared from your consciousness. But just as the wind blows across the desert, scattering and obliterating any trace of the footsteps of all who have passed through its great expanse, the soul of the desert remembers that they once were there. Gethyn realized that like the desert, so too had her soul remembered and recorded the imprints of all who had journeyed across her landscape.

As the day turned into late afternoon, she said her goodbyes, promising to come back and visit soon. Hordes of people began the long walk back through the garden and to their apartments in the city. Gethyn and Zendor stopped to pick a piece of fruit by the River of Life. Afterward, they walked up the bank and through the tall stone wall with its grand arches until they came to the garden exit. Neither spoke as the colors spilling across the sky said it all—the end of the day was just as glorious as the beginning had been.

"How was the reunion?" asked Clarence, opening the glass door for Gethyn to pass through.

"You know, I never realized until today how many people loved me and have been praying for me," she said as though she still couldn't believe it.

Once inside her cabin, the young woman slipped into the comfortable, clean white robe and summoned Jesus. Scarcely before His name had left her lips, He was there. He took His usual place, and she hers, and they talked until the wee hours of the morning.

22

Day Six

Bright and early the next morning, Gethyn left the tall skyscraper and walked across the street to the luxurious garden. It was a tranquil place to take a leisurely walk or sit and meditate. She was supposed to meet Zendor at the River of Life, but as the young woman looked around, her guardian was nowhere to be seen. Two little girls were talking in whispers and giggles on the riverbank, and Gethyn recognized them as being Arie-Ann Tucker and Dolly Jemison whom she'd met a few days back at the outdoor amphitheater.

Arie-Ann's countenance was like a continuous fountain overflowing with perpetual curiosity and delight. She wore an ankle-length dress of blue gingham overlaid with a white pinafore and a flowered bonnet tied loosely under her chin and that rested on her back. Gethyn had seen the little girl who was as delicate and agile as a butterfly many times as she flitted and fluttered around the garden going here, there, and everywhere, never seeming to stay put in any one place for long. The word "stranger" did not exist in her vocabulary as she greeted everyone she met with a warm, friendly smile and a ready "How do you do?" It wasn't so much Arie-Ann's smile that made Gethyn feel like a bee drawn to the sweet nectar of a flower, or the smattering of freckles across the bridge of her snip of a nose, but her big brown puppy dog eyes. They were always dancing with laughter, leaving everyone she met with a merry heart. One chance encounter with her was all it took to be smitten.

Dolly, on the other hand, had hair the color and texture of corn silk, which fell evenly to the middle of her back. Like Arie-Ann, she was six years old and though not as extroverted as her friend, she did speak up when she had something to say. The little girl's eyes were sea-green with amber flecks and were framed by a fan of dark blonde lashes. She wore a steel gray homespun dress with white collar that hung loose on her tiny frame.

Gethyn had learned Arie-Ann and Dolly hadn't known each other during their life on Earth and had only met and become best friends after having arrived in Paradise. Since finding each other, the two had become inseparable. They had much in common to talk about as in life both girls had been traveling west on wagon trains with their families, looking for a new beginning. Arie-Ann contracted cholera and was buried on a lonely trail halfway to Oregon, while

Dolly had drowned after the overloaded wagon she was riding on capsized during a ferry boat crossing in Missouri. Many years later, they were reunited with their parents and in time met their siblings, some of them for the first time.

The girls made it a point to keep up with those who came after them and would wait eagerly at the outer gate of Paradise upon learning one of their relatives were coming, no matter how many generations removed they might be. Reunions at Homecoming Park were always a source of great pleasure and joy for the girls. Having experienced only six short years of life on earth, the girls were delighted at having no shortage of aunts and uncles to learn from and cousins to play with. They came to the reunions often, both of them loving being a part of God's ever-expanding family.

Arie-Ann held a bouquet of colorful flowers at her side with one hand and Dolly's hand with the other. "Hi, Gethyn!" chirped the little girls simultaneously in melodic singsong voices.

It never crossed the young woman's mind to wonder where their parents or guardian angels were as she had come to realize no harm could come to any of God's children from inside the protective walls of Paradise.

"We're going to summon Jesus!" Arie-Ann volunteered enthusiastically. Both girls loved spending time with their Lord and Savior and always looked forward to seeing him.

"Can I join you?" Gethyn asked the children.

"Of course, you silly goose," said Dolly, after which all three giggled.

No sooner had they summoned Jesus with their thoughts than He was there with them. Arie-Ann and Dolly knew Jesus was always being summoned but couldn't understand how He could be in so many different places at once. For now though, He was with them, which was all they cared about. Arie-Ann's dark chocolate braids bounced every which way as she jumped up and down, her eyes now having grown to the size of silver dollars.

Gethyn, wearing jeans and a T-shirt, stood beside the two little girls in their homespun dresses. By now, the difference in their clothing didn't seem unusual to the young woman.

Jesus's blue eyes sparkled, reflecting the joy of His spirit. "Good morning my beauties," He said, in a voice that had a timbre unlike any other.

"Good morning, Jesus," the six-year-olds said in unison, giggling nervously.

Jesus laughed too, and the girls ran and hugged Him around the knees.

"We wanted to share the first fruits of our day with you," said little Dolly, looking up at the beautiful man.

"And give you these flowers," piped up Arie Ann, with Dolly nodding her head in agreement.

Taking the flowers the little girl offered, Jesus smelled the bouquet and showed His pleasure with a warm, gracious smile. "Come then," He said.

Like Gethyn, the children had been told they must eat of the fruit every day or risk becoming very ill. They accepted the instruction without question or complaint and came to the garden every day to pluck one of the twelve varieties of fruit that grew by the River of Life. As most six-year-old little girls who are best friends do, they enjoyed mirroring each other in everything they did, so both chose a piece of fruit that was pale pink and yellow in color.

The four of them found a comfortable spot by the river and reclined on its soft, green velvety bank. After giving thanks to the Father, they ate the delicious fruit.

Afterward, Dolly tilted her face up toward the Lord's and in a voice too sweet to resist made a request. "Abba, please tell us a story."

Jesus tucked the girl's blonde hair behind her ears and looked into her beautiful green eyes, enchanted by the rare purity and innocence that emanated from her soul essence. He drew Dolly upon His lap and waited for her to get settled before starting. Arie-Ann and Gethyn sat together at His feet, both eager to hear His words.

In a voice that commanded their complete attention, Jesus spoke. "It is written: 'Then the Lord said unto Moses, Go in unto Pharaoh, and tell him, Thus saith the Lord

God of the Hebrews, Let my people go, that they may serve me..."

Jesus had a way of telling the story that left them hanging on every word. Before it was over, He had told not one, but three stories. He didn't mind though as He loved spending time with the children and was delighted at having been summoned.

"Bye, Jesus," Dolly said, exchanging hugs and kisses with the Lord.

Arie-Ann took the exalted man's hand and looked up at His wondrous face. "The next time we get together, will you tell us the story again about the five thousand people you fed with five loaves of bread and two fishes? That's one of my favorites! What's really amazing is when you tell the story, it comes alive, and I can see it as clear as day, just as though I was really there!" she said, practically in one breath.

Jesus smiled and bent down, hugging Arie-Ann affectionately. He kissed the top of the little girl's head and replied, "A splendid story it is, and someday, when 'Thy Kingdom Comes,' I will take my beauties all the way back through time with me to that very day so you can experience the feeding of the five thousand firsthand. Would you like that?"

Gethyn found herself enthusiastically shouting "Yes!" along with the little girls, scarcely believing her ears. *Wouldn't that be something?* she thought, and then reminded herself, *Of course with God, everything is possible.*

Jesus laughed, and his voice was like music to their ears.

"There's a puppet show at the children's learning center about to start," said Arie-Ann, tugging on little Dolly's sleeve.

The Lord saw the enthusiasm in the little girl's eyes and was pleased. He was well-aware that puppet shows could be found in many different areas of Paradise and knew it was the perfect way for young children to learn about God who had died before being old enough to read stories from the Bible for themselves. Jesus bid both girls good-bye, watching as they skipped merrily away, their contagious giggles trailing behind them like a kite string.

Alone with Jesus, Gethyn said, "I know you usually meet me where I live later in the evening, but it's a beautiful day in Paradise, and there's no one I'd rather spend time with than you. Can you stay awhile, Lord, or must you go?"

Pleased, He smiled at the young woman, answering, "I will stay for as long as you wish."

As He stood before her in His white linen robe and sandals, Gethyn thought how noble and dignified He looked. Her gaze met those of her Lord and Savior's, and her heart melted from her intense love and adoration of Him.

23

Gethyn and Jesus walked up the riverbank until coming to the tall retainer wall running parallel to the river. They followed it downstream for about a quarter mile and then walked through one of the stone archways that was beautifully adorned with bougainvillea in vibrant colors of purple and deep red.

The Lord led the young woman down a new path. It was one she'd never been on before, the border of which was sparkling white quartz. To the right and left were flowering trees such as dogwood, coral, jacaranda, and crepe myrtle, mixed in with pine, maple, aspens, and Chinese elms. Gethyn found it amazing how Paradise had the perfect soil and climate to grow any species of tree, flower, or plant and how they all seemed to complement and enhance each other.

That's how it should be with people, she thought silently to herself then jumped when the Lord answered, "You're right. It would be a much better world if people brought out the best in each other. Unfortunately, many are unwilling to share their time, blessings, light, or truth with those who are different, believing the sun only comes up for them alone."

Gethyn saw something ahead and pointed. "What is that?" she asked curiously.

Jesus looked over at the girl walking beside him and smiled. "Come, I will show you."

Entering the long cylindrical structure, the Lord explained how this type of tunnel was favored during the Renaissance period for being cool and shaded as well as moderately dry during a rain shower. They were constructed of strong flexible willow stems called withies and wooden slats. Arches placed in intervals were made by weaving willow stems as though weaving a basket and then connecting the arches together with long wooden boards. Honeysuckle, wisteria, and other flowering vines were planted at each arch until the entire structure was blanketed in fragrant beauty. The withy tunnels had been popular long ago for being a passageway where couples could walk and talk privately.

Gethyn and the Lord enjoyed their walk through the long tunnel and talked casually of many things. Once on the other side, wide flagstone steps led to a sunken garden. Everywhere the young woman looked, there were exotic flowers, fountains, and architectural wonders. While sitting on the outer wall taking in the absolute wonder of it all, she realized that each time she thought there couldn't possibly be anything more God could give her to enjoy, He surprised her. It made Gethyn think of her earthly father and how he loved nothing more than giving her gifts, even when there was no occasion. He always called them "just because" presents. She smiled, thinking how both her father on Earth and her Heavenly Father always seemed to know which things would give her the most pleasure without ever having to ask.

The morning spent with Jesus was a memory Gethyn knew she would savor forever, but she was a little disappointed upon discovering that the path they were on led out of the garden as she wasn't ready for their time together to end. Once her foot touched the gold-paved thoroughfare, she turned to the right and began walking towards the New Jerusalem. God's holy city sat regally atop the mountain like a King on his throne.

The young woman had only walked two steps before Jesus called out, "Are you tired of my company so soon?"

She ran back to where He stood and threw her arms around His neck. "Tired of you? Never my Lord!" Never!"

The exalted man stroked her hair, saying, "Very well, my beauty. There is something else I would like to show you."

Gethyn didn't ask questions as just being in His presence was enough. The young woman knew whatever Jesus had in mind was bound to thrill, fascinate, or leave her speechless, but she was totally unprepared for what she saw.

Up ahead was a colorful hot air balloon perched on top of a grassy knoll. Her jaw dropped and her turquoise eyes sparkled like sunlight on the water when she realized what they were about to do.

Jesus helped the girl into the basket and, once she was situated, untied the ropes that anchored the balloon to the ground before climbing in. In normal circumstances, a valve would be opened, allowing fuel to ignite with the burner, heating the envelope, and causing it to rise in the air. But in this instance, the Lord's energy was more than sufficient to power the balloon.

The young woman stood mesmerized by the panoramic view before her, knowing she had never even remotely seen anything as breathtaking in her life. Her eyes took it all in— the golden city, the Garden of Eden, and the River of Life. They continued to ascend, and as though by tacit agreement, neither spoke for the longest time. Each seemed to know words would only serve to mar the occasion, and neither was willing to compromise the beauty of the moment. Gethyn had questions, but they could wait for a while as she didn't want to ruin the mood trying to comprehend and dissect the answers given. The young woman didn't want to think or do; she just wanted to *be*.

Once they reached the desired altitude, the Lord slowed their ascent, causing the colorful balloon to catch an air current and lean into the wind. Jesus was pleased to see Gethyn relaxed and enjoying herself as He wanted her to experience all the pleasures Paradise had to offer.

Leaning against the railing, the young woman breathed in the exotic fragrance that permeated the air, letting it consume her. The sun glinted off her hair, and a friendly breeze bent down to kiss her face. *I feel like I've died and gone to Heaven*, she thought blissfully then laughed inwardly once it dawned on her that she had. Well, she wasn't really in Heaven yet, but Paradise was the next best thing.

After a few minutes of silence had passed, Gethyn looked at the Lord standing beside her in his spotless white robe and sandals and saw He was obviously enjoying the view as much as she was.

"It's beautiful, Lord," she commented, sighing deeply. "I hadn't planned on asking you questions, but I can't seem to help myself. Do you mind?"

Smiling at the tall, willowy young woman, Jesus answered, "I do not mind, child. What would you like to know?"

He loved Gethyn, finding her soul essence pleasing and her spirit like a flower on its tippy-toes reaching for the sun. Since she arrived, He could see her striving to take everything in and learn from everyone she met.

"How was the world created?" she asked, aware millions of people before her had probably asked Him the same question. "Was it made in a week like it says in Genesis of the Bible or are the scientists correct in their big bang theory?"

The deified man looked far across the horizon as though searching for the right words to answer. "Let me ask you this, Gethyn. Have you ever met a person who was really good at something? Say writing music, singing, or maybe woodcarving, cooking, or gardening?" The young woman shook her head yes, and Jesus continued. "God instilled one of His own personality traits into the heart of all mankind—a burning need to create. A need is stronger than a desire. A desire wants, while a need has to be satisfied. Someone who ignores their ability to create in the way he or she was gifted will never experience or understand the sheer and utter joy Heavenly Father felt when creating the world and everything in it. God loves creating so much that He wants everyone to know how it feels to make something from nothing, whether it is sewing a dress, building a cabinet, composing a song, or inventing something that never existed before. Whenever someone creates, Father says, 'That's my boy,' or 'That's my girl.' Just like earthly parents see themselves in their children, so too does God see Himself in His. Don't forget, He made man in His own image.

"Here's something I bet you didn't know. God doesn't just create. He *has* to create. It's part of who He is. Many people think that once He created the world, he retired. However, it isn't true. He's an artist with an unlimited imagination that cannot be contained, and as such, He is always creating something new for His children to eventually discover.

Before beginning a creation, He sees it in its completed stage in His mind and cannot rest until He has labored over it and brought it into being. The Bible is accurate, my beauty. As any artist will tell you, a masterpiece is not created in one sitting. It can take weeks, months, even years to create something of great importance. God's creation was not a single work of art, but a body of work that encompassed the whole universe. Each brush stoke was carefully thought out, each detail deliberate. Now as far as the scientists and their big bang theory, in a sense they are right as well. You might say the created world was the result of an *explosion* of God's thoughts upon the canvas of space and time."

Gethyn listened intently to every word Jesus was saying, appreciating how He explained things in a way she could comprehend. "That's amazing! I never thought about it that way!" The young woman rested her head against His shoulder, knowing there was nowhere in the world she would have rather been at that moment than with Him.

The two spent the afternoon casually drifting wherever the gentle wind currents carried them. Sometimes they talked and at other times fell into a comfortable silence. Although it had not been raining, at one point the most glorious rainbow Gethyn had ever seen appeared, stretching its band of colors across the New Jerusalem and the garden.

Jesus pointed to it and asked, "Do you see how the rainbow is comprised of many individual colors yet it represents a whole?"

The young woman nodded yes.

"So too are God's children," Jesus continued. "He created them in many colors, yet together, they represent the whole of mankind. Like the rainbow, one is not meant to stand out more than another. Each is beautiful. When God sees them come together as they were meant to be, it takes His breath away."

As it neared sunset, wisps of clouds moved slowly across the sky, trailing banners of pink and dark indigo behind them. The serenity of being up in the balloon combined with having Jesus's complete undivided attention led Gethyn to initiate conversations that pertained to things she had always found puzzling.

"Lord, how can God be everywhere at once?"

Jesus knew the young woman longed for the council of His wisdom and knowledge and was happy to shine a light on the myriad of questions she asked. As her Shepherd, He never tired of leading Gethyn to the well of truth so she might drink her fill until satisfied. There were many things that could not be easily explained, however, as the human mind was unable to comprehend the immense knowledge, wisdom, and power of Almighty God.

Jesus turned to face Gethyn, His stance noble and princely. "You are not alone in asking the question as most people seem to have trouble understanding omnipresence. 'All-knowing' and 'all-powerful' are concepts more easily understood by mankind. Everyone has met someone stronger or more intelligent than themselves, but no one has experienced being in more than one place simultaneously. For most, it's hard to imagine something they can't relate to personally."

Jesus gazed at the young woman, whose hair shone gold in the last embers of the sun and fell around her shoulders like a shawl. He thought it would make more sense if he offered the explanation in the form of an analogy, so after forming His thoughts, He spoke. "Gethyn, when you are standing on the ground your vision is limited to what you can see directly in front of you or around you. You have no idea what is happening down at the River of Life or in the New Jerusalem unless you happen to be in one of those places at the time. Is that not true?"

The young woman shook her head up and down, answering, "Yes."

The Lord made sweeping motions with his arms. and continued. "From this vantage point, however, what you were unable to see before is now possible. Correct?" The Lord looked into the young woman's eyes, which were as clear and blue as a cloudless sky. "When we speak of God's omnipresence, it doesn't necessarily mean He's *physically* present everywhere, any more than it means you're physically present everywhere right now because you're looking down at the garden and the city from this hot air balloon. Now that's not to say He isn't in all places at once, for He Is. In the broader sense of the word, what it means is that from His unique vantage point, the whole universe is present before Him, just as all of Paradise is present before you right now."

Gethyn tilted her head slightly to look into the handsome face that was framed with chestnut-colored hair. As though a lightbulb came on in her mind, she answered, "Of course! I see now!"

The exalted man spoke the words, and the wind guided their gradual descent. Gethyn hated to see their time together end as she had enjoyed having Jesus all to herself. Attempting to further prolong the inevitable, she asked, "Lord, may I ask one more question?"

He answered, "Yes, child. What would you like to know?" The young woman hemmed and hawed for a moment or two, as though uncomfortable or afraid to ask what was on her mind. "Lord, I know you're the only perfect person who has ever lived, but once I'm in Heaven, will I become perfect too?"

Jesus was not surprised by her question as he had read her thoughts. "Gethyn, let me answer by first asking you a question. What do you think 'perfect' means?"

The young woman thought for a moment or two before answering. "I think it means without sin."

The Lord corrected her, saying, "No, you're mistaken, but it seems most people have the same misconception. Actually, when someone is perfect in the biblical sense, it means they have reached full spiritual maturity. That is why churches, testimonies, Bible studies, and workshops continue here in Paradise. You see, whether a person lives to be a ripe old age or whether their life is cut short, they will continue striving for knowledge, wisdom, and understanding until they reach their full potential. That is why as on Earth and likewise in Paradise, when 'Thy Kingdom Comes,' even the most wise and learned man who has ever lived will still be as an infant in comparison to God's standard of perfection. Spiritual maturity is a process of evolution. It takes more years to acquire than there are grains of sand on the ocean floor."

Once the hot air balloon was safely on the ground, Jesus helped Gethyn out of the basket. As they walked up the mountain toward the city, the young woman looked at the lights of the spirits flickering in the distance and was reminded of a summer spent at her aunt and uncle's house in Georgia. She remembered that she and her cousins had chased fireflies on many warm summer evenings, but that was long ago in another life.

They stopped in front of the high-rise where the young woman lived. They embraced, and the radiant man kissed the girl on each cheek.

"Good-bye, Lord. I had such a wonderful time. Thanks for spending the day with me and for answering my questions," she said.

Jesus waved, and as though a vapor, He vanished.

The young woman stopped to greet Clarence, who stood holding the glass door open for her.

"Hi," she said. "I just had the most marvelous day with Jesus." Immediately afterward, she felt foolish, like someone who drops names to sound important, and the thought humbled her.

Gethyn went through the lobby with its atrium full of exotic plants and trees, past the built-in coves where people sat talking, and around to the elevator. When it arrived, she stepped into it and looked out the three-sided windows at the city, regal and resplendent in its evening clothes. The young woman played and replayed in her mind all she had seen and learned that day.

While I may never be perfect, it was a perfect day the Lord made, she thought. The car began its ascent, and Gethyn let the energy of her spirit rise to the level of her spiritual understanding. Once the elevator door opened, she reached into her jeans pocket for the golden key. At the door with the placard reading "Gethyn Fields," the young woman smiled and just for the fun of it clicked her heels together three times, saying, "There's no place like home."

24

Day Seven

An hour before sunrise, Gethyn heard a persistent knock on the front door. Puzzled, she crawled out of bed to answer it and was surprised to find her guardian angel standing there looking as though it had seen a ghost. Also with the angel was its tiger-eyed friend, Tanniz.

"What's the matter, Zendor," the young woman asked, concerned.

Words toppled like dominoes from the creature's mouth. "Something important has come up, and I won't be able to meet you in the garden this morning," Zendor said quickly in a voice riddled with nervous tension.

Still asleep, Gethyn mumbled, "What's happened? Why are you so upset?" She looked first at Zendor then at Tanniz while waiting for a response.

Tanniz stood silent as Zendor answered, "I don't know, but the Association of Angels has been summoned to meet at the assembly hall, and we are all required to attend. Meetings are only called every once in a blue moon, and when they are, it usually means there's a breach of security somewhere that needs to be addressed."

Reassuring the young woman, Zendor added, "There is no need for you to be alarmed though."

Gethyn watched as the towering angel opened the door to leave.

"God be with you," Zendor called out.

Gethyn reacted quickly, responding, "And with you as well."

With that, the two guardians turned and hurried quickly down the hallway to the elevator, leaving the young woman, who was now wide awake, puzzled as to what this new development meant.

It was a couple of hours before sunrise, and the city was unusually congested. Like five-o'clock rush hour traffic on Earth, angels were walking or flying in from all corners of Paradise and beyond. In no time at all, the assembly hall was filled beyond capacity with multitudes of celestial beings who had been summoned to appear, some of whom filled varying roles in the government of God.

Zendor had telepathically gotten word of the mandatory meeting just an hour before and decided to make a quick stop at Gethyn's apartment to inform her of the change in plans. On the way, the guardian ran into Tanniz, who, having already informed Jace, agreed to go with Zendor to fill

Gethyn in on the developing situation as they knew it. That being done, the two hurried to the meeting place. They flew above the gold-paved boulevard and once at the assembly hall were able to secure seats in the mezzanine section.

A buzz of nervous excitement filled the cavernous room as more and more angels came in and found seats. Not knowing why the meeting had been called, the celestials questioned each other in hopes that someone knew what was going on. They had only been seated approximately ten minutes when a loud rap of a gavel brought everyone's attention to the podium on the stage. There was a collective gasp as the angels saw before them a magnificent warrior who was ten feet tall, with eyes blazing and wearing a long tunic that came down to the knees as well as an armor breastplate. It was none other than the mighty archangel Michael, Field Commander of the Army of God. When the magnificent creature spoke, its voice was deafening.

"There is trouble in Paradise!" the archangel announced loud enough for everyone to hear.

Those five words ignited a wildfire of panic, as though a lit match had been dropped carelessly on dry brush in the middle of a drought.

But Michael's thunderous voice quickly doused the flame. "Silence!" the warrior commanded, and everyone quickly obeyed.

"I was with a regiment of soldiers stationed at an undisclosed encampment in a star field several thousand miles southeast of here when we heard chatter on the airwaves of a plan to overtake a convoy of guardian angels headed for Paradise. I hurried here at God speed to alert you that a terrorist cell has been detected and identified and are in fact en route as we speak. The regiment is monitoring the enemy's movements from a safe distance, and I have come to gather reinforcements before making a move. From what we have learned, it seems an angel of the second hierarchy belonging to the first choir of the dominions has fallen into temptation and been corrupted by Satan's lies. It has abandoned its duties and been coerced by the adversary to bring havoc to our home. Not only has the angel fell victim to Satan's seductive tactics but it has also encouraged lower-ranking angels to join in the mutiny."

Many voices rang out, "Who is the traitor!"

The archangel answered, "It is Bazari!"

There was a collective gasp of disbelief followed almost immediately by a multitude of angry voices.

Again, the warrior had to silence the crowd before continuing. "Bazari and the other recruits have disguised themselves as benevolent guardian angels. They fell in behind a convoy coming from Earth sometime after it had passed the border station. It is their intention to overtake the guardians and steal the precious spirits of God's children. They know the guardians will be defenseless as they are forbidden to let go of the spirit cradled in their arms until releasing them to Jesus at the River of Life.

"It is their sole intention to keep the spirit children from reaching the river. They know the human's spirits can't be claimed legally, as Jesus already purchased their freedom from the grave with His blood, so the next best thing is to devise and enact a cunning plan to prevent them from having their spiritual eyes opened. Satan does not want the Earth children to drink from the River of Life, for once their spiritual eyes have been opened and they have eaten of the fruit that ensures their survival on this realm, they are forever in the loving hands of the Lord for all eternity."

A voice in the crowd called out, "Why would they attempt such a thing? Don't they know God is aware of everything that happens in the universe? Not a blade of grass grows or raindrop falls that He is not cognizant of. Surely they must know they will be captured and what the ramifications of such a revolt would be!"

Angels began shaking their heads in agreement and mumbling to one another.

Before Michael could answer, another voice interjected, "Why would one of our own do something so foolish?"

Michael surveyed the assembly hall and the angels assembled before answering. "Bazari and the others have been duped and are merely pawns in the hands of the adversary. Satan has a way of searching out the vulnerability of others, which is clearly the case here. He has appealed to their pride and ego, convincing them of their ability to get one over on God. It is a sick game, as Satan knows they will never get away with the ill-considered plan. The Dark Prince laughs at their stupidity yet encourages them on the remote chance they might be successful. As you know very well by now, skirmishes with evil spirits are to be expected, and true to form, every few years we must deal with Satan's antics in one form or another. However, we cannot let the guardian angels or the innocent spirit children get caught in the middle of a conflict. We must take action!"

Angry voices filled the assembly hall, shouting, "Tell us what to do!"

Standing fierce and posed for battle, the archangel answered, "First, we need two choirs of angels to reinforce the outer gate of Paradise and several others to guard the twelve gates of the fortress walls of the city, ensuring none of the criminals manage to get past our army and defile the New Jerusalem."

Thousands of hands sprang up, offering to volunteer.

Michael looked out at those assembled, exuding a countenance of confidence and control. "We will beat Bazari and the other traitors at their own game. Just as the band of fallen angels is posing as guardians on their way to Paradise, we will have several hosts of armed angels posing as guardians on their way to Earth. No one will suspect anything out of the ordinary. We know the traitors are in the rear of the procession so as to keep the dim, waning light of their spirits from alerting the rest of the convoy. While they may have thought it was a clever tactical maneuver, it was not. They have failed to see the fatal flaw in their plan and that their strategy actually works to our advantage.

"Here is what we will do. Those of you posing as guardians headed to Earth will pass their procession but will circle back and come up behind them, careful to keep a safe distance. The archangels and I will take another route, meet up with my regiment, and then wait until everyone is in position. Make sure to have your swords concealed well inside your robes, and while en route, do not communicate by way of telepathy. It is imperative that neither the real guardians nor the enemy know what is about to happen, as panic would only serve to exasperate the situation and cause pandemonium. Once the order for attack is given, those of you disguised as guardians will quickly move in from the left and the right with swords drawn and station yourselves in front of the terrorists, cutting them off from the rest of the convoy. That is when I will position my regiment at the rear, sealing off the only remaining escape route. Once the enemy is engaged in battle, a band of soldiers will form a military escort around the real guardian angels and whisk them away, ensuring they deliver the spirits of the Earth children safely into the waiting arms of Jesus."

Once the battle plan had been outlined, Michael looked out among the faces of the Association of Angels and asked, "Are there any questions?"

A hand shot up. "How will we know when to make our move?" an angel asked.

Michael responded, "Good question. Once you have circled back, you will stealthily creep up behind Bazari and the others and wait for the sound of Gabriel's horn. The impostors will no doubt put up quite a struggle but will be no match for the army of the Lord."

When all questions had been answered, Michael shouted out his orders. "Bazari must be stopped! We must hurry! Follow me!"

The assembly hall vacated quickly with celestials scattering in every direction. Several choirs of angels ran to the inner wall of the New Jerusalem. They formed a tight circle around the holy city and posted reinforcements for those already standing guard at each of the twelve gates. They were determined not to let anyone or anything desecrate the holy city. At the same time, two large flocks of angels flew to the main gate and, using their bodies as a barricade, stood poised with swords ready for battle.

Zendor, Tanniz, and the other guardian angels were not soldiers; it was not their calling or God's purpose for them. They were guardian angels—angels of the lower third hierarchy. Their responsibility and duty was to see to the needs of their charges. There would be a notification once the enemy was apprehended and order was restored in the heavens.

Several hosts of angels assembled at the outer gate of Paradise and began their descent down the golden stairway with its thousand steps. Once they had all gathered on the landing area, they checked their weapons and then said a prayer for protection. Lastly, they changed their forms so as to appear as benign guardians.

The multitude of angels extended their wings, lifted off, and fell quietly into a *V* formation. They proceeded in a southerly direction towards Earth, all the while chanting, *"Holy, holy, holy is the Lord God Almighty. All of creation is full of His glory."*

The sky was pitch-black as there were no stars in this realm of space, the only light being that which the creatures projected from their spirits. They wasted no time as their mission was of a serious nature. It was critical they apprehend Bazari and his followers before the takeover could be executed.

After traveling quite some distance, a trail of light that looked like an arrow pointing north appeared in the distant horizon. The host of angels took note of the convoy, their senses on high alert. There was no telepathic chatter nor sound of wind rustling the feathers of their wings as they flew through the otherworldly silence. As the light from the approaching caravan drew closer, the hosts kept their eyes straight ahead, daring not to look to the right or left. Appearing as innocuous as possible, they passed within feet of the other convoy. They traveled a short distance past the convoy before banking their wings to the left and circling back. They did not make a sound or create a shadow as they crept up on the unsuspecting impostors. Once in position, they waited for the signal.

All of a sudden, Gabriel's horn sounded loud enough to wake the dead. Like the Red Sea parting, a host of angels numbering in the thousands quickly divided down the middle and surrounded the procession headed towards Paradise. With deliberate and calculated precision, one group cut through the convoy as easily as a knife slices through pie, putting a wall of separation between the guardian angels and the criminals.

The real guardians stopped and turned around in fright upon hearing Gabriel's horn and the mighty archangel Michael give a command to "Charge!" They hovered in place, mouths agape in disbelief, but could not see through the impenetrable barrier of angels who stood between them and Bazari's gang. In the blink of an eye, royal soldiers appeared, quickly whisking the convoy of guardian angels, along with God's spirit children, away from the battle that was about to take place.

With the guardians safely on their way to Paradise and Bazari and his followers surrounded, Michael, Raphael, Uriel, Gabriel, and a whole regiment of soldiers on horseback came galloping up out of nowhere. Bazari as well as the other fallen angels suddenly changed into hideous, grotesque, misshapen forms as whatever beauty their soul essence might have once possessed was now gone.

Michael bellowed, "Seize them!" There was the sound of metal swords clinking and clanking and a deafening roar of angry voices as the opposing forces met in a battle of will.

Provoked, God stepped into the theater of war. Space was transformed from what had been minutes before a calm sea of tranquility into a wild and raging tempest. Mighty rolls of thunder crashed violently throughout the heavens, the sound so loud that it was heard on Earth, causing some people to wonder if the End Times were upon them. Fingers of blue and silver forked lightening pointed accusingly at the traitors, and cold, stinging hail pelted them at every turn. Still, the cell of terrorists fought against God's army and His high-ranking hierarchy of angels.

Then the Lord and all His glory rode into the midst of the military campaign on a majestic black stallion, wearing a long white tunic with a royal blue velvet cape draped over His shoulders. On His head were many gold crowns, and in His hand was a jewel-encrusted sword. God smiled approvingly, moving aside to allow His Son to take charge.

The storm retreated suddenly, taking its arsenal of weapons with it. The exalted man got off His steed and handed the reins to a soldier who stood nearby. He walked into the fray, sword poised and ready to do battle.

In a loud, commanding voice heard above the cacophony of noise, the Lord demanded, "Who here dares to harm God's spirit children?"

Fighting ceased at once. Soldiers and angels retreated to the outskirts of the circle to allow the Lord to enter the battlefield. There was an eerie silence as all eyes turned to look at the band of traitors standing alone in the circle. It wasn't the first time Jesus's heart had been broken by betrayal.

The Son of God strode over to where the leader, Bazari, stood and asked, "Why?" It was a rhetorical question as Jesus already knew the answer. The Lord saw into the angel's spirit and saw that its integrity had been compromised, its soul corrupted.

The angel likewise looked into the eyes of the deified God-man and saw it was too late for remorse or forgiveness. Penetrating blue eyes bore into Bazari and then the others, each falling where they stood, unable to withstand the presence of the Lord.

With the revolt now over, the criminals were taken into custody. Bazari tried desperately to escape Raphael's iron-fisted grasp. The once-appointed angel of God screeched, sneered, and shouted vile threats of retaliation to any who would listen. In contrast, the others surrendered quietly, knowing that even if they could escape, there was nowhere to run and nowhere to hide. Raphael turned the captives over to Michael, who tethered the traitors together. The mighty warrior took a long length of rope and tied a loose knot around each of their necks, beginning with Bazari.

Once they were secure, the rope was tied to Michael's saddle horn.

The regiment of soldiers positioned their horses into two receiving lines facing each other and then extended their swords forward and at an angle, forming a military canopy for the King of Kings and His mighty archangels to pass through. They sat tall and proud atop their horses, breastplates polished and gleaming. The Son of God was a vision to behold as He rode through the canopy on His sleek black stallion with head held high and gold crowns in place. As He passed before them, each soldier hailed, "All glory and honor to the King!" The mighty archangel Michael, leading Bazari and the small band of fallen angels, followed the Lord, who in turn was followed by Raphael, Uriel, and Gabriel.

The Lord turned to face the multitudes. "Bring the traitors and meet me at the outer gate of Paradise." Like a shooting star, He shot across the sky on his stallion, followed closely behind by God's royal army and several hosts of angels.

Gethyn and Zendor had been walking around the city all morning. Although Zendor put on a good show of trying to act normal, the young woman could tell something was on the guardian's mind. They had been listening to life stories at the amphitheater and were just leaving when without a word of explanation, the angel whisked her up in its massive arms, spread its wings, and headed toward the skyscraper where Gethyn lived. It happened so fast that the young woman wasn't sure if her imagination was playing tricks on her or if she had indeed just felt the exhilarating sensation of flight.

Landing on the sidewalk in front of the tall skyscraper in a matter of moments, Zendor hurriedly ushered Gethyn past Clarence, through the lobby, and to the elevator. Once inside the cabin, Gethyn's euphoria was interrupted by her guardian's voice.

"I don't have time to explain right now. Just stay put and don't leave this apartment until I come back. Do you understand?" said Zendor emphatically.

The young woman had never seen the angel look or sound so serious, but before she had time to respond, it went to the window, opened it, and stepped out onto the ledge. Then, spreading wings that spanned twenty feet, Zendor took flight.

Gethyn ran to the window and stood watching until her guardian was out of sight. She couldn't imagine what was going on, her only clue being what Zendor had told her earlier that morning about there possibly being a breach of security. Soon, different scenarios played out in her imagination.

Is it the end of the world? she wondered, not being able to conjure up anything else in her mind that could interrupt

231

the safe haven of Paradise. Everywhere she looked, there were angels flying as fast as their wings would take them, as though being chased by time and worried it would catch up to them. Gethyn felt a foreboding current in the air and shivered involuntarily.

Members of the Assembly of Angels who had not been present at the battle gathered quickly at the outer gate of Paradise after being summoned telepathically. All had come to witness Bazari's fall from grace and those who had foolishly followed him, as it wasn't something that happened every day. They had not come to celebrate but to hear the Lord pronounce a death sentence upon the criminals.

It was common knowledge that without the guiding light of God, the once-valued angels would be forever lost. They had chosen their fate and each were aware of the dire consequences their actions would demand if caught. No one, including the Lord, could kill Bazari or the others as they were angels, albeit fallen ones, and were not subject to death or extinction. However, there was a fate much worse than death that awaited the criminals.

Angels numbering in the hundreds of thousands, possibly as many as a million, flocked to the outer gate and waited for the axe to fall, so to speak. The Lord, followed closely behind by the archangels, came galloping up to the landing and dismounted, as did the archangels. Not a word was spoken as they walked up the golden staircase with its creamy white banister.

Jesus spoke at length before excommunicating the fallen angels from Paradise and pronouncing them enemies of God. He untied the rope around their necks and then forced them to descend the long stairway. The Lord followed the criminals to the landing area and then, with His intense blue eyes, gave them a preview of the full measure of His wrath to come and the eternal damnation that awaited them. As the criminals cringed and writhed on their bellies in agony, their forked tongues darted in and out of their mouths like serpents.

The multitude of angels watched as the Lord extinguished the light in the spirits of Bazari and the others, casting them into outer darkness to await the Judgment. Without God's light to guide them, they would be lost, and their souls would forever live apart from God in a hell of their own choosing. It was a lesson for all to remember.

25

As Bazari and the likes of him were being expelled from Paradise, the procession of guardian angels carrying the spirits of God's children hurried quickly down the gold-paved boulevard with its tree-lined tributaries. It was approaching daybreak, and their only thought was of getting to the River of Life that ran through the Garden of Eden located in the center of the New Jerusalem. By the time they reached the riverbank, Jesus was already there in his pristine white robe, His face not revealing the slightest hint of what had just transpired. At precisely sunrise, He commanded, "It is time now for the spirits of God's children to awake."

Outside the garden, various choirs of angels were resuming their duties, and the telepathic grapevine was abuzz with celestials discussing the dramatic sequence of events.

As she had promised, Gethyn remained in her cabin until Zendor returned. Her eyes widened once she heard the startling account of events and was shocked to learn what Bazari and his converts had conspired together with Satan to do.

The young woman besieged the angel with her questions and fears. "What if one of my family or friends had been taken prisoner!" she cried.

"Don't be afraid," said Zendor, trying to discourage any thoughts of worry or panic. "Bazari never had a chance. God is and has always been in control, but every once in a while, Satan has to be reminded of that fact. Remember, Romans 8:38–39 says that neither death nor life nor angels nor principalities nor powers nor things present nor things to come nor height nor depth nor any other creature shall be able to separate us from the love of God, which is in Christ our Lord."

Zendor had things to discuss with the Lord and walked with Gethyn to the door. Once alone, the young woman sat in the comfortable chair by the fireplace, mulling over everything Zendor had said. In the end, she knew the guardian was right. God was in control, and those things that were over her head were under His feet. Knowing faith and doubt cannot coexist together, she let go of the thoughts troubling her and was immediately relieved of the burden she carried on her shoulders.

It had been a week since Gethyn first arrived in Paradise, and the young woman was feeling stronger every day. She thought of her new friends, Lottie and Clarence, and how they had each found their purpose. The red-headed beauty wondered how long it would be before she discovered something meaningful to do as well, secretly hoping it involved her passion for writing or her love of children. It was not unusual for Gethyn to fall asleep wondering when she was going to find her purpose. Then one night, she heard a prompting from her spirit, whispering, "You need not go in search of your purpose as you will not find it. Trust in the Lord and it will find you."

Having some free time and not really having a destination in mind, Gethyn left the high-rise and began wandering the gold city streets aimlessly. By some quirk of fate, the young woman bumped into Jace and silently hoped she wouldn't blush again or appear starstruck in his presence. The cowboy was good-looking enough to have been in commercials or movies and seemed genuinely happy to see her.

"Howdy, ma'am," he said, tipping his straw hat.

Gethyn curtsied and in her best southern accent returned the greeting. "Why, I declare, if it isn't the dashing Jace Covington."

They both laughed, and as the young man began to speak, he unconsciously polished the toe of his boot on his jeans leg.

"Now that the excitement is over, do you have any plans for the rest of the day?" he asked, testing the water between them.

"No," she replied honestly. "Zendor begged off, saying he had things to discuss with the Lord, so I'm on my own."

Gethyn saw a slight smile on the cowboy's lips.

"Tanniz did the same," remarked Jace. Taking her by surprise, the dashing cowboy looped his arm through hers and said, "Well then, pretty lady, I reckon you and me are just stuck with each other. Would you like to see what's down the yellow brick road?"

They both laughed. Gethyn felt a warm, tingling sensation come over her and fought the urge to give in to it. *What would Dave think?* she wondered to herself. *It's only been a week, and here I am off cavorting with someone I barely know.* Although it was true that Jace was virtually a stranger, the young woman knew with every fiber of her being that she didn't want him to be and felt conflicted by the tug of war going on in her heart.

Jace thought for a moment before making a suggestion. "Ma'am, I know of a little country church not too far from here, if you'd like to join me for service."

Gethyn looked into brown eyes the color of molasses and could almost see them begging her to say yes. She felt like an anvil going down in quicksand and pulled her eyes away from his before she disappeared altogether. She told herself no but was surprised to hear her voice answer "Yes, I'd love to go."

As the two fell into step, Gethyn began analyzing her decision. *This is not a date*, she told herself. *It's not like we're going to the movies or out to eat. We're going to church, for heaven's sake.* As the battle between her heart and mind waged on, the young woman was only vaguely aware that the tall cowboy was talking.

Gethyn found Dave in her thoughts and brought him to the forefront of her mind. She secretly pined over the fact they had been so close to being married. The invitations would never be mailed nor would she ever wear the beautiful gown she and her mother had chosen together. As she reluctantly followed the trail of breadcrumbs to where they led, the young woman realized her dad would never walk her down the aisle and she would never see the look of love on Dave's face as he stood waiting for her to join him at the altar. There would be no wedding vows made or a holy covenant between the two of them and God. It was not the ending she had hoped for. Once she had traveled down that road and back, she abandoned the thoughts that tortured her by the wayside.

Gethyn snapped back to the present as though being suddenly awakened from a trance. Before her was unimaginable beauty, and she was reminded of the conversation between her and Lottie about the healing power of beauty. As her friend before her had done, the young woman surrendered her pain, trusting beauty's adept hands to make something "purdy" grow in the barren soil of her heart.

Jace led Gethan down a lovely yet remote garden path that she had never seen before. Everywhere the two walked were flowers and plants of varying hues and scents, reminding them of God's creative genius and diversity. They passed through a grove of live oak trees with Spanish moss hanging from its boughs, and they came upon a quaint-looking little white chapel nestled among several mature magnolias. The fragrance of the blossoms evoked memories of Gethyn's grandparents' house.

The young woman had seen many churches like this one when passing through small, postage stamp–sized country towns on her way to somewhere else. They all seemed to be made of clapboard, with double doors, stained glass, a bell tower, and a tall pointed steeple pointing the way to Heaven. She had always wanted to stop and go inside one of them and had at many times imagined herself sitting on one of the smooth wooden pews singing standards from a red bound hymnal.

There was not a soul in sight as they walked up the steps to the double doors. Before entering, Jace reverently removed his cowboy hat, and then the two of them walked down the center aisle and took a seat in the third row. The interior looked exactly as the young woman had imagined.

"Where are all the people?" asked Gethyn, having expected to see a congregation.

Jace turned his face towards hers and smiled. The young woman didn't know if it was his even white teeth or the dimples that rivaled the depths of the Grand Canyon that she found irresistible.

Taking her hand, the cowboy playfully answered, "I reserved this chapel especially for you, little lady."

Gethyn giggled, liking this man more than she knew she should.

He patted the top of her hand with his other, chuckling as well. "I'm just kidding. For convenience's sake, most people like to attend one of the bigger churches in the city. I do too, but sometimes I like to slip away by myself and come here. There's something about worshiping in this little country chapel that takes me back to my simple Oklahoma roots. The one I went to back home was full of salt-of-the-earth people who were unpretentious, humble, and worked hard for a greenback dollar. Most were farmers or ranchers who worked from daylight 'til dark. You know, not a one of them would have thought twice about helping one of their neighbors, even if it meant they themselves would go without."

Gethyn looked sideways, meeting Jace's gaze again, and saw in his soul essence the same qualities he attributed to his neighbors. She had to admit, good looks aside, there was much to admire and respect about the man.

Had the young woman met the ruggedly handsome cowboy before Dave, she knew she would no doubt have been attracted to him just as she was now. Gethyn had to keep reminding herself that she was dead, and any romantic notions concerning Jace were pointless, regardless of her fiancé. The truth of the matter was there would never be a holy union with Dave, Jace, or anyone else. Not only that but the blessing of children she had hoped for someday was a dream she would have to put to bed. Like a vinyl record with only one song called "What If," it continued to play over and over until the young woman couldn't bear it anymore. She pulled her hand away from Jace's, reminding herself that that part of her life was over and that her soul must find a new song to sing.

Even though the two were the only ones in the church, Gethyn still whispered as though someone might hear their private conversation. "Do you think we should go?"

Jace slicked back his auburn hair with one hand. "No, ma'am," he whispered back. "As long as we're here, we might as well call on the Lord and let Him minister to us."

Gethyn agreed. They summoned Jesus with their thoughts, and the lovely little chapel was instantly bathed in the light of His presence. The exalted man stood in the aisle, smiling at the young couple seated to his left.

"Gethyn, Jace, how wonderful to see you today. Isn't this a lovely, little, out-of-the-way place to come worship?" Jesus surprised them both when he added, "I come here myself at times when I want to be alone and pray."

Jace sat up a little straighter on the hard wooden pew. "Yes, sir, I was just telling Gethyn how much I love coming here and how it reminds me of my church back on Earth. I know there's nobody here except the two of us, but we were hoping to hear a sermon. Would you mind?"

The noble-looking man smiled graciously, responding, "It matters not if there are two people or two thousand gathered in my name. If one of my sheep calls, then I must go to him." The deified man in the white robe and brown sandals walked with dignity to the altar. He rested His hands on either side of the podium before beginning His lesson.

Gethyn sat mesmerized by the Lord. She tried to imagine Him standing in the boat on the Sea of Galilee preaching to the people gathered on the shore. It seemed surreal that He was standing in front of her talking about how the meek would inherit the Earth. The beautiful young woman wondered how long it would be before she believed the life she was experiencing was really real. She had to admit there were times when she felt like Alice in Wonderland and wondered if she had accidentally fell down the rabbit hole.

The Lord's voice was both charismatic and appealing, his timbre unlike any other. Both Jace and Gethyn hung on every word, taking them to heart.

When the service was over the exalted man walked Gethyn and Jace to the church doors and bid them Godspeed. "God be with you till we meet again," He called out as the couple began walking up the garden path.

Gethyn turned around and called out, "Yes, Lord! Till we meet again!" A song of the same title had been one of her favorites and had even been sung by her brother,

Emmit, at her funeral. Had she known, she would have been pleased.

Jace took Gethyn a different route on the way back, and as they came out of the garden, they could see the city all aglow on the distant mountain. They stepped off the gold-paved boulevard to take a seat on a bench overlooking one of the tributaries. While it was still fresh on their minds, they began discussing the sermon they had just heard.

The topic had been about the meek inheriting the Earth, but Gethyn wasn't exactly sure what being meek meant. "Surely Jesus hadn't meant people who were pacifists, weak, or timid would inherit the Kingdom of God?" she wondered silently. She was confused. Thinking Jace might know, Gethyn asked him.

The cowboy sitting beside her looked like a movie star, although when he spoke, it was evident he was much more than a pretty face; he had depth and character. The man responded, "I reckon I have a purdy good idea." He crossed his leg, resting the weathered straw hat on his knee.

Gethyn looked at Jace's blue jeans and blue chambray shirt, glad to be wearing comfortable clothes as well. "Could you explain it to me?" she asked. As she waited for him to answer, she began tallying up his virtues. The young woman thought him to be the most polite man she had ever met. He always called her "ma'am" and answered "Yes, ma'am" or "No, ma'am," "Thank you," and "Please." She was sure his mama had been proud of his good manners.

"We used the word 'meeked' on the ranch when describing a horse that has been broken into a bit. What it means is that once a horse has yielded its power by accepting the bit, the rider can then harness its strength and guide the horse to do whatever he wants him to do. So I reckon in terms of people, once a person yields or surrenders to Jesus, the Lord can then redirect their strength and guide them in the direction they need to go. When Jesus says the meek shall inherit the Earth, I believe he is referring to those who willingly surrender and accept Him as the Lord of their lives so He may direct their path."

Gethyn was enlightened by the explanation and thanked Jace.

The cowboy looked across the distant horizon and said, "You know, those despicable angels bent on defiling God's holy city and preventing the spirit children from reaching the River of Life this morning are perfect examples of those who are not meek. Their actions proved the immaturity of their spirits. They let pride and ego direct their actions until they had lost their desire to surrender to God's will. Those who say 'My will be done, and not yours, Lord' aren't going to inherit anything except a one-way ticket to Hell."

As time passed, their conversation turned to other topics. Without even being consciously aware of it, they had tuned out their surroundings and the people in it until they were the only two in Paradise. When the day finally turned to dusk, Gethyn and Jace walked up the mountain and through the inner gate of the New Jerusalem. They leisurely strolled down the gold city sidewalks enjoying the lights, just as any other young couple who were in no hurry for the night to end.

26

Day Eight

Once awake, Gethyn pitter-pattered around the cabin, reflecting on all the things she had learned and all that had happened since arriving in Paradise.

Has it really only been a week since I died? the young woman thought to herself. So much had transpired and she was still trying to process it all.

In a sense, every day was an adventure into the unknown, and Gethyn was finding her new life stimulating, exhilarating, and liberating. Bouts of homesickness were becoming less frequent as the young woman became more acclimated to Paradise. Occasionally during quiet times alone, there were pangs of longing for those she had left behind on Earth, but it was comforting to know that for everything she had lost, something had been gained. While her parents, brother, and friends were temporarily lost to her, she was thrilled to be reunited with her grandparents and other relatives as well as having made new friends. Although she would never accomplish the dreams she had while living on Earth, it didn't matter, for she was beginning to envision the new Earth, a place called Heaven, and the opportunities that awaited her. Gethyn remembered a quote she had read once by Marsha Norman. It said, "Dreams are illustrations…from the book your soul is writing about you." The young woman knew her story would continue to unfold in Paradise and then in Heaven, where hopes and dreams planted in its fertile soil would come to life.

The young woman left the apartment and walked down the corridor to the elevator. By now, she had met many people who lived in the high-rise, and they chatted amicably while making the descent to the lobby.

Clarence opened the door for Gethyn, and she stopped to talk for a few minutes as had become her custom. The young woman smiled as she saw Arie-Ann, Dolly, and her childhood friend, little Stevie, holding hands and skipping toward them on the sidewalk.

"Where are you children off to this morning?" she asked, giving them all a beautiful smile.

"Hi, Gethie!" exclaimed Stephen, his baseball hat askew. "We're goin' to the garden to look for butterfries!"

The two girls giggled, and then Arie-Ann, the worldly one of the three, spoke up. "He's trying to say 'butterflies,' but it comes out wrong because he's missing a front tooth."

Gethyn smiled. "Oh, I know exactly what he's saying. Stevie and I go way back, don't we, Stevie?"

The boy's head nodded up and down like a bobblehead doll. "Yep. Gethie is my bestest friend in the whole wide world."

Remembering how she had to strain her neck to see Zendor's face, she knelt down until she was at eye level with the children. "Now you do know there are no butterflies in the garden or anywhere else in Paradise, don't you?"

Dolly, with her long corn silk hair and sea-green eyes, put her hands on her hips and answered for all of them. "Of course we know, you silly goose. We're just playing make-believe."

Playing along, Gethyn asked, "And what will you do if you find any make-believe butterflies?"

Arie-Ann looked at the young woman as though she were daft, answering, "We'll catch them with our invisible butterfly nets."

They all had a good laugh—the children, Gethyn, and Clarence. The trio waved good-bye then skipped across the street, leaving joy and laughter in their wake. Gethyn watched little Stevie and marveled at his zest and vitality, all the while silently praising God in her heart for restoring the boy's health and childhood.

"Well, I guess I'd better go find Zendor," Gethyn told Clarence.

"Okay, we'll see you later. Have a great day!" he answered.

The young woman crossed the wide gold-paved boulevard and headed for the garden entrance. She loved being in the sanctuary and found it to be as beautiful and peaceful as she had always imagined it would be. Gethyn couldn't believe Adam and Eve had once lived here, eating the same fruit that grew on the banks of the River of Life as she did every day and had enjoyed the same flowers, trees, and pathways. She was reminded of a conversation she had with Jesus during one of His evening visits. Gethyn had asked Him about the one thing she had found missing from the garden: the Tree of Life. She had listened intently as the Lord told her humans would not be allowed to eat from it until "Thy Kingdom Come," as the fruit of its branches gave eternal life.

"Lord, I don't understand," she had said. "There are people in Paradise who are hundreds, if not thousands, of years old. If we won't be eternal until we are in Heaven, then what are we now?"

Jesus had smiled when she asked, pleased with her desire for truth and knowledge. "Because you are a human being, you require daily sustenance to maintain your temporary body just as you did on Earth. In Heaven, after Father has reunited your physical body with your soul and spirit, He will also restore the Tree of Life to the garden. You will only need to eat from it once, as after you have tasted its fruit, you will never grow weak or tired again. Eternity will course through your veins, giving you endurance, stamina, and superhuman capabilities unimaginable."

Zendor had been sitting on the low-hanging branch of the ancient oak tree by the River of Life waiting for her, and he hopped down when she approached on the pathway. The colossal angel smoothed his robe and fluffed his feathers a little then met her halfway.

"Isn't it just the most beautiful day?" Gethyn gushed.

"That it is," replied the angel, smiling. As blue and yellow sparks burst from the angel's pale amethyst eyes, Gethyn realized how much she had come to love Zendor and felt safe and comforted in the knowledge that she and the winged creature had a bond that would last for all time.

"Do you have any plans for us?" asked the redhead as she walked over to one of the fruit trees.

While she was making her selection, Zendor suggested, "Well, I thought we might see what's happening down at Martyr Field, as it's not too far from here."

Right before taking a bite of the sugary sweet fruit, Gethyn asked, "What kind of sports do they play there?"

For a moment, her mind envisioned a football game between the angels and the saints with Jesus as referee. The thought caused her to smile.

"They don't play sports there, Gethyn," Zendor informed her. "It's where all those who have been martyred and persecuted in the name of Jesus gather. Every day, people and angels alike come to the field to pray with them and to ask God to avenge their blood. Hearing their testimonies of faith is very powerful and inspiring, as they refused to denounce Christ even as they were being tortured and killed."

The two walked for a good ways until coming to a huge outdoor arena, larger than any football stadium Gethyn had ever seen. Actually, the size and architecture of the structure reminded the young woman of the Roman Colosseum. Gethyn heard a loud thunderous sound emanating from inside that frightened her, but she soon realized it was the result of thousands of voices shouting as well as people stomping their feet.

As the two entered and looked for a place to sit, they saw that the bleachers were filled to capacity. Then like an answered prayer, Lottie's voice was miraculously heard over the commotion. "Honey-chile'! Zendor! Come over here! I got room for you!"

Gethyn and the towering angel excused themselves as they stepped over feet in an attempt to reach the old black woman. "Thanks, Lottie! This place makes me think of the days of the Romans and gladiators!" the young woman exclaimed.

"I reckon so, but thank the Lawd they ain't feeding Christians to the lions today."

Another loud roar went up through the crowd, with people expressing their enthusiasm by clapping, cheering, and stomping their feet as loudly as possible. Curious about running into her friend in such a strange place, Gethyn felt compelled to ask Lottie about it. She waited for the cacophony of noise to die down and then leaned over.

"I'm surprised to see something could drag you away from tending your garden," she teased.

"Honey-chile'," Lottie said, bumping her shoulder against Gethyn's good-naturedly, "I do lots of things besides plantin' flowers. I go to church, I meditate on scripture, I talk with the Lawd, visit with my chillun, and other things, including coming to this here place."

Persistent, Gethyn asked, "Why here?"

The old black woman took hold of Gethyn's hand and squeezed it as her muddy brown eyes looked into those that looked like a tropical ocean. "I comes to this place causin' it keeps ol' Lottie humble. There's two reasons I come, to tell you the truth. The first one is to remind myself that my toils and troubles on the Earth was nothin' compared to them out there on the field. And the second reason I come is just in casin' I begin to think I's really some-um' and start gettin' all high and mighty. Sometimes we all need to be knocked down a peg or two. Comin' here reminds ol' Lottie what real love and sacrifice is so I never forget."

Gethyn threw her arms around the old black woman and hugged her. Their eyes turned to the field where hundreds of thousands of people walked around the inner perimeters of the arena, waving as though part of a parade. Zendor, who sat on the other side of Gethyn, told her the names of each martyr, explaining how each person had died a horrible death at the hands of those who did not possess the milk of human kindness.

The young woman learned the first persecution of the church took place in the year 67 under the sixth emperor of Rome, whom many atrocities were directly attributed to. He had no compunction about having Christians dressed in shirts made stiff with wax, fixed to axletrees, and then set on fire to illuminate his garden. His insanity included sewing people up in skins of wild beasts and then feeding them to the dogs. Years later, another emperor blamed Christians for any form of famine, earthquake, or pestilence, and as such ordered them slain. Zendor pointed out one man named Ignatius who died in AD 108 after being thrown to the lions by the current emperor of that time. As the Christian met his fate, he said "I am the wheat of Christ. I am going to be ground with the teeth of wild beasts, that I may be found pure bread."

As one martyr after another passed in front of them, Zendor schooled Gethyn on the many evil, bloodthirsty emperors and rulers of long ago. She learned over the centuries that there had been no shortage of ways employed to torture and kill people for their Christian beliefs. The young woman felt sick upon learning how believers were burned at the stake, beheaded, devoured by beasts, and thrown off precipices. Others had their brains dashed out with clubs, were boiled in oil, had hot plates of brass pressed to tender areas of their bodies, or were pressed to death with weights. As if those acts weren't cruel or torturous enough, she learned others were sawed in half or had their limbs pulled apart.

As Gethyn listened to the individual stories of the Christian martyrs, she wept openly. Even as a child, she had wanted to heal the wounds of the world, but the crimes inflicted upon these courageous believers could not be bandaged, at least not by her. Jesus was the only one with the power to heal them and make them whole again. At first, her heart was broken by the testimonies she heard, but after a while, righteous anger replaced her tears. When the crowd stood up to honor the martyrs as they passed, Gethyn rose too. Her voice blended in with the deafening roar that erupted throughout the stadium, as she, Lottie, Zendor, and others raised their fists, shouting, "Avenge them, oh God, for their blood runs like a river of sorrow down through the ages."

As the day wore on, a cloud of conviction hung over the arena as everyone present stood united in their quest for justice. For several hours, Zendor and Gethyn prayed fervently along with thousands of others gathered at Martyr Field. By the time they said good-bye to Lottie and made their way toward the young woman's apartment, her voice was hoarse. While Gethyn's spirit had initially felt weak and faint by the horrendous stories of the martyrs, she soon rose to the occasion, asking for God's wrath and vengeance to visit those who had so grievously and wrongfully persecuted and slain innocent men, women, and children.

Zendor saw the young woman to her door, and once inside, she immediately knelt by the bed and prayed. Afterward, she went to the closet for her white robe. After what she had witnessed, she not only wanted to feel clean; she *needed* to feel clean. Gethyn removed her jeans and T-shirt and slipped into the robe Jesus had given her.

Jesus is right, she thought to herself. The longer she was in Paradise, the more she wanted to rid herself of earthly things. The clothes she had been wearing since her arrival no longer felt comfortable against her skin, for they had come to symbolize the sin-filled corrupt world from which she came. Thinking of the martyrs, Gethyn felt both sick and angry all over again. She thought of the depths of inhumanity and depravity man was capable of committing against one another, and it didn't bide well with her soul.

27

Gethyn summoned Jesus with all her heart as she needed the comfort and reassurance of His words. At once, His presence was before her. "Oh Jesus," she cried, falling into His arms.

The beautiful man held her while she sobbed uncontrollably, and when at last the tears subsided, He placed gentle hands on her delicate shoulders and held her at arm's length away from Him. He looked deep into her troubled blue eyes, and although He knew the young woman's thoughts, He let her speak her heart.

"My child, what grieves you so?" he said with compassionate concern.

"Zendor and I went to Martyr Field today, and I was overwhelmed and horrified by what I heard and saw. Please tell me there will be a just punishment for those who committed such cruel and unnatural crimes against God's children." Gethyn looked up into the Lord's eyes and found the answer there: the day of reckoning would come.

The radiant man embraced the girl and kissed the top of her head. "Let's sit and talk for a while, and I will tell you of things to come."

Gethyn curled up in her chair, and Jesus took the other. Once both were comfortable, the exalted man spoke.

"After the millennial reign of Christ, Satan will be loosed from prison where he will once again try to deceive and entice man into revolting against God. Rather than the battle he expects to take place, God will intervene in a climactic, cataclysmic way. Satan, along with his army, will be consumed by the full fury of God's fiery wrath and will dwell for all eternity in terror, pain, and torment in the Lake of Fire and Brimstone.

"The books will then be opened, and as written in Revelations 20:12, the dead both great and small will stand before God. The first book opened will be the Book of Records, containing the works of both believers and unbelievers. What is written there will determine the just rewards given to those found innocent after having been cleansed by the blood of Jesus. On the other hand, the degree of punishment merited for those whose deeds have not been forgiven will be given as well. Another book will be opened called the Book of Life, and those whose names are not written in it will die a second death.

"Many people don't understand why God doesn't punish people right away for their crimes. There is good reason, however. You see, once a sin has been committed, it causes a ripple effect as the circle of corruption widens. It not only widens but it filters down from one generation to the next, continuing to contaminate and ruin lives until the end of time.

"God is keeping a tally of everyone who has ever stumbled and fallen as well as one for those who caused the fall. Those who are defiant and unrepentant, who refuse to confess their sins and beg for mercy, will eventually stand before God Almighty at the Great White Throne for judgment and sentencing. I assure you those who have not been born twice will die twice and be forever separated from God. They will be found guilty, punished, and consigned to the Lake of Fire. However, their stripes will not be as severe as the one who gave them a platform to commit sins against themselves and others. Woe be to the pornographers and those who deal in human trafficking in that day of reckoning. Woe be to those who have persecuted and slain someone who believed in me. The day of their judgment draws ever nearer."

Gethyn was in no hurry for the Lord to leave as she loved learning from the Master Himself. During the day while exploring the garden and the New Jerusalem, the young woman would think of questions to ask Jesus during their visits. She thought back to when Jesus told her about her death, yet she still kept coming back to one question.

While He was there, she decided to ask, "Lord, how does God decide who's going to die and when? I mean, it seems like it would get really complicated, there being so many people and all."

Although the circle of radiant light surrounding Jesus gave Him an otherworldly appearance, His countenance remained down to earth. The deified man looked upon the girl with the red-gold titian hair, heart-shaped face, and blue eyes that were always curious to see with clarity. He smiled at Gethyn, who was curled up in the chair with feet tucked beneath her, like a wide-eyed baby bird huddled in its nest waiting to be fed.

"While it is true everyone's days are numbered, God's prior knowledge of the particulars of a person's demise is due to His being omniscient and omnipresent. Being the Alpha and Omega, it is only He who has the ability to see the past, present, and the future simultaneously," the Lord informed the young woman.

"People perish every day from disease, old age, accidents, murder, and suicide, yet for some reason, many choose to believe God sits on His mighty throne dictating whose day it is to die and how. What they don't realize is most often, it is they themselves who choose the manner in which they will part from life on Earth, as God the Father is the Creator of life, not a mad conductor orchestrating death.

"Many die of their addictions. Have you ever known any procrastinators, Gethyn? They drink, smoke, or use drugs, knowing their vices bring increased risks of contracting cancer, emphysema, cirrhosis of the liver, hepatitis C, or

HIV. They tell themselves, 'I will quit someday, but not today.' Theirs is a slow, lingering death of their choosing, not God's. He wishes people to live a long, abundant life. Others choose food as their weapon of choice, clogging their arteries with fatty food. They ignore warning signs of high blood pressure, diabetes, and out-of-control cholesterol levels. I've heard them make resolutions to begin exercising and eating healthy yet give up easily. The Father and I weep when they die of heart attacks and strokes, knowing their lives didn't have to end that way.

"How about the risk-takers who seem to have a death wish? They perform dangerous and unnecessary feats for the thrill of the adrenaline rush they get by tempting fate. They enjoy playing Russian roulette with their lives, and even when injured, they continue pushing the envelope. Other risk-takers are those who join gangs or become involved in various criminal activities, knowing there is a strong likelihood of being gunned down on the street, either by others like them or the law. Yet they maintain they have no choice because they were born into that life. While true they may have been born into that life, it is their choice whether they stay in it or leave. Everyone has a choice.

"War kills a lot of people. Sometimes war is necessary, sometimes not. Father especially hates war led by arrogant men with no tolerance for religious differences. God and religion are two different things. There are those who have religion yet do not know God. War kills a lot of people, righteous and unrighteous alike. Some die honorably in service, proudly protecting the rights and freedom of their fellow countrymen, while others spill blood for its own sake in the hope of propagating hatred. There are martyrs who choose to subject themselves to torturous deaths rather than renounce their religious beliefs, while others quietly kill themselves after finding the pain of living unbearable.

"Some people find themselves in the wrong place at the wrong time, helpless to escape the circumstances that have befallen them. They belong to the group of innocents—those who are too young, old, weak, or naïve to protect themselves. In the case of murder victims, they do not choose to die nor are they allowed to choose the manner of their deaths. Death is imposed upon them against their will. Aborted fetuses fall into this category as well. Although God is angered and sickened by man's inhumanity to man, He cannot interfere with one's free agency, even when it is used to commit evil deeds.

"Some deaths are the result of living in an imperfect, natural world. There are people who die in tornadoes, hurricanes, tsunamis, and earthquakes, while others are struck by lightning or drown in a flash flood. Too, death can come as a result of someone growing old, their body literally wearing out.

"In the end, most people die from choices they themselves make at some point in their lives, and it is that decision, not God's, that sets their death in motion. It was your choice, my beloved, to drive home even though you knew you were tired and driving conditions were not favorable. Once you fell asleep and your car went over the side of the mountain, gravity took over, and there was nothing or no one who could save you. Not Zendor, not me, not even God. God cannot reverse laws He Himself made and put into effect.

"God weeps when one of His children dies, especially if it could have been prevented. However, like any father whose child falls and skins its knee, He picks them up, dries their tears, and comforts them. Then He carries them home, knowing the pain will soon be forgotten and that many new adventures await them."

When it was time to part, she told the Lord how much she loved Him and how she never wanted to live apart from Him or God. They embraced, and He kissed her on both cheeks and she kissed Him as well.

Once Jesus had gone, Gethyn stood at the window in her clean white robe, letting her light shine for all to see. She felt each time they were together, her spirit glowed a little brighter from having received the light of His truth. And it was true.

28

Day Nine

Before Gethyn was even awake, there was a light tapping at the front door. She rose from bed and upon opening it found Philena standing there, smiling demurely. Gethyn was still having trouble wrapping her mind around the fact that Philena McClary, who was younger than her, was in fact her fifteenth great-grandmother. To the titian-haired young woman, it seemed life and death were as two old friends whispering mysteries of untold things back and forth between the veils of secrecy each wore.

"Hi, Philly," Gethyn said, opening the door to allow the girl to come in. Although surprised, she motioned for Philena to come in and while doing so stole a quick glance out the window, trying to gauge the time. The sun was just beginning to crest, and soon the sky would be filled with shades of lavender and rosy pink.

"Art early, thee knows. But alas, 'tis something thee desireth to show ye. The day wilt get busy before long, and I hope to prevail upon ye to walk with thee this bright and early morn."

Gethyn had nothing else planned, and a walk in the city before everyone was awake sounded nice.

"Where are we going?" the young woman asked once they had greeted Clarence and gone through the heavy glass doors of the skyscraper.

Philena's light green eyes crinkled in a smile. "'Tis a surprise. Ye wilt have to wait and see." The Quaker girl looped her arm around Gethyn's as they strolled down the sidewalk, Philena in the plain clothing of the Quakers and Gethyn in her comfortable faded jeans, T-shirt, and tennis shoes.

It was nice having the city to themselves. It was quiet, their footfall being the only sound. Gethyn admired the architecture of buildings as they passed, wondering about the day when God would finally proclaim "Thy Kingdom Come." The young woman tried to imagine people engaging in various forms of commerce, not only in and around the city but on the new Earth as a whole.

I wonder what I'll be doing then? she thought to herself. In her mind, Gethyn thought about all the exotic places she had yearned to see—Paris, London, Greece. Although she had not lived long enough to experience traveling abroad, it filled her heart with immense joy to know that in

Heaven, she would have unlimited time to go everywhere and do everything she had ever dreamed of. Gethyn tried imagining what it would be like to live in a world without crime, pollution, sin, sickness, or death—a place where she could go everywhere her heart ever desired without fear of conflicts, wars, or time running out. The one thing she looked forward to most was a world where there was no hate, greed, or ulterior motives in people's hearts, where everyone genuinely loved and cared about each other. As the young woman walked arm in arm with Philena, she gave herself over to embrace whatever new and wonderful things the day had to offer.

Gethyn didn't know how far they had walked before they stopped in front of a large complex comprised of many buildings, some of which were several stories high. Philena steered the young woman toward one of the larger buildings, and they climbed steep steps before entering its massive doors. Inside was an enormous gallery with a domed ceiling where thousands of beautifully framed paintings of children, all wearing white, hung. Some were of a single child, while others depicted two or more children. There were also paintings of babies sleeping peacefully, and as Gethyn looked upon them, she felt a little pang of regret upon knowing that she would never experience having a child of her own. She moved around the gallery, struck by how the artist had managed to bring out the best feature of each child, whether it was their smile, eyes, or dimples.

Each painting was a brilliant masterpiece, but what amazed Gethyn most was how the beauty and simplicity of each child's innocence was so perfectly captured.

"Philly, these paintings are so lifelike! I wonder if they were inspired by real children?" exclaimed the young woman.

The Quaker girl whispered quietly, "Aye," as though afraid of disturbing someone. "I know for certain these paintings are of wee ones who once lived on Earth."

Gethyn looked at Philena and asked "How do you know?"

Without hesitation, the girl answered, "Because I hath seen them here."

The tall, willowy redhead stopped to look at her friend, her eyes wide in astonishment. "All these children are here in Paradise?"

The Quaker girl's green eyes twinkled in delight as she took Gethyn by the arm. "Come, I wilt show thee."

The two of them walked down a long glass hallway that opened up into another building. They found an elevator and let it take them where they needed to go. When the door opened, Gethyn saw a nursery large enough to hold several hundred infants and was told there were several more floors containing thousands more. There were many men and women in the room as well, walking with babies or sittings in rockers singing soft lullabies as they rocked a little one to sleep. Guardian angels were there as well, watching over innocent babes.

As the two of them passed row after row of bassinettes, Gethyn asked, "Who are these babies, and why are they here?"

Philena's hands found the deep pockets in her plain olive dress and in her gentle, soft-spoken way answered, "These wee souls were stillborn or died in infancy and art a-waiting for thine parents to arrive and claim them."

Gethyn took in the information before firing a volley of questions. "But what if a child's parents aren't believers? What will happen to them? Will they stay in this room forever?"

The Quaker girl had anticipated the question and had looked forward to the moment when she could share the answer with Gethyn. Facing her, Philena took Gethyn's hands in hers. "No. If that be the case, the wee one mayest be adopted. Those who were unable to bear wee babes of their own on Earth shalt be able to experience the joy of being a parent, and those who lost their wee ones for whatever reason shalt be reunited and have the opportunity to raise the babe they thought was lost, nary to be separated again. The men and women ye see here art not the birth parents of the wee ones, but they find purpose in comforting the spirits of the babes until someone comes forth to claim them."

After touring the floors where the babies were kept, Philena showed Gethyn where the toddlers lived and then the young children. As was the case with the infants, volunteers and guardians provided love and nurture to God's innocents. The surroundings were bright and happy, and it was evident each child was thriving in their environment.

On one floor, Gethyn saw a charming little freckled-face girl with red braids. She noticed the child was wearing peasant clothes with a babushka on her head that was tied under her chin. The young woman went over to the miniature table and chair where the girl was preparing for a tea party. As Philena was preoccupied with another child, Gethyn asked if she could join the child for tea.

The voice of the little girl had an enchanting musical quality and very sweetly, she answered, "I am preparing for a visit from the Lord. I'm sure He won't mind if you join us, and neither will I."

Although she couldn't speak the language, Gethyn recognized the girl's dialect as being Russian and understood everything that was said. She smiled, and took a seat in one of the child-sized chairs.

"I am Gethyn. What is your name?"

The pint-sized girl answered, "Anya Nicolin."

Before their conversation went any further, Jesus appeared and was graciously showed a seat by the child. Anya seemed pleased to serve make-believe tea and cookies to Gethyn and the Lord but could not be persuaded to sit with them.

"*Nyet, spasiba.* (No, thank you.) You are my guests, and I want you to feel welcome."

The Son of God was most pleased as he looked upon the child who had the heart of a servant. After the make-believe refreshments were gone, Jesus said, "Come," calling for the child.

She climbed onto His lap, and He asked "Anya, would you like to hear a true story?"

She nodded her head, replying, "Da," which meant yes in her native tongue.

The man who was a friend to children everywhere spoke. "Anya, did you know someday I will host a wedding banquet for my bride, and all who receives an invitation will dine with me?"

The child's eyes grew excited, and she asked, "When will that be, Lord?"

Jesus smiled, playfully tugging on one of the girl's braids. "Not until my bride is ready, but the day is drawing near."

By the time Gethyn and Philena were ready to leave the complex, they had played and interacted with several of the children, although Gethyn had developed a special feeling for Anya. Maybe it was because they both had red hair, although she thought it was more than that. Whatever it was, she felt drawn to the five-year-old.

"Will you come back to see me?" the child asked, leaving Gethyn's heart a puddle of mush.

She knelt in front of the girl and, looking deep into her clear blue eyes, answered, "Of course I will."

"*Po-russki?*" Anya asked, meaning "When?"

The young woman took the child in her arms and held her for several minutes. A kind of love the young woman had never experienced before took full possession of her and filled her heart to overflowing.

"I will come tomorrow and the next day and every day after that, forever and ever," said Gethyn, giving the child an Eskimo kiss.

At the same time, a smile was sweeping across Anya's face. A single tear found a corner of her eye to sit in, and she asked, "*Vy obeshchaete?* (You promise?)

"Yes, I promise," Gethyn reassured, giving the little girl another tight squeeze before she and Philena headed for the elevator.

The two young women chatted all the way back to the high-rise, as though having been energized by the children. At Philena's door, they stood talking for a few minutes and then hugged each other.

"Thank you for taking me to see the children. I enjoyed them so much! Do you go there every day?" asked Gethyn.

The young Quaker girl smiled demurely, putting her hands in the pockets of her long dress. "Aye. Ever since I've been here, I hast gone to see the children most every day. I nary had a chance to be a mother to thy Samuel, so I find pleasure in mothering the wee ones at The Nursery. Usually I come in the morn', mind ye, but sometimes at noontime or later in the day, but always I go. I couldn't help notice ye seemed to hath taken a shine to wee Anya Nicolin."

Gethyn tucked her hands in the back pockets of her blue jeans and smiled. "I wonder if her parents are believers."

The Quaker girl knew what was on the young woman's mind and touched her arm gently. "Wee Anya hath been in Paradise almost as long as I have. Nary a soul hath come for the child as yet, so I would be given to think nary a soul ever wilt. Would ye be having thoughts of maybe someday adopting Anya?"

Gethyn looked down at her tennis shoes, rolling the thought around in her mind. "I don't know. I guess we'll have to wait and see how life writes the rest of the story," she stammered.

Even as she said the words, the young woman realized how true the statement was. Her present life was just a continuation of the previous one, but with it came new opportunities for growth. She and God were still coauthors of her unique story, and as such, she still needed His counsel when making decisions affecting her life.

Once she and Philena had finally said their goodnights, Gethyn walked the short distance to her sky-cabin. She subconsciously went to the window and looked across the horizon. Sunset would be coming soon. The young woman's mind wandered, and she found herself thinking of Philena McClary. Who would have ever thought her fifteenth great-grandmother would have become her best friend? Suddenly remembering the old adage "Sometimes life is stranger than fiction," Gethyn thought how true it was. Next her thoughts turned to Dave and then to Jace Covington and how she liked spending time with him. The good-looking cowboy was someone she liked considerably, yet the young woman was still having difficulty trying to sort out the role he was to play in the rest of her life. She let the romantic wishful thinking go and turned her thoughts to the child she had met that day. There was something haunting about Anya's eyes that made her want to swoop the girl up into her arms and protect her.

Gethyn went to the narrow clothes closet and retrieved the robe that hung there. Then she removed her jeans and T-shirt and slipped into it. She was feeling confused about her feelings for Dave, Jace, and Anya and decided to summon Jesus. He was the one friend she had always been able to trust and who had always given good counsel. In the blink of an eye, the Lord stood before the young woman, His light illuminating the room. He was as handsome as ever in His white linen robe and sandals, and His chestnut-colored hair cast a lustrous sheen.

"Hello, Gethyn. I'm so glad you called on me."

The girl brushed her long red hair aside and hung her head. "Lord, I would like to talk to you about love."

29

Jesus embraced the girl and kissed her cheeks. Like before, He placed wood and kindling in the stone fireplace and then lit it with the intensity of His gaze before taking a seat in His usual place.

"Now, my beloved, what would you like to know about love?" the Lord asked in a voice both soft and gentle.

Gethyn tucked her legs beneath her and pulled a throw blanket that hung from the side of the chair over her legs as though she were cold.

"I don't know where to start, Lord. My heart feels as though it's being pulled in three different directions, and honestly, I am so confused that I don't know what the right thing to do is anymore. I guess I'll start with Anya Nicolin, a little Russian girl I met today. I don't know anything about her life. I only know there is something about the child that made me fall in love with her from the instant I laid eyes on her. Philena told me the girl has been here a very long time and that most likely Anya's parents weren't believers as no one has ever come for her."

The Lord looked into the heart of the young woman sitting across from him, pleased with the genuine love and compassion He saw there.

"Philena was right about Anya's parents in that they weren't believers. Their names were D'mitri and Elizaveta Nicolin, and they sold their souls for money. They never acknowledged God in anything, nor did they reach out for me when I found them wallowing in a quagmire of depravity. I revealed myself to both of them, offering to cleanse them of their sins and wickedness if only they would confess and repent, but they would have no part of it. Gethyn, have you ever seen a cat wallowing in a patch of catnip? Catnip to a cat is an aphrodisiac and rolling around in it renders them into a heightened state of euphoria. That's how D'mitri and Elizaveta were about sin. They loved their sinful nature and did not want to be clean or righteous. Even when the Holy Spirit convicted their hearts, they continued to choose wrong over right."

Gethyn listened intently, and when the Lord paused for a moment, she asked, "What happened to them?"

Jesus looked into the young woman's blue eyes and replied, "They were poor but honest Russian peasants, scrounging by the best they could. D'mitri worked as a chimney sweep, and Elizaveta sold potatoes on a street corner. Pretty soon, Anya came along, and times grew even harder. One day, D'mitri foolishly stole a watch from a wealthy family he serviced and got caught. Although he gave the timepiece back, word got around that he was a thief, and he lost all his customers. Pretty soon, the three of them were on the street. Quite by accident, they stumbled upon an abandoned, dilapidated old gypsy wagon hidden in the woods outside Moscow and moved in.

"Satan got a stronghold on their hearts, and D'mitri and Elizaveta hatched up a scheme to rob patrons coming out of taverns. As one would exit the establishment, Elizaveta would engage them in suggestive conversation. Then her husband would come up behind the fellow, whack him on the head with a club, and ransack the man's pockets. They became very good at their ruse, both thinking themselves very clever. D'mitri thought it a much easier way to make a living than doing hot, dirty chimney work, and for her part, Elizaveta didn't miss coming home bone-weary from standing on her feet all day trying to sell a few measly potatoes. They laughed as they pocketed the spoils of their evil deeds, treating themselves to nights out on the town while their child went hungry."

"What about Anya? Where was she while all this was happening?" Gethyn implored of Jesus.

The Lord shook His head in disgust. "They tethered the poor little child with a rope that was only long enough for her to go outside and relieve herself. It was for her protection, they told themselves. As her parents' escapades grew more frequent, Anya was left alone for longer periods of time. She was dirty, hungry, and starved for attention, but

275

even so, she loved her mother and father, not because they were good or kind but because she had a forgiving heart. Whether right or wrong, they were all the poor child had.

"One night, a group of men came out of the tavern right as D'mitri and Elizaveta were fleecing a gentleman and saw them. They yelled 'Thieves!' Of course, D'mitri and Elizaveta fled the scene of their crime with the patrons of the tavern in hot pursuit. The couple ran down the cobblestone street under the cover of darkness as it was a moonless night, all the while looking back over their shoulders. They ducked into an alleyway between two houses and crouched down against the wall of one of them. They heard the angry crowd of men run past and sighed in relief at not having been caught. But justice always prevails, whether in one life or the next. All of a sudden, they heard a loud crack above them. What they didn't know was that the pounding of their footsteps on the cobblestone had loosened icicles hanging from the eaves of the house. Just as they looked up to see what made the noise, icicles ten inches long fell like daggers into their foreheads, killing them instantly. Not surprisingly, even in death, they would not let go of the rubles clutched in their hands. D'mitri and Elizaveta were disposed of like garbage, but no one knew there was a child waiting in an old gypsy wagon in the woods for their return."

Gethyn was angry, and her teeth clenched as she listened to the story. She wanted to know yet was afraid to ask what had happened to Anya. As the Lord began to speak, the young woman steeled her heart for the worst.

"It was a week before Anya was discovered. The girl was near-death, having gone with scarcely any food, water, or warmth. A peasant named Viktor Borovsky was passing through the area and heard a faint cry coming from the woods. Curious, the man followed the sound to the wagon that was well-hidden from view of the main road. When he found Anya tied up like a dog, he wept with compassion. There was no one else around. He already had a large family of his own to care for, so he did the only thing he knew to do. He carried the child to the first house he came to and laid Anya tenderly on the doorstep. He knocked loudly on the door and left, sure the owner would come out to investigate. No one did, however, or at least not in time to help. Unbeknownst to the kindly peasant, the house was unoccupied. Anya's guardian angel prayed and comforted the child as best it could, but there was nothing it could do to save her. There was a heavy snowfall that night, and when exposed to the elements, little Anya froze to death."

The Lord and Gethyn both wept.

After a few minutes had passed, Jesus said, "While it might seem like a cruel twist of fate, it actually turned out to be the best thing for Anya."

Puzzled, the young woman looked into the Lord's deep blue eyes for explanation, and He answered the unspoken question He knew was in her heart. "You see, she will never be hungry, thirsty, cold, afraid, or alone ever again as she has found shelter in the arms of God's mercy and grace. Sometimes things happen that can't be understood by man, like Anya's death. She had already suffered more than her share, and had she lived, she would have been an orphan left alone to face insurmountable challenges. God had watched her life unfold and was horrified by the circumstances she had to endure. Bound by laws He himself had made, God could not prevent the outcome, but He could bless her with the life she deserved once she was no longer earthbound."

"Lord, my heart tells me to bring Anya into my home and give her a mother's love, but at the same time, something tells me to wait—that the time is not right yet. There is a heaviness that tugs on my heart, although I can't pinpoint exactly what it is. Until I do, I can't go forward. Of course, I haven't been here very long and realize I'm an infant in terms of all there is to learn about God and myself.

"On Earth, I felt confident of who I was, but death has changed everything. It seems now I'm unsure of my purpose and what direction my life is going. I can't tell if adopting Anya is my purpose or if I'm supposed to do something else. Can you tell me?" the young woman asked.

The Lord crossed His ankles and folded His hands in His lap. "Child, your purpose is the same here as it was on Earth. Purpose is the external expression of your soul's passion to glorify and edify God by using the blessings, gifts, talents, and abilities given you to help others. A person does not have but one purpose to discover, but many over the course of eternal life. It is not for me to tell you the desires of your heart, how you should honor God, or who you should share your blessings with, but I will tell you this. You will unequivocally know your purpose is true at such time when your body, soul, and spirit are one in agreement. Only then will you be able to move forward with unwavering conviction."

The Lord noticed the fire had died down and rose to add more wood and kindling. Once the flame had spread and was burning steadily, He sat back in the chair with his arms on the armrests.

Gethyn's forehead creased, and though Jesus knew what she was thinking, He let her speak.

"Lord, I want to talk with you about Jace Covington. I find myself drawn to him, yet whenever we're together, I feel as though I'm betraying my fiancé, Dave. I'm confused and don't know how I'm supposed to feel."

Jesus stood and then walked back and forth in front of the fire, his hands behind his back. He stopped in front of Gethyn's chair.

"Child, look at me."

The young woman obeyed and saw sparkling blue eyes more beautiful than any she had ever seen before.

"Though you were engaged to marry, you were not bound in covenant. Therefore, you should not feel you are breaking any sacred vows or commitments by having a loving relationship with Jace, or anyone else for that matter."

The Lord saw a slight change in the young woman's countenance, as though relieved by His words.

"Now I want you to listen carefully to what I am about to say."

The young woman answered, "Yes, Lord," and waited for Jesus to continue.

"Even if you and Dave *had* been married, upon your death, the covenant between you would have been dissolved."

Gethyn gasped in disbelief, but she held her tongue.

The Lord continued. "God created marriage between a man and woman for many reasons. The man's role has always been to provide and protect while the woman's is to bear children and nurture the family. They were designed to love and care for the other through all the circumstances of life 'until death do them part.' On Earth, marriage serves a purpose, but outside of Earth, that purpose no longer exists.

"While there is no marriage or giving of marriage in the afterlife other than between me and my bride, it does not mean loving, meaningful relationships that existed on Earth between couples devoted to one another won't continue in Paradise or Heaven, for some will. Those who truly embodied being one in spirit may find each other again and resume a relationship if they so choose, but it is not uncommon for a man and a woman to go their separate ways once death has dissolved their bond of matrimony.

Without the built-in genetic urge to propagate in order to ensure the survival of the species or the concern over physical needs and survival of themselves and/or family, people are free to devote their time to others areas of interest and higher levels of spiritual growth. You and Jace are free to love one another if it is your desire, but there will never be a physical consummation of your feelings."

The young woman felt a tinge of disappointment. "Why won't there be physical love, Lord? We have temporary bodies, and in Heaven, we'll be resurrected with our earthly body."

The Lord looked at the girl sympathetically, knowing she felt slighted by her fate. "Gethyn, on Earth there is a purpose for physical consummation within a marriage, but unfortunately, its purpose has become distorted by man's lust of the flesh. While it was designed to be pleasurable and propagate the species of man, it reflects something much deeper in meaning, which I'm not sure you understand. You see, in a marriage, being intimate not only means the most vulnerable, loving, trusting, deepest part of you wants to connect with the most vulnerable, loving, trusting, deepest part of your spouse, but that the two of you, having come together as one in spirit, seek an intimate relationship with God. The physical consummation between a man and his virgin bride represents a blood covenant between the two of them and God. That is why intimacy is so sacred and shouldn't be taken so lightly.

"The romanticized physical demonstration of what most refer to as "being in love" belongs in the natural physical realm. It is an illusion of love and in reality has nothing to do with love. My child, it was never the physical you that loved others, but rather the longing of your soul essence to connect with the soul essence of another. You see, when physical attraction is taken out of the equation, love flows freely through an open-ended conduit between you and those you come into contact with. This kind of love has no conditions, no preferences, and no type. It is honest and pure. Its only purpose is to give and receive love. In the context of time eternal, a person will love completely until their whole essence becomes a living, breathing expression of love. You will love without thought or effort because it will be impossible for you not to do so. 'Being in love' does not satisfy or last forever, but 'being love' does.

"So while it is true that you will never experience physical intimacy as those on Earth do, I promise that what you have lost dims in comparison to the spiritual expression of God's love that you will experience someday when 'Thy Kingdom Comes.' You will not be disappointed or long for what you missed as you will have a personal, loving, intimate relationship with your Creator that will fulfill you in ways more wonderful than you could possibly imagine. Wait and see, child."

30

Day Ten

The sun rose and light filtered through the window, but Gethyn did not jump out of bed with her usual enthusiasm to greet the day. She felt lethargic, as though she was coming down with the flu. Just making the effort to sit up was too much, and the young woman fell back against the pillows, feeling weak and faint.

What is wrong with me? she thought, unable to comprehend what was happening.

As the hours passed, Gethyn's health became worse. The light faded, and the room became a dark tomb. She felt as though she were near-death, but by then, she didn't have the strength to question how that was possible. Lying there unable to move, all the young woman could do was grab hold of thoughts as they passed through her mind. One by one, those she had come to love and think of as family came to mind. There was Philly, whom she adored and thought of more as a sister than as her fifteenth great-grandmother. Gethyn had learned a lot about her descendants from both her and her grandparents and was fascinated by the rich history of those who had walked the Earth before her.

Tears welled up in her eyes as she thought of Anya, the little Russian girl she hoped to adopt someday. "Oh no! I promised to go see her today!" Gethyn cried. The thought of disappointing the child grieved her heart, and though she tried, she could not will her body to rise out of bed. Finally, the young woman resigned herself to the fact she could do nothing but lie there.

On the second day, Gethyn's thoughts became delirious. She was feverish and sweating profusely yet at the same time shivering and cold. Gethan felt as though she were bobbing up and down in a river, being carried by a swift current downstream. Her arms flailed wildly as she struggled to stay afloat in the water that only seemed to take her further and further away from those she loved. She saw Dave and Jace and desperately reached out to them, but they were unable to save her. The next thing she thought of was Zendor.

Where is Zendor? she asked herself. *If ever I needed my guardian angel, it is now!* In her mind, she saw the nine-foot creature and the look of terror in its eyes. There was something else as well, which she perceived of as guilt.

Why would the angel feel guilty over something that wasn't its fault? Zendor didn't make me sick. Something in Gethyn's subconscious mind remembered the celestial being's reluctance to talk about her death, and before the thought vanished, she reached for the puzzle piece and held on to it. Jesus had said there were sometimes two answers to a question. Had the creature not wanted to talk about her death because it felt guilty for not saving her?

Then she wondered, *Why didn't my angel save me? Isn't that what guardians do? Wasn't Zendor supposed to be my protector?* Her questions were replaced by thoughts of Zendor's soft-spoken nature. Gethyn had seen the angel's pale amethyst eyes light up when it talked about the day she was born and all the other stories it had shared with her of their life together on Earth. The guardian loved her as though she was its own child, of that the young woman was certain. Gethyn felt she knew Zendor well enough to know that had there been any way possible, the angel would have prevented her death. All of a sudden, she realized its refusal to talk about her death wasn't because of feelings of guilt, but rather feelings of *anguish*. What tortured the angel wasn't that it *hadn't* saved her, but that it *couldn't*. It was Zendor's fear of Gethyn not understanding the subtle difference that kept the angel from being able to speak to her of her death.

Within her delirium, there was a bubble of clarity, and in it the young woman remembered the predawn hours of that Easter morning. Something had kept telling her not to attempt to drive up the mountain, that it would be covered in fog and would be dangerous. In her stubborn determination to get home, however, she hadn't listened. Now Gethyn realized it had been Zendor trying to warn her and protect her from harm. Though her death was no fault of the angel's, it felt it had somehow failed her. Gethyn's heart swelled with emotion, and she wanted only to see Zendor again and assure the creature of her love.

The enormous angel sat praying by the young woman's bedside although she was unaware of its presence. Tears rolled down its cheeks, as the thought of losing the girl again was unbearable. All of a sudden, Zendor knew what needed to be done. The guardian hated the thought of leaving her side, but willed itself to go. Wasting no time, it went to the window, opened it, and took flight.

Clarence happened to look up from his station at the front of the skyscraper, but he could not ascertain who the celestial being was who had leapt from the window ledge high above. All he saw was the wings and feathers of an enormous angel flying fast and furious toward the garden.

The gravely ill girl neither knew her guardian had been there or that it had left. Her thoughts turned to Dave and then to Jace. They were so different from one another in looks and temperament, yet both shared a common desire to live in the will of God. Gethyn saw the light of God in each of them, and it was that light that had drawn her to the beauty and love of each of their soul's essence. In the deepest part of the young woman's heart, she knew that if she survived this strange malady that had suddenly afflicted her, she would not have to choose between Dave or Jace.

Love in the spiritual realm was not either/or. Simply put, it just *is*. Closing her eyes to worldly perceptions, she saw with spiritual clarity how love was actually quite simple. It was only humans trying to lean on their own understanding who inadvertently made love complicated. She knew now it was the earthbound part of her that held her back and kept her from experiencing the fullness of love.

As she lay shivering in bed, Gethyn realized something else. The people in her life, whether from the past, present, or future, were like gentle, loving waves washing over her soul on the great ocean of time, but without the strength of the current, she would never reach her destiny. No matter how long she continued taking in the love that surrounded her, there was no man, woman, or child who could fill the bottomless void within her soul that longed to be filled. In the last moment of lucidity before losing consciousness, Gethyn saw the face of the only one who could and called out His name. "Jesus."

When Gethyn came to, the Lord was at her bedside, exuding love and compassion. He smiled and then touched her cheek tenderly.

"Thank God you've awakened, child, as I thought I was going to have to raise you from the dead."

The humor was lost on the young woman as she was too ill to grasp his intent.

"You're here," she said in a feeble voice.

"I always come when I am called," the Lord answered while tending to her needs.

"Please don't leave me," Gethyn implored, reaching for the sleeve of His robe. Once the words were out of her mouth, she suddenly remembered asking the same thing the morning she had died and how Jesus had stayed to comfort her. The exalted man read her thoughts and reassured the young woman.

"I promised then never to leave you just as I promise now. I love you, Gethyn, and want you with me always."

The young woman looked into His bright blue eyes, knowing His word was everything.

"What happened to me? Why am I so sick?" she wanted to know.

The Lord wiped her brow with a cool cloth, answering, "You forgot to eat of the fruit. Remember me saying a human cannot survive in the spiritual realm for long without eating the sustenance provided?"

Gethyn remembered suddenly. She and Philena had gone straight to The Nursery and did not stop at the garden. "Is Philena sick too?" the young woman asked in a shaky voice.

The Lord tucked the covers around her before answering. "No. She went to the garden before ever coming for you the day before yesterday. Once, years ago, Philena forgot to eat the fruit and became as sick as you are now. Believe me, she has never forgotten since."

Gethyn was beginning to feel marginally better and managed to sit up against the headboard with the pine tree and full moon her daddy had carved. Jesus tucked a pillow behind the young woman's head to make her more comfortable before sitting on the edge of the bed.

"I'm glad to see you're regaining a little strength," the Lord said. "You know, you have your guardian angel to thank for that."

Gethyn's eyes widened. Puzzled, she said, "Zendor?"

The exalted man pushed a tendril of red hair out of her face before taking her small hand in His. "Yes. Zendor decided to check on you after not seeing or hearing from you all day yesterday. When you didn't answer the door, Zendor flew around to the window, opened it, and came inside, only to find you lying in bed sick and half out of your mind. Not being able to save you on Earth is something that has weighed heavily on Zendor's mind, and the creature is bound and determined not to ever let anything happen to you again. While praying over your bedside, Zendor had a revelation. Realizing the cause of your sickness, your guardian rushed to the garden to get sustenance for you. Once back in your cabin, Zendor ground some fruit into a pulp and managed to get you to swallow a little of it. The angel stayed with you until you called for me. Zendor is down in the garden as we speak, praying for your recovery.

"Gethyn, I knew before Zendor ever arrived that you were ill. I could have healed you easily, but I thought it served a greater purpose for your guardian to minister to you."

The young woman threw her arms around the deified man's neck. "Oh Jesus!" she cried. "I need to talk with Zendor right away!"

The Lord summoned the angel with His mind, and Zendor appeared before its Master on bended knee.

"Rise Zendor," Jesus commanded, and the angel obeyed. "I summoned you on behalf of Gethyn. It is she who wishes to speak with you. I will leave the two of you to speak in private, but should either of you need me, just call out my name." With that the Lord vanished into thin air.

When the guardian angel turned toward the young woman, she looked up and saw its tear-streaked face.

"Come sit with me, Zendor. I want to talk with you."

The winged creature went to her and sat on the side of the bed. "You scared me so bad, Gethyn. I thought you were going to d——" the angel said before stopping itself.

"Die? You thought I was going to die?" the young woman asked. The very words made the angel tense up and turn inward, and as sick as Gethyn was, she sensed it. "Zendor, I don't know if a person can die from not eating the fruit, although there were moments when I felt so sick that I wanted to. I don't know what would have happened if you hadn't come looking for me. The Lord told me what you did and how you prayed and received revelation telling you what was wrong and what you should do. He told me how you went to the garden for fruit, mashed it up, and made me swallow it. I don't remember any of it, not even your being here earlier, but I just want to thank you personally for taking care of me until the Lord came."

The angel sat with wings folded behind it and head bowed as though afraid to meet her gaze. Although still weak, Gethyn had things she wanted to say that couldn't wait.

"Zendor, I love you with all my heart. While I was out of it, several things went through my mind, and one of them was you. I know how much you love me. You were there when I was born, and you were there when I died, and I know for certain you would have saved me Easter morning had it been possible. I don't ever want you to think I would be angry or hold you responsible for something you had no control over. Since coming here, I've learned death is not the end of the world. Jesus told me when I first arrived in Paradise that it is not important how one dies but rather how one lives, and the longer I'm here, the more I realize how true it is. It was because of His death that the grave couldn't hold me. Death deserves no mention, as life is all that matters. I live because He lives in me."

31

Day Thirteen

Zendor had insisted Gethyn stay home a couple more days, leaving her side only to go down to the garden to carefully select a choice piece of sugary sweet fruit. The guardian stood by while she ate, watching as its charge gradually regained her strength. Philena heard about Gethyn's illness through her own guardian angel, who in turn had learned of it through the telepathic grapevine. She stopped by to see her grandchild, even though separated by fifteen generations. She and Zendor fussed over Gethyn like old mother hens, each trying to outdo the other in caring for the girl.

There was a slight tapping on the door, and when Zendor opened it, there stood little Stevie in his shorts, T-shirt, and baseball cap turned backward. The angel ushered the child in and laughed as the boy bounded over towards Gethyn like a puppy dog running to its master. He hopped up on the bed, plopped down beside her, and then began talking a mile a minute.

"Gethie, I heared you was sick, so I decided to come cheer you up. I heared a new joke. Do you wanna hear?"

Gethyn nodded yes, and the child asked, "Why did the dog jump into the water?"

Not even waiting for two seconds, Stevie asked, "Do you give up?" after which the young woman smiled and said yes.

The little boy beamed, shrugged his shoulders and put the palms of his hands face up. "'Cause he didn't want to be a *hot* dog."

They both looked at each other and giggled.

Little Stevie stayed with Gethyn for the better part of the day, telling jokes, stories, and singing songs just as she had done for him before he died. "Don't worry, Gethie. The Lord said pretty soon you'll be well enough to go outside an' play again. Hey! Do you 'member this song?

> On top of spaghetti, all covered with cheese
> I lost my poor meatball when somebody sneezed
> It rolled off the table and onto the floor
> And then my poor meatball rolled out of the door

"Gethie, get well please! If you'll get well, I'll go to the garden and look for us some wooly worms. 'Member that time when you snuck one into my room and let it crawl up my arm? You weren't there, but Mama almost died before I did when it came crawling out from under the sheet the next day. All she saw was its head, but that was 'nough for her to go runnin' outta the room hollering to Daddy that there was a snake in my bed."

Gethyn pictured Mrs. Bowers freaked out over a harmless wooly worm and giggled along with him. The young woman looked at the boy with the missing front tooth and through him relived the innocent joy of being six years old again.

Once they had settled down, the boy grew serious. "Gethie, I couldn't tell you back then, but I guess it's okay now. If I hadn't died, I was gonna ask you to marry me when we growed up."

Even though she still felt slightly ill, the young woman was deeply moved and reached out to hug the child. Little Stevie let her hold him for a minute before pulling away.

"I guess it's too late now though," he said, sounding defeated.

Gethyn smiled tenderly at her childhood friend and playfully tugged on his cap. "I'm afraid so. You waited too long to ask, mister. Now maybe if you'd asked me when we were five…"

The two lapsed into a fit of laughter. Even Zendor joined in, and before long, lightning bolts and fireworks were exploding all over the room.

After the boy left, Gethyn fell into a deep sleep, and when she woke was happy to find that she felt a lot better. Stevie's spirit had seemed to breathe its zest for life into hers, and afterward, she felt well enough to get out of bed and go sit by the window in one of the overstuffed chairs.

Before the day was over, she had other visitors. Arie-Ann and Dolly dropped in as well as Lottie, who stopped by to bring a bouquet of flowers.

"I brung you some purdy flowers, honey-chile'. You need some healin', and like we both know, beauty's one-a God's natural remedies."

Her grandparents came, as did Jace. Even Clarence made an exception, leaving his post in front of the high-rise to come up and see about her. There was one person who didn't come though, and it was the one person Gethyn wanted to see the most: Anya Nicolin.

"Zendor I've *got* to go see Anya! I promised to come see her every day, and that was four days ago!" the young woman wailed.

Philena offered to go to The Nursery with her, but the guardian was hesitant to let Gethyn out of its sight.

"Why don't you just come with us? That way you don't have to worry," the young woman said. The towering nine-foot angel beamed, happy to be included.

Clarence had missed seeing the beautiful young woman with the red-gold hair and was delighted to see her come walking through the lobby of the building with Zendor and Philena. He quickly opened the heavy glass door for them to pass through.

"I'm so glad to see you're up and about. We all missed you," the uniformed doorman said.

"I missed you too, Clarence," Gethyn said, kissing him on the cheek. "I felt as though I was on the vacation from hell," the young woman joked.

The gray-haired gentleman smiled, happy to see the girl acting like her old self.

"I'll tell you what, Clarence. I wouldn't wish what I've been through on my worst enemy!" she declared. "I don't remember the pain of dying the first time, but I can't imagine it being any worse than the excruciating pain I've been in the last couple of days."

The doorman greeted other patrons before turning his attention back to Gethyn. "Well, I'm glad you followed the light and found your way home."

Turquoise blue eyes sparkled in the morning light as the young woman nodded. "Me too," she said.

Gethyn breathed in the intoxicating air deeply, drinking in the grandeur of the magnificent city—the New Jerusalem. People from all walks of life were going about their day free from worry. The young woman had never seen anyplace as beautiful as Paradise and felt privileged to live there. The three walked down the sidewalk, enjoying the brisk morning air and losing themselves in their own private thoughts. Gethyn longed to see Anya and hold the child in her arms again. She forced herself to walk and not run, as she needed time to contemplate what she would say to the little girl once there.

Finally the trio arrived at the complex and climbed the steep steps to the massive front door of the building. After going inside, they proceeded through the lobby and down the glass hallway that connected them to the tall skyscraper known as The Nursery. Gethyn's heart raced while waiting for the elevator, all the while secretly wishing she had wings like Zendor so she could fly to the girl's side. Once the car arrived, the three stepped inside.

The elevator doors opened, and Gethyn saw Anya standing at the window looking out. Her red hair was plaited in two heavy red braids, and she looked like a little ragamuffin in the simple peasant dress and babushka. Knowing Gethyn wanted to be alone with Anya, Philena went in search of a set of twins she had befriended some time back while Zendor talked with Anya's guardian, Ryelle.

The young woman approached the tiny figure by the window who had yet to see her. Softly she called out, "Anya."

The Russian child turned, and Gethyn saw the child's face was a cloud of confusion, anger, fear, and pain.

Tears immediately sprang into Gethyn's eyes, and she immediately dropped to her knees in front of the child. "Oh, Anya, I have missed you, honey."

The little girl stood as silent and stiff as a toy tin soldier, arms firmly planted at her sides, not willing to budge.

"I can see I've hurt you deeply, and I'm so, so sorry. It was unintentional," insisted Gethyn, attempting to plead her case. "I know I promised to come see you every day—"

Before the young woman could finish, Anya curtly fired off, "Then why didn't you," in her native tongue.

Though Gethyn had never studied Russian, she understood the child perfectly. "Silly me, I forgot to eat of the fruit that grows by the River of Life and have been very ill for the past four days. I think the reason I got well as fast as I did was because I knew you were waiting."

The five-year-old fell into the young woman's arms, and both of them sobbed. "I thought you didn't come because I'm *bespoleznyi* (worthless). Nobody ever loved me, not even my parents. I just thought you decided I was unlovable too."

Gethyn felt as though she had been kicked in the stomach and found herself gasping for air, while at the same time her heart shattered into a million tiny pieces. She held the child out in front of her by the shoulders so she could look into her eyes.

"Oh, Anya, please do not talk as though you have no value. It isn't true! You are a princess! The precious daughter of a King! Don't you know He loves and values you so much He bought you with His own blood? It is because of His love that you and I are both here. And, might I add, I love you."

The two of them fell into each other's arms again and cried until all their tears had been exhausted.

Gethyn called Philena and Zendor over, as they had been anxious to meet the little girl who had stolen the young woman's heart. Ryelle came as well, and once introductions were made all around, the five of them had a splendid tea party. They were having so much fun that before long other children and their guardians joined in. Joy and merry laughter permeated the room.

When it was time to go, Gethyn took the child in her arms and held her for the longest time.

"Will you be my mother?" the child asked in her tiny voice.

Gethyn wanted to answer yes right away, but she held back. She looked into the girl's cloudy blue eyes, hoping she could find the words to make the child understand what she was about to say.

"Anya, I would love nothing more than to adopt you and take you home with me right this minute. Before I can be your mother though, there are still some things I need to learn and sort out. You see, while you have been in Paradise a long time, I am new here and still getting oriented to life after death. I *want* to be your mother more than you know, and I *will be* someday. I promise you that. In the meantime, I will come see you every day, and when the time is right, I will bring you home with me for good. Can you wait for just a while longer?"

The peasant child went to a faraway place in her memory, recalling how she had waited for parents who never came back. She also remembered how she had laid on a stranger's doorstep waiting to be found, but instead of being rescued, she had died cold and alone underneath a blanket of snow. It seemed as though she had been waiting all her life for life to begin, and now she was being asked to wait again.

"Please don't leave me," Anya pleaded with her eyes.

Gethyn remembered saying those same words to Jesus and how His answer had brought such peace to her heart.

"I promise never to leave or forsake you, child," the young woman said sincerely.

The pint-sized five-year-old relaxed somewhat. With a little trepidation in her voice, she asked, "After I'm adopted, can I call you Mama?"

Gethyn thought her heart would burst right then and there.

"I would consider it an honor and privilege, Anya," she said, tears welling up in her eyes. She thought of her own mother and instinctively felt a kinship with her. As any expectant parent, Gethyn looked forward to giving life to this child. Not only that, she anticipated being born into a new life as well.

"I will see you tomorrow," Gethyn said, as she forced herself to let go of the little girl who had so quickly become a part of her. The two of them walked hand in hand to the elevator followed by Zendor and Philena.

As she pushed the elevator button, Anya pretended to scold the young woman, saying, "Don't forget to eat your fruit in the morning."

Gethyn laughed and replied, "Believe me, I will *never* forget again."

The child giggled, knowing in her little heart she was loved by this woman who had red hair and blue eyes just like her. Anya tugged on her T-shirt. "Since you are a child of God, are you a princess too?" she asked.

"Absolutely," replied Gethyn. The young woman saw the little girl's brow crease as though pondering some deep analytical question.

"What is it, sweetie?" Gethyn asked.

With all the sincerity of an innocent five-year-old, Anya asked, "If we are princesses, will we get a tiara to wear?"

The elevator doors opened, and Zendor held them while Gethyn answered the tiny girl's question.

"Oh yes, Anya! Someday, when 'Thy Kingdom Comes,' we will all be clothed beautifully and given jeweled crowns to wear by the King Himself. For now though, I must go make preparations for you."

By the time the young woman stepped into the elevator and looked back, she saw that the dark, haunting despair she had once seen in Anya's eyes was gone and that it had been replaced with hope. Gethyn blew a bouquet of kisses to the child who stood waving good-bye, but before the doors had fully closed, the young woman was already missing the little girl.

32

Five Years Later

Earth

In the five years since their only daughter's death, the Fields had gone through the many stages of grief and had ridden a roller coaster of emotions. Thank God for their faith as it had been the lifeline they held on to while struggling to stay afloat in the sea of their grief. Joe and Mary Ann knew that had the Lord not been with them through the days, nights, weeks, and months after Gethyn's death, they would have been consumed and swallowed by the dark abyss of pain and sorrow.

At first, Gethyn's parents were shocked by the news of Gethyn's unexpected death. While Mary Ann had been anticipating planning her child's upcoming wedding, the thought of planning her funeral had never entered her mind. For a while, life and the living were hidden behind a distorted blur of tears, and though well-wishers spoke kind words of well-intended encouragement, the Fields were too numb to hear. The only sound that would have brought them out of despair would have been the sound of their daughter's voice.

Once they came to grips with the reality of Gethyn's death, a profound sadness fell around them, much like the fog that clung to the mountaintop they lived on. Over and over, they were hit by one enormous tsunami wave of tears after another and were left feeling as though they'd never be able to put the pieces of their lives back together after such loss and devastation. They were in excruciating pain to the point of its being almost unbearable and were sure they would lose their minds from the heartbreak of being separated from their child. Though the couple had each other, it was a lonely time. Things that had once occupied their hands and their minds no longer held any interest. There was an endless litany of questions as well as many what-ifs that tortured them, such as "Did she know how much she was loved or why couldn't it have been me who died instead of her? The thing that haunted her mother most was that Gethyn had died alone. While she had been there at Gethyn's birth, not being there to comfort her daughter at the end of her life was something she found hard to accept.

Shock, sadness, and guilt finally gave way to anger, and Gethyn's parents demanded an answer from God as to why their daughter had been killed in such a horrific way. No matter how loud their screams, their demands went unanswered. When anger didn't work, they tried bargaining with the Heavenly Father to bring their child back, although that failed as well. "Why would Gethyn, who was young, kind, and loving die when there were evil people in the world who did not deserve to live? Where was the justice in that?" they wanted to know.

Time after time, they hit a brick wall, unable to find any logical answer, until at last they slipped into a deep depression. They thought about their daughter constantly and the things they had done or places they had gone together as a family. No matter how much they longed to catch a glimpse of Gethyn in any of the familiar places, she was never there. Her parents found it hard to enjoy their lives or each other, and there were many times each of them would have liked to crawl into their own bed of sorrow and never come out. It was hard putting on a smile and pretending to be okay for their friends and family. They were not okay. Although they discovered life would go on with or without Gethyn, for a time they found the world to be colorless and void of joy. The couple suffered bouts of insomnia, fatigue, and loss of appetite. Nothing and no one gave them a moment's happiness, and every holiday and birthday served only to reawaken memories of Gethyn, which in turn was a reminder that she was no longer with them.

In the beginning, the Fields felt they would never wake from the complex nightmare of Gethyn's death. In time though, the intense, painful feelings of loss subsided, and they were able to reenter and function within a social network. As the years passed, their feelings became more tempered with good memories rather than the profound sadness they had initially felt, yet there were still moments when they were suddenly overcome with raw emotion.

The final acceptance of their daughter's death did not mean their lives had returned to normal, for their lives would never be the same as before. Joe and Mary Ann managed to forge a path forward with the help of the Lord, however, and were eventually able to talk about Gethyn without experiencing the wrenching pain that had gripped them before. However, it was not until their son, Emmit, married and their first grandchild was born that they were able to experience true joy again.

As with any parent who has ever lost a child, the Fields never forgot Gethyn. She lived on in their hearts, thoughts, and dreams and was just as much a part of their daily lives as she had been from the day she was born. Thinking of her now brought a smile rather than tears, and whatever anger, blame, or depression they had felt before had long ago dissipated. They took wise counsel heard on a television show and made a conscious decision to celebrate her life and to thank God for the twenty-two years they were blessed to have shared with Gethyn rather than attend her funeral every day for the rest of their lives.

Gethyn's brother, Emmit, had gone through his own grieving process as he had been very close to his little sister. He was ten when she was born and was always told to protect her. She was an easy child to love. Looking back, Emmit realized he had never gone through a stage where he didn't want her to tag along. Because of their age difference and gender, they had little in common, yet he enjoyed entertaining Gethyn and watching her face light up in a smile. When she was little, he encouraged her to walk and talk, and he played with her for hours on end. She in turn idolized him. Although her parents were always available and her love for them undeniable, it was Emmit she was most likely to turn to when she had a problem. Their bond was close, and in a sense, they were like twins separated by ten years. They spoke the same language, and their souls were intertwined and inseparable.

With Gethyn gone, Emmit felt as though he had lost his identity. He was no longer an older brother; he was an only child. There was no one for him to protect and no one to love and idolize him in return. Before her birth, he had been a lonely ten-year-old boy; but once she came, the house was filled with the music of laughter and joy. With her death, Emmit felt like that sad, lonely child again.

His parents, who had always been pillars of strength, crumbled. Seeing the pain in their eyes, Emmit put his own grief aside, feeling he must be strong for them. He tried consoling them but found he could not. No one could. While friends and family rushed to comfort his mother and father, no one seemed to notice his pain and loss. In a sense, Emmit felt invisible and would continue to feel that way for a long time to come as he dealt privately with his grief.

Gethyn's death made Emmit question not only "Why?" and "What if…" but "What now?" As he turned his thoughts to the future, he realized they would share no more camping trips or talk late into the night of their hopes and dreams. He would never have a brother-in-law or get the opportunity to be a good role model to the nieces and nephews he had looked forward to having someday, nor would Gethyn be there to spoil his children. The thought of not growing old together was the most painful, and painful too was the realization that once their parents died, there would be no one left to share holidays and birthdays with or help him keep the family memories alive. Her death made Emmit question his own mortality, and he resolved to draw closer to the Lord.

Gethyn never knew what an inspiration she had been to her brother during the short time she lived and how he had been most proud of her dream of becoming a missionary with Dave. She was all about helping make the world a better place to live, and she did, just by being in it. Emmit realized his sister had given all of herself away to others until there was nothing left to give. While he had always considered himself her role model, he now saw with perfect clarity that *she* had been his. He embraced her dream of becoming a missionary, joining an outreach program that traveled all over the world carrying the banner of Christ and teaching people how to live and work together in peace, harmony, and love. He met his wife, Amanda, on one of his missions, and eventually, they were blessed with four children. They named one, a beautiful girl with titian red-gold hair and blue eyes, Gethyn.

33

With the passage of time, Gethyn began to mourn the loss of her earthly life less, finding ample reasons each day to celebrate the new one she had been given in the spiritual realm. In the first few years, there had been crippling pangs of guilt whenever she experienced any type of sensory pleasure, as she was keenly aware her loved ones were grieving her absence deeply. With her passing, the young woman knew her parents would not permit joy or pleasure of any kind to visit them for a long time to come, and if they would not, how could she? For a long time, Gethyn wrestled with whether she was being disloyal to her family by moving on. Although her family were Christian, the shock of losing their only daughter had catapulted them into a place they hadn't foreseen. In a sense, they had died and were buried with Gethyn, and it would take a long time before they were ready to crawl out of her cold, dark grave and live again.

Ever since arriving in Paradise, the young woman had felt an invisible tug-of-war going on within her, although she hadn't known what it was. One morning, she woke to discover it gone. With perfect clarity, Gethyn realized now what the uncomfortable feeling had been. It was her and her family trying desperately to hold on to one another. What each hadn't realized though was that by prolonging the inevitable, they were also prolonging their own grief and sorrow, as it was impossible for Gethyn to be in two places at once. She couldn't go back and comfort them, and they couldn't come to her, at least not yet. It wasn't until each of them was able to accept her death that her family could be truly present on Earth, which in turn allowed Gethyn to be truly present in Paradise. Now the young woman's spirit was free to soar without a sense of guilt for those left behind, and her family could move on as well. Of course they would never forget one another, not even for one day, for love lives on in the heart and in our memories and follows us from one life to the next.

One day, while Gethyn was home in the cabin, she curled up in her favorite chair to spend time daydreaming. Seeing the southwest patterned blanket draped over one arm of the chair, she reached for it and spread it over her legs. The young woman closed her eyes and began going over in her mind all the things Jesus had said about Heaven. As happy as she was in Paradise, she couldn't wait until it was time to go to her eternal home. Gethyn began remembering how as a Christian her goal and intent had always been on *getting* to Heaven, but now it suddenly dawned on her that she had never seriously stopped to consider what life would be like once she actually *got* there. From her newfound perspective, she wondered how she or anyone else could spend their whole life planning for the trip of a lifetime without first trying to learn all they could about the place they were going. Gethyn remembered how her family had always obtained brochures from a travel agency anytime they went on vacation, wanting to know everything from A–Z about their destination. They asked questions about the weather, the accommodations, and how they would get around once there. They wanted to know about recreational activities and what kind of entertainment was available as well as points of interest to see. A lot of time was devoted to preparing for each of their trips in order to know what to expect beforehand.

At one time or another, Gethyn had had a vague curiosity about what Heaven would look like; but like many people, her image of the afterlife consisted of God and angels, with lots of singing, reciting of scripture, praying, and very little else. She hadn't been able to get excited about being an unembodied spirit floating around forever in a place that was supposed to be home but didn't look or feel like home. The thoughts were not comforting and had given Gethyn a sense of anxiety and dread for the boring life she perceived as waiting for her on the other side of death's door. As such, she had chosen to relegate thoughts of Heaven to somewhere far in the back of her mind. Now she knew that the Heaven people think of as going to when they die does not exist yet. It will be on the new Earth. Just as her body passed away and would one day be resurrected, so too would the heavens and Earth pass away and be resurrected. With newfound clarity, Gethyn realized that God created man to live *on Earth*, not as an unembodied spirit floating around. He gave human beings *physical* bodies to live in a *physical* world, and once they are resurrected, they will again be in their *physical* bodies. A *physical* body needs to live in a *physical* place. God can live anywhere, but humans can't. Therefore, once Heaven comes into being, God will live among man on the new *Earth*, the *only* place humans can exist in their *physical* bodies.

God's whole creation is a masterpiece that He called "good." A true artist does not throw away a valuable painting that has been damaged but rather restores it with loving care to its original condition. Once the stain of sin has been removed, Earth, mankind, the animals, and the heavens will finally be free of the curse. There will be no more violent weather outbursts, no danger from wild beasts, or fear of mankind. Life eternal will begin in the perfect world God originally designed and created for us, and Heaven and Earth will live together harmoniously.

While Gethyn's mind had never before been able to fathom Heaven, now her imagination raced toward her future with open arms and an eager heart. She felt an intense longing for the world to come much like a child longs for Christmas to arrive.

Even though the red-headed beauty was evolving and maturing daily, in some ways she had become as a little child. She finally understood the reason Jesus loves the hearts of little children so much. It is because they believe without seeing. Their imaginations have no boundaries or limits, allowing them to go to places most adults have forgotten exists.

Gethyn's eyes, the color of the Caribbean Sea, opened a little wider in awe and wonder, as her knowledge expanded and her understanding of God's ways grew. No longer earthbound, Gethyn was free to embrace the life she had with open arms. She was no longer as a bird tethered to a cage; she could fly and soar to heights unimaginable.

Gethyn was awakened by a persistent knocking on the door. It jolted her awake and immediately brought to mind the time years ago when Zendor arrived at her door in the predawn hours to announce there was a breach of security somewhere in the universe.

"Had another angel turned traitor?" Gethyn wondered, jumping out of bed. For a moment, a pang of fear pierced her heart, but she quickly dismissed it. She had come to know and accept that God is in control, not some of the time, but all of the time. With that understanding, came the knowledge that fear and faith cannot coexist together. Like weeds in fertile soil, she pulled all doubt from the garden of her heart to make room for fruits of the spirit to grow.

The young woman padded to the front door in bare feet while at the same time raking fingers through her tousled red hair and wiping the sleep from her eyes. Opening the door, she saw that it was Zendor, but the creature did not appear upset or worried about anything as it had before. To the contrary, the angel looked radiantly happy. It stood smiling in its unusual way, showering Gethyn with yellow and blue sparks and multicolored ribbons of lights.

"Please tell me what is so important that it couldn't wait until morning?" Gethyn asked, stifling a yawn.

Zendor pointed to the window where one tendril of pink light stretched across the sky. "It is morning," the angel said. "It's going to be a beautiful day in Paradise, and I was thinking that maybe you'd like to do something different."

The celestial paused, fascinated by watching curiosity travel from the young woman's imagination to her blue eyes and then spread over the contours of her face.

After a minute of silence between them, Gethyn spoke. "Are you going to tell me what you have in mind or am I going to have to pluck one of your feathers out," she teased good-naturedly.

Zendor walked past her and stood by the window. "I thought I'd take you flying over the city and garden, but if you'd rather go back to sleep…" He turned and pretended to head for the door.

"Yes, yes, yes!" Gethyn answered.

"Yes, you'd rather sleep?" Zendor teased.

The young woman looked up at her guardian and emphatically stated, "I mean no! I don't need any more sleep. I'm awake, and I want to go flying!"

A hailstorm of sparks and lightning bolts shot from Zendor's eyes. "Oh, I almost forgot." The guardian walked out the front door for a moment and came back carrying a picnic basket. "I thought we could have a picnic at the waterfall where I took you on your first day."

Gethyn smiled and nodded her head enthusiastically in agreement. Curious, she asked, "What's in the picnic basket?"

The angel opened it, and both laughed as it reached in and produced fruit from the trees that grew on the banks of the River of Life.

The young woman giggled and said, "But of course!"

Zendor again walked to the window and opened it. The solitary ribbon of pink light had now expanded to include blue and purple streamers, and together they cast a soft glow over the golden city and the garden within. The winged creature put one massive arm around Gethyn's waist and held the picnic basket with the other.

"Are you ready?" the creature asked.

With her heart racing a mile a minute, Gethyn answered, "I've never been more ready."

In an instant, Zendor ducked out the window, and they were in the air. The titian-haired beauty felt like Wendy on her way to Neverland with Peter Pan. Her eyes were as bright as the stars, and her face was full of childlike wonder. With the angel's massive arm holding her to its body and its protective wings around her, it was easy for Gethyn to imagine having wings of her own. The young woman could feel the strength of the creature's wings as they steadily climbed higher and higher above the city. Finally, Zendor leveled off and maintained a steady altitude. The view was too beautiful for words. Gethyn looked down upon Paradise, and her heart ached with love for her temporary home. Just then, she looked directly below and saw a beautiful pink cloud shaped like a heart. Tears filled her eyes, for she was reminded of the red leaf valentine she had found in the woods by the cabin at Lake Lone Pine. She knew without a doubt that God had left it that day especially for her to find as a reminder of His love, just as He had placed this pretty pink valentine in the form of a cloud in the sky for her now. Zendor saw the cloud too. Without warning, the creature tucked its wings tight to its body and did a nosedive. Before Gethyn could protest, they pierced the heart-shaped cloud. Zendor pulled up and then hovered in place. Gethyn was filled with the sensation of being inside the womb of God's love. She heard His heartbeat and felt herself floating on a gentle ocean where time was endless. Love and emotion rose and fell over and around her until she was lost in the rhythm and sighs of its powerful euphoric embrace. The titian-haired beauty had never experienced such pure intimate love and could have stayed in that moment forever if it were possible.

Gethyn did not want to leave the loving caress she experienced while enveloped in the heart-shaped cloud. Eventually though, the winged creature brought them out and tipped its wing to catch an air current. Holding on to Gethyn, they leisurely circled the New Jerusalem like seagulls looking for a glint of sun reflecting off a fish. It was not fully morning yet, and Gethyn enjoyed the twinkling lights of the jeweled city as well as the soft glow of light cast by humans and angels alike as they began to move around the great city that sat on a mountaintop below. After a while, Zendor flew over the garden and at one point took them so close to the ground that the young woman could see their shadow. She inhaled deeply, taking in an intoxicating breath of the sweet fragrance that permeated all of Paradise, as it was a smell that did not exist anywhere else in the universe. Gethyn had never felt so alive, so liberated, so loved, or so at peace. God had given her wings in the form of Zendor, and she was flying.

Zendor landed with ease beside the jungle path. Holding on to Gethyn's hand with one hand and the picnic basket with the other, Zendor led the tall redheaded beauty to the ancient waterfall. They swam and played in the cold pool of water for the longest time and then rested on one of the smooth flat rocks. Gethyn ate a delicious piece of sugary sweet fruit Zendor had packed for her, which fortified her energy.

The young woman loved this special place, but all too soon, it was time to go. Zendor collected the picnic basket, and the two began climbing down from the flat boulders. Just then, they heard voices coming from above. Looking up, they saw a man and a woman on the cliff high above. Gethyn held her breath and stood as though paralyzed, as she watched the couple perform a perfectly synchronized swan dive into the pool of water below, making barely a ripple. The redhead was sure she had never seen anything so profoundly eloquent and beautiful. The man and the woman surfaced quickly and then swam to the edge of the basin and climbed out. They found a smooth flat boulder and lay down on its warm surface and talked quietly among themselves.

Considering their athleticism, Gethyn was surprised to see that they were much older than she had at first thought. Both were gray-headed, but seemed to possess strength and agility beyond their years. The man was lean and fit and wore no more than a loincloth. The older woman's clothing consisted of a bra type garment hidden beneath long flowing hair that hung down her back and over her small breasts. In addition, remnants of uneven lengths of skins were pieced together and worn as a short, low-slung skirt exposing the woman's smooth belly.

Something about the couple puzzled Gethyn. It was as though the thought was submerged in muddy water and she couldn't tell where it was going. Leaving the ancient waterfall and the couple behind, Gethyn and Zendor walked down the jungle path.

All of a sudden, the young woman stopped dead in her tracks. She looked at her guardian, her blue eyes as deep as the ocean and as wide as the sky and exclaimed, "Zendor! That couple at the waterfall didn't have belly buttons!"

The angel looked down at the beautiful girl with pale amethyst eyes and laughed, sparks and curlicues raining down on her. "Don't you know who that was?"

Gethyn thought for a moment and was almost afraid to speak the words. "Adam and Eve? Are you telling me *that* was Adam and Eve, Zendor?"

The celestial being chuckled again, saying, "Well, who else do you know without belly buttons?" Gethyn shook her head and shrugged her ivory shoulders. "I guess it never occurred to me that they would be in Paradise, seeing as they're the ones who caused the fall," the young woman answered incredulously.

As they walked, Zendor talked to Gethyn of that time long ago in the history of mankind. "It has been said that once Adam and Eve sinned, they hid from God. They did not have Jesus's promises of forgiveness and redemption as people have today. They felt hopeless, full of despair, and self-loathing after realizing what they had done. God loved

Adam and Eve and enjoyed the close relationship they shared. When He came to the garden and didn't find them, He went looking for them until He found them hiding. Even knowing what they had done, He did not reject them but rather promised to one day send someone who would strike back against the sin and evil that threatened His creation, His people, His plan. He was faithful despite their sin, promising a solution. He covered their nakedness with animal skins to hide their shame and guilt. The animal sacrifice was the blood atonement for their sin. Much later, Jesus became the sacrifice for the world, and it was His blood that became the atonement for all of mankind's sins.

"Adam and Eve were forgiven Gethyn, but even so, they *had* to be cast out of the garden. The curse that followed and fell over the heavens and Earth affecting every living thing was so that man would never forget that things are not how God intended for them to be. Mankind needs that constant reminder in order to recognize their brokenness and their desperate need for redemption. Let me ask you this. If you did not have pain, how would you ever know when you were hurt or needed a doctor? The curse is much like that, Gethyn. The Earth groans, the heavens wreak havoc, and mankind bemoans all that is wrong in the world. But the truth is that the curse is deep-rooted within each person, a thorn in man's side so He will seek help. If humans were allowed to live in their sin with no consequences, they would never seek God. In that light, you can see that in actuality, the curse is an act of God's grace."

Gethyn was happy to know that Adam and Eve were forgiven and that they would never be cast from their garden home again. She asked Zendor if they ever came into the New Jerusalem but was told the couple was shy and usually kept pretty much to themselves. They were rarely seen, so the fact that she had seen them at the waterfall was an extraordinary event, Zendor said.

They took the same route through the jungle as they had on Gethyn's first day in Paradise, passing through groves of ancient trees and exotic plants. The young woman's mind wandered, and she could almost imagine long-tailed monkeys watching them or the sound of colorful macaws and toucans in the trees overhead. Of course, Gethyn knew the jungle did not contain any wildlife or birds presently, but she looked forward to seeing them up close on the new Earth.

Gethyn and Zendor saw glorious sunlight on the path in front of them, which meant the clearing was just ahead. A thought came to the young woman, and she wondered if other people came here too. Then she imagined the delightful laughter of Anya, Stevie, Arie-Ann, and Dolly, swimming and splashing in the pool at the base of the waterfall, and made a promise to herself to bring them here someday.

As they stepped onto the gold-paved boulevard, the angel put its arm around Gethyn and once again they were in the air heading towards the New Jerusalem. It had been a day to remember. The gentle rhythm of Zendor's wings in motion lulled the woman/child to sleep. Once at the high-rise, the winged creature flew through her window and delicately tucked Gethyn into bed, reminding the guardian of when she was a child. Zendor sat by her bed for a while, content to watch the steady rise and fall of her chest, and then quietly flew out the window and disappeared into the night.

34

The young woman was exuberant each morning upon meeting Zendor in the garden by the River of Life. As she ate the special sustenance that allowed her to live in the spiritual realm, she was filled with joyous anticipation of all the day had to offer. It was as though she was determined to hold each day hostage until it relented and gave up all its secrets.

Whether she was with Zendor, Philena, Grammy, Grandpa, Jace, Anya, Lottie, Clarence, Arie-Ann, Dolly, little Stevie, or the hundreds of other people and celestials she had met in the years since arriving in Paradise, she loved each of their soul essences completely and unconditionally in bold vibrant technicolor. Her world *was* paradise, both literally and figuratively; and by now, she wouldn't have gone back to Earth had the option been available to her. She had been sending prayers and thoughts daily to her family and friends who had been left behind and knew it was only a matter of time before they would be reunited. She could wait. In the meantime, she was happy and content with the rich fullness of her life.

One day in particular stood out in her mind. Gethyn remembered waking that morning to an unusually bright and glorious day. Feeling convicted in spirit, she quickly dressed in her white robe and summoned the Lord. The young woman could not imagine a life other than one living in the will of God and found it imperative to seek His assurance and blessing before making decisions. Gethyn was writing profusely now, inspired by her surroundings and the love that flourished here. She was writing children's stories and reading them aloud to the children she had come to love at The Nursery, and she had begun a novel about the new world to come. She didn't know whether she had found her purpose or if it had found her, but she approached each new day with an open heart, ready and willing to take the next step towards evolving into the person she was meant to become. Her heart, soul, and spirit were in agreement and confirmed what she already knew: today was going to be a pivotal day in her life.

After speaking with the Lord, Gethyn changed back into her faded blue jeans and T-shirt and raced across the street to the garden. At once, she was enveloped in a wonderland of woodsy scents and flowers that exuded heavenly fragrances. She was in a hurry to find her guardian. She spotted Zendor waiting for her at their favorite spot. The winged creature smiled, and sparks flew from its pale amethyst eyes. Before the young woman could even speak, the angel held out a piece of fruit.

"You're never going to let me forget to eat my daily sustenance again, are you?" She laughed.

"Not for a trillion years at least, but after that, you're on your own," Zendor joked.

Gethyn punched the guardian playfully on the leg, and it grimaced, pretending to be in pain.

"What would you like to do today?" Zendor asked.

The young woman was bursting at the seams to tell Zendor her plan but found herself vacillating between blurting it out or keeping it a secret a while longer.

"Are you going to tell me or am I going to have to hold you down and tickle it out of you?" Zendor asked, with a hint of mischief in the pale amethyst eyes that looked back at her.

"You wouldn't dare!" Gethyn said, her voice clearly going up an octave.

"Oh I wouldn't, would I?" responded Zendor.

Gethyn squealed and took off running with the angel in pursuit. It quickly caught up with the girl, held her down, and began tickling her. She laughed and squirmed on the ground until finally crying uncle.

"Okay, okay, I'll tell you!" She laughed as the guardian helped her to her feet. "I'm ready. It is time. Today is the day I'm going to adopt Anya and bring her home, and I want you to be there with me when I tell her."

A single tear suddenly formed in the corner of the angel's right eye, and its countenance changed. Gethyn saw its sweet vulnerability, and her heart melted into a puddle.

"You have always been with me, and I see no reason why you shouldn't share one of the most memorable days of my life. What do you say?" she asked.

Zendor felt honored to have been invited and in a soft, humble voice answered, "Never, since the day you were born, have I been so excited and honored to witness a child being placed in the arms of its mother. You were always more than just my charge, Gethyn. You were like my own child, and in a sense, through you, I will be a grandparent. You have given me pleasures unimaginable."

Zendor knelt down and they hugged each other.

"Well, what are we doing standing around here burning daylight? Let's go!" the young woman said.

Their spirits were light as they walked down the city sidewalk toward the complex that housed The Nursery. They hurriedly climbed the familiar steps, walked past the gallery where paintings of the youngest of God's children hung, and then down the glass corridor to the next building. As Gethyn contemplated the look on Anya's face upon hearing the news, she was suddenly struck with the realization that there *were* butterflies in Paradise. Although not a one could be found in the garden, there seemed to be several fluttering around in the young woman's stomach.

Gethyn, sometimes accompanied by Zendor or Philena, had been coming to spend time with Anya every day for the past five years. The young woman never missed a day since the time she had grown gravely ill, and the love between her and the child had only deepened with the passing of time. Anya was no longer haunted by fears of being alone or unloved and blossomed a little bit more each day into the happy go-lucky child she was meant to be.

When the elevator doors opened, the young woman saw the child she had come to love serving imaginary tea to three other children seated around the small round table. Seeing Gethyn, the tiny girl with long, red braids scampered over to greet both her and Zendor as they stepped onto the floor.

"*Privet!* (Hello!) I'm so glad you're here," she said in Russian.

Anya looked back over her shoulder and saw that her friends had gone in search of something else to do.

"I have just prepared some tea. If you will be seated, I will serve you," she said, holding an imaginary teapot in one hand.

"No tea today, Anya. We aren't planning on staying." Gethyn was savoring the anticipation and could barely contain her excitement.

The child was puzzled as she looked first at the young woman and then up at the towering angel. "But...why?" Anya stuttered.

Gethyn knelt in front of the little girl, looked into the blue eyes that looked back into her own, and said "Because if you still want me as your mother, I am ready to adopt you today. I think it's time you come home. What do you say?"

The child's eyes filled with tears of joy, and she leaped into Gethyn's arms, almost causing the two of them to tumble over backward. "*Da, da, da!* Oh, yes!" she cried.

After saying their good-byes, Zendor and the girl's guardian, Ryelle, followed Gethyn and Anya back to the high-rise. As though it were Christmas morning, the little girl's eyes were all aglow with the sights and smells of everything around her, and she was also full of anticipation for what was to come.

They saw Clarence standing in front of the building in his pressed gray and black uniform, hat with "The Landry Hotel" embossed across the front, and black wing-tipped shoes that were buffed and polished to a high sheen.

"Well, now, who is this little lady?" he asked, smiling down at the tiny girl.

"I am Anya," she beamed.

"Anya is my daughter," Gethyn said for the first time, liking the way it sounded on her lips.

"You're just as beautiful as your mother," Clarence told the child, after which the little girl grabbed him around the leg and hugged him. As though by tacit agreement, Zendor and Ryelle kissed their respective charge's good-bye, with the promise of meeting them in the garden the following morning.

Gethyn and Anya walked through the beautifully decorated lobby of the high-rise with its atrium and sitting areas. Everywhere the child looked, she pointed, exclaiming, "*Eto krasivo!* It's so beautiful!"

They stepped into the glass elevator, and while it ascended, Anya delighted in taking in the spectacular view of the New Jerusalem.

After walking down the long corridor, they came to Gethyn's cabin. The young woman smiled when she saw that the Lord had changed the placard on her door. It no longer said "Gethyn Fields" but rather "Gethyn Fields and Anya Nicolin-Fields."

The new mother reached into her jeans pocket and pulled out a gold key. It was not her key, but one Jesus had given her for Anya.

"This is your key, sweetheart. Would you like to open the door?" Gethyn asked in a soft-spoken voice.

The child's eyes grew big as she looked upon the gold key in Gethyn's palm. After a moment, she took the key and opened the door to her new home, the first real home she'd ever had. It was warm and cozy, unlike the cold, damp, garbage-strewn gypsy wagon she and her parents had lived in outside of Moscow. Anya knew love abided in this place, and now so did she. Tentatively, she looked around the one-room cabin, familiarizing herself with each chair and painting. She saw the bed and, admiring the beauty of the antique quilt, scampered over to touch it. Then she noticed the headboard Gethyn's daddy had made and traced the carving of the pine tree and full moon with her finger, just as her mother had done countless times as a child. Anya walked around the table and envisioned future tea parties with her friends. The child looked out onto the screened-in back porch and saw the twin beds positioned on opposite sides. Eventually, she discovered the tall, narrow closet and opened the door. Inside was Gethyn's white robe and, beside it, a smaller one made especially for her.

"Oh, Mama, it's beautiful!" the child said excitedly. "Can I put it on?" she pleaded.

"Yes child."

The young woman took both robes off their hangers and laid them on the bed.

"I think we should get out of our earthly rags and put on the clean robes of righteousness."

After they had changed, Gethyn sat down in one of the oversized chairs and pulled her daughter onto her lap.

"I think we should invite Jesus to celebrate this monumental day with us. What do you think, Anya?" the new mother asked.

"*Da*," the girl said in a matter-of-fact tone. "Maybe I should serve tea."

Gethyn imagined the smile on Jesus's face and hugged the five-year-old. "I'm sure the Lord would like that very much, honey."

35

Thirty-Two Years Later

One day Gethyn was alone with her thoughts in the cabin she shared with Anya. She stood at the window overlooking God's holy city and felt her heart overflow with joy for all that was before her. The young woman was thankful for the life she shared with the impish five-year-old Russian child with long red braids and blue eyes that she had adopted years earlier. Their soul essences had not changed with the passage of time, but each day, their spirits grew a little brighter, casting a glow through the window where they lived for all to see. Right now, Zendor and Ryelle had taken Anya with them to The Nursery so she could visit friends who were still waiting for parents to arrive from Earth or to be adopted.

All the questions relating to why Gethyn had died had long since been buried. The young woman had come to realize that the why did not matter and that the real issue was "What now?" Her thoughts were often of her loved ones on Earth, and every morning, she religiously rose and prayed for them as well as for all mankind. The deep wound Gethyn had felt once by being suddenly separated from her family and friends had long since healed, and now thoughts of them were not in the context of the past but rather the future. Instead of looking back, she looked forward to seeing them, trusting completely that in God's time she would.

Gethyn no longer mourned the loss of Dave or the wedding that never took place as she knew now that when a spark of love is created, it can never be extinguished. When she looked back upon the girl she had been all those years ago, she realized the romantic feelings she had felt then were just a dim shadow of love, only a pale imitation. Over the years, Gethyn's soul connected with hundreds of humans and angels and would continue making connections forever.

The young woman's mind roamed like a buffalo grazing leisurely on prairie grass. She lingered on a thought until content and then moved on to another. Gethyn had come to love the fact she owned no possessions in Paradise other than the clothes on her back and the robe of righteousness given her by Jesus. In truth, she had not missed the clothes, car, cell phone, television, or other material stuff she had enjoyed on Earth, as none of them held value to her anymore. She was living in the kind of environment she'd always envisioned as a girl—a world where loving relationships healed. There was no commerce in Paradise as nothing was being bought or sold. The only commodity being exchanged was love. Love for God and those He loved was all that really mattered here. As Gethyn stood at the window, an old saying she heard once as a child suddenly came to mind. She couldn't remember the words exactly, but it was something like "It is only when you discover that God's love is all you have that you discover God's love is all you need." *It is so true*, the young woman thought to herself.

Opportunities, potential, and purpose that had been lost at the time of Gethyn's death had been restored in ways too wonderful to describe. She was discovering in exciting new ways that through God everything really was possible. The hopes and dreams she had on Earth seemed small in comparison to the unbridled ones that roamed free on the open plains of Heaven's horizon just waiting to be lassoed and saddled. Every day the young woman's spiritual consciousness was raised while in the company of the Lord or one of His apostles. Gethyn found her perspective changing and becoming more aligned with those of her Creator. Additionally, she found she longed for the fulfillment of *His* desires rather than her own and looked for ways to glorify and edify Him. With each new day came the realization that she was a citizen of Heaven, who for the time being had been given temporary shelter in Paradise.

Gethyn and Anya had many wonderful fireside chats with Jesus over the years. One evening, Anya asked, "Lord, will there be animals in Heaven?"

The exalted man smiled and answered, "Oh yes! Father is very fond of animals and will bring many of them back. He might even add some new animals, Anya! Not only does He enjoy them but He has also seen how humans have taken to them as well and vice-versa. As any loving father, He would not withhold gifts He knows would please and delight His children. Have you ever noticed that not only were animals with Adam and Eve in the garden, but there were animals with Noah in the Ark and with me at my birth?"

The little girl's voice grew excited, and in her native tongue, she answered excitedly, "*Da!* That's true!" Then her face lit up again as she thought of another question. "Will there be dinosaurs, Jesus?"

The question made the Lord smile. "I wouldn't be surprised," He said with a hint of mischief in His eyes. "Yes, animals great and small will once again roam the Earth, but there will never again be reason to fear them. The lion will lay down with the lamb, so to speak."

Gethyn was as excited as Anya to learn this. Recalling how her friend Philena, who was actually her fifteenth great-grandmother, missed her cat named Kip, she couldn't wait to share with her what the Lord had said.

"Jesus, if there will be animals in Heaven, then why aren't there animals in Paradise?" Anya wanted to know.

The girl's curiosity melted the Lord's heart, and the love in His heart for her swelled. "Paradise is a spiritual realm in which animals cannot live. Though they have a body and soul, they do not have a spirit. You see, God made humans in His image, giving them a spirit in order that they might communicate and have a deep relationship with Him. While animals, other than my Father's horses, do not inhabit Paradise, many of them will be resurrected once 'Thy Kingdom Comes. Once they are resurrected, they will be reunited with their souls and live among men in peace and harmony for all eternity on the new Earth."

Gethyn looked out the window across the New Jerusalem, content in her daydreams. The young woman thought of the pleasures waiting in Heaven that Jesus said had to be seen and experienced to believe. He promised she wouldn't be disappointed and even added "Believe it or not, I am looking forward to Heaven just as much as you are."

It was a thought the young woman had never considered before, but she found it intriguing. "What do you look forward to the most, Jesus?" Gethyn asked with genuine interest.

"I look forward to my wedding and the Marriage Supper. The preparations have been underway for quite a long time, and I long for my bride," the Lord said, giving the beautiful girl's hands a squeeze.

The morning was still young, and with each passing day, Gethyn had come to appreciate the beauty and simplicity of Paradise more and more. As the young woman watched people on the city streets below going about their business, a revelation came to her. Everyone *walked* in Paradise. There were exceptions of course. Angels had the option to fly, and the Lord could materialize wherever He was needed, but there were no cars, buses, trains, planes, or any other form of transportation. Gethyn recalled that when Jesus was alive on Earth, He had walked everywhere He went. After years of walking through the garden and down the gold-paved streets of the New Jerusalem, she had come to understand that when you walk you can't help but notice people and your surroundings. With perfect clarity, she saw the reason Jesus never ran or seemed in a hurry to get somewhere. Walking gave Him the opportunity to stop, talk, teach, minister, touch, and heal. The young woman remembered that while alive, she had passed nameless, faceless people on the street every day while speeding by in her car in a hurry to get somewhere. On Earth, most people lived self-centered lives, focusing on their own personal agendas—where they had to go, what they had to do, what was important to them. Now Gethyn realized how arrogant that way of thinking was, as what is more important than people and relationships? It made her wonder how many opportunities she had missed to make a difference. Gethyn knew she couldn't change the past, but now as she walked around the city limits of Paradise, she made a point to stop and take time to offer pretty bouquets of love to passersby, each handpicked from the meadows of her heart.

After a while, the young woman drew away from the hypnotic lure of the window. Curling up in her favorite chair, she closed her eyes. It didn't seem possible that thirty-seven years had passed since she had died in the predawn hours of Easter morning. Gethyn calculated that had she lived she would be fifty-nine years old, but in the spiritual realm, she was still twenty-two. Her daughter, Anya, born in 1771, was 239 years old in physical years; but in Paradise, she was still a child of five.

The young woman remembered someone on Earth saying that people in Heaven would all be thirty-three years old and asked the Lord if that was true.

"No," He had replied. "When people are reunited with their physical bodies they will be the same age as they were at their death, but with the ravages of sin, disease, and death removed, they will appear much younger. Not because they are younger but because they will be filled with vitality, strength, enthusiasm, curiosity, opportunity, potential, and unlimited time to do all they ever dreamed of. Health will be restored, and all infirmities will be gone, not only for the old but also for the physically and mentally handicapped as well. Everyone will be whole."

Her curiosity stirred, Gethyn asked, "Even if old people can do one thousand push-ups in Heaven, won't they be disappointed if their bodies don't look as young as they feel?"

Jesus shook His head no. "On Earth, humans judge each other by their physical beauty, but in Heaven, there will be no vanity or ego, and the beauty of a person's soul is all one will see when they look at others or themselves.

"Gethyn, did you ever notice how on Earth children couldn't wait to be older but then once they *were* older longed to go back and relive their childhood? If you really think about it, it is the life experiences associated with certain ages that people really crave. In Heaven, neither youth nor old age will prevent people from experiencing life to its fullest. Therefore, age will not matter.

"Let me ask you this. How interesting do you think it would be if you lived in a world where everyone was thirty-three? Wouldn't you miss the laughter of little children at play or miss asking the advice of someone you respected who had lived more years than you? It takes all kinds of people to make the world go round, not just on Earth, but in Heaven too. Children teach us to be curious, to laugh, to imagine, and to not take life so seriously, while teenagers remind us to have dreams for ourselves. The middle-aged and elderly are wise and have valuable lessons to share as well. You see, with every age, there is something worthwhile to learn. Who would you teach and who would you learn from if everyone were the same?"

"On Earth, a person may live to be hundred years old, but that is young when compared to how long they will live in eternity. In reality, they haven't even *begun* to live and experience all life has in store for them, as one day in Heaven will be as a thousand years on the old Earth. Time will go on and on without end. People will never stop learning or evolving into the person they were created to be. In a very real sense, everyone, whether they are an infant or a hundred-year-old grandmother, will remain forever young in the context of time eternal."

Once the Lord had finished His explanation, Gethyn smiled at the Lord, saying, "I see your point."

The young woman stayed at home all day in quiet reflection, remembering all that the Lord had taught her over the years. She was happy and content and wept tears of joy, thinking of all her blessings.

Gethyn spent a lot of time thinking about the Lord. It was He who had come to Earth to save the world from sin and the grave. She thought of how He had always been faithful to meet her at every twist, turn, corner, and crossroad in her life, always offering words of encouragement and hope. The young woman knew Jesus was her one true love and had exceeded all expectations by satisfying every need, dream, hope, and desire of her heart. To bask in His adoration and devotion was what she lived for. He soothed all doubts and fears, was loving, kind, compassionate, and perfect in every way. It was *His* name, not Dave, Jace, or any other name that lingered on her lips, for Jesus alone was the lover of her soul.

Once Zendor and Ryelle had dropped Anya off, Gethyn listened as the little girl chatted about her visit at The Nursery and how they had run into Jace and his guardian angel, Tanniz, on the way home. She was a delightful child and had bloomed like a geranium on a window ledge since being adopted by Gethyn. Her eyes were no longer haunted, and she was no longer afraid of being unloved and unwanted. She had found her way home and into the arms of her *true* mother.

After sharing the events of the day with one another, the two of them changed into their clean white robes and summoned the Lord, as was their nightly custom. As always He was there instantly, a look of wondrous grace lighting up His handsome face. He started a fire for the three of them and then took a seat across from Gethyn and her daughter. He smiled at the two, cozied up together in the large overstuffed chair. The young woman thought she saw an extra twinkle in Jesus's bright blue eyes and then wondered if it was just her imagination. Usually the Lord's custom was to wait and let Gethyn and Anya tell Him what was on their hearts, but this time, He was the first to speak. The exalted man looked at the beautiful redhead with the heart-shaped face sitting across from Him, knowing the profound effect His words would have and what her reaction would be even before He spoke.

Jesus smiled and then said the words the young woman had known would eventually come. "Gethyn, your mother is on the way to Paradise."

36

Morning had not yet broken when Gethyn and Anya rose from their beds. The little girl made up the twin bed on the screened in porch, while her mother made the one in which her parents used to sleep. She pulled up the heirloom quilt and smoothed it out, and then Anya joined her to kneel and pray. They exited the high-rise hand in hand and walked down the wide, gold-paved boulevard. They passed through the thick inner walls of the New Jerusalem with its twelve glittering foundations, each one a different precious gem, and headed toward the massive outer gate of Paradise. Gethyn had entered through it years before carried in the arms of her guardian angel, Zendor, although she had no memory of it. Until today, the young woman hadn't had a reason to go to the gate and was overly anxious about getting there in time to welcome her mother, who would be arriving soon.

Gethyn and Anya encountered others heading in the same direction, assuming rightly that they were going to the gate in hopes of getting a glimpse of a loved one as well. As the mother and child walked down the main thoroughfare, they talked quietly amongst themselves.

"Do you think she is going to like me?" asked the tiny girl with the long red braids.

"Like you? Mama's going to *love* you!" Gethyn exclaimed. "She was so looking forward to me getting married and having children, and I remember how I used to dream of seeing the look of love in her eyes when I put my first baby in her arms."

Anya stopped and looked up into her mama's eyes. "But I'm not a baby. I'm five years old."

Gethyn looked down at her precious daughter. "Anya, you are *my* baby, and once I introduce you to my mother and after she recovers from the shock of learning I *have* a child, she isn't going to care if you're a newborn or thirty! I promise she's going to take you into her arms and love you just as though you were born to me. Do you understand?"

Like the sun breaking through on a cloudy day, a sudden smile appeared on the child's face. The little girl tilted her head and answered, "*Da, Mamulya* (Yes, Mama)."

"She will be a wonderful grandmother, you wait and see," Gethyn emphasized. "Surely my brother, Emmit, married and had children, or at least I've always hoped so for my mother's sake. I've always felt if she had a grandchild to love and spoil, then maybe it would take some of the sting out of losing me. Anyway, she was always good with children. In fact, you might even say she was a kid magnet. When I was little, whether she was teaching me to read or how to tie my shoelaces, she was always kind, patient, and loving. She taught me so much about love, Anya and I knew that when I became a mother, I wanted to be just like her."

"*Vy?* (Are you?)," Anya asked.

Gethyn paused before answering. "I hope so, but soon you can answer that question for yourself."

The young woman squeezed the child's hand as they continued walking down the thoroughfare with the tributaries and shade trees running along each side. Though the perimeter of Paradise was quite a distance from their high-rise in the city, neither grew tired nor felt the need to stop and rest as they made the long journey on foot.

Upon arriving at the massive outer gate, they found what appeared to be a receiving line on both sides. The sense of anticipation among the people waiting there was palpable. The young woman's heart beat rapidly at the thought of seeing her mother who would be ninety-one years old now. *Will I recognize her?* Gethyn thought to herself. *Oh course you will*, she chided herself. *It is not the outward appearance that will draw you to her but rather the essence of her soul.*

It was a couple of hours until sunrise when someone gave a shout and then another. "They're coming! They've just touched down in the landing area." The crowd erupted into a hail storm of hallelujahs followed by a downpour of "Thanks be to God!"

Gethyn and Anya got caught up in the excitement of the moment and were laughing, crying, and shouting for joy. Everyone's spirit was light while waiting for the guardians to climb the golden stairways' one thousand steps. As the first guardian angel stepped into Paradise, the crowd immediately quieted down. There were hundreds of thousands of guardians arriving. As they passed, everyone attempted to see who they carried in their arms and if it was the person they were waiting for. You could tell when a loved one was recognized as a shout would emanate from the crowd, "Praise God! John's long journey is over!" Although the name of the person was different each time, the refrain was one heard over and over again.

All of a sudden, an enormous angel pushed through the hordes of people, wavy black hair cascading down one side of its face and down its muscular back until it reached Gethyn and Anya.

Surprised to see her guardian, the young woman asked, "Zendor, what are you doing here?"

He looked down on the titian-haired beauty and smiled, silver-streaked lightning and blue and yellow sparks shooting from pale amethyst eyes. "I saw Jesus while in the garden and asked where you were. He told me your mother is arriving this morning." The celestial being took Anya and hoisted her onto its broad shoulders so she could see above the crowd. "I knew you and Anya would be here, so thought I'd come wait with you. You don't mind, do you?"

Gethyn punched him playfully and responded, "Of course not. I'm glad you're here to share this day with us, but I don't know how I'm ever going to find Mama among the thousands and thousands of guardian angels filing past."

Without missing a beat, Zendor answered, "Oh, that's easy. I know your mother's guardian, Amsul."

The young woman looked up at the nine-foot towering angel, and tears welled up in her blue Caribbean eyes. "Have I told you today how much I love you, Zendor?"

The angel met her gaze and chuckled. "No, however, you're going to love me even more when you see what I have brought for you and Anya."

The redheaded child pulled on the angel's black mane of hair and squealed, "What is it?"

Laughing, Zendor said, "Well, hold your horses, little lady, while I get it out."

The angel reached into the fold of one of its wings and brought out a piece of fruit for each of them. "I didn't want to take any chance that either of you would forget your sustenance today of all days," Zendor explained.

Gethyn took a piece of fruit, and the angel handed one up to Anya. "I don't know what I would ever do without you," the young woman said while taking a bite. It was sugary sweet, and she was soon nourished and energized. The creature beamed from ear to ear in its own unusual way, happy to be appreciated by the girl it had loved and cared for since first being appointed her guardian.

They continued watching the procession until all of a sudden, Zendor saw Amsul. "There they are!" Zendor bellowed.

Gethyn looked in the direction her guardian was pointing and saw a magnificent celestial being with long curly blonde hair. The winged creature was at least as tall as Zendor, which made it difficult to see who was being carried protectively in its arms. Gethyn strained her neck trying to glimpse the woman she believed to be her mother, but all she could see were a few tendrils of hair that were as white as a snow-covered mountain. The last time Gethyn had seen her, she had been a healthy, middle-aged woman. Even with Anya around its shoulders, Zendor lifted Gethyn up with one arm high enough for her to see the woman in Amsul's arms. As she gazed upon the small figure lying deathly silent in the guardian's arms, it was hard for her to reconcile the last image of her mother with the one of the frail, wrinkled woman being carried through the streets of Paradise. It had been so long, and Gethyn couldn't be sure from what little could be seen. However, she trusted Zendor. If the celestial being said Amsul was her mother's guardian angel, then there could be no doubt. It had to be her.

The procession of guardians made their way quietly towards the River of Life in order to meet Jesus by sunrise. Gethyn knew that once the convoy of celestials had brought the spirits of God's children to the banks of the river, the

Lord would open their spiritual eyes. Just as His voice was the last they heard before dying, His voice would be the first they would hear upon waking in their new life. The young woman remembered seeing Jesus's blue eyes upon her arrival and how He had given her the special sustenance to eat, staying with her and answering her questions until she had regained her strength.

Gethyn's mother would go through a period of orientation just as she herself had done. During that time, she would finally meet and get acquainted with her guardian angel, Amsul, and see the temporary home that Jesus had prepared especially for her. Knowing her mother had been earthbound for ninety-one years, the young woman held on to what Jesus had once told her. He had explained that at some point, the elderly began looking forward to moving on and making the transition from one life to the next. While Mary Ann would no doubt miss her husband, son, and grandchildren, maybe seeing Gethyn again after so many years would soften the blow of being separated from those she loved and left behind on Earth.

Once the angels had all filed past the welcoming committee, there was nothing for the crowd to do but disperse. It would be a few days before those arriving would be ready to meet the friends and relatives who were eager to embrace them. Not only was she eager to talk with her mother and catch up on the lives of her earthbound family but she was also equally excited to share with her how her own life had been unfolding since arriving in Paradise on Easter morning many years before. If there was one thing Gethyn had learned over the years, it was that there was plenty of time. Neither of them was going anywhere anytime soon, and when they did, they would be going together.

Though Gethyn's mother was in every waking thought, the young woman had no choice but to go about her life as usual. She and Anya prayed for those on Earth in the mornings before heading for the garden for their daily sustenance. Generally, they would meet up with Zendor and Ryelle, although sometimes they went their own way. Gethyn and Anya would stop and visit with Lottie, and the old black woman would teach the child about making "purdy" things grow. Mother and child especially enjoyed visiting children at The Nursery. Anya would play with her friends while Gethyn rocked babies who were either orphaned or waiting for their parents, and she would read stories she had written to the older children. Sometimes she borrowed Philena's father's violin and took it to The Nursery where she would play soothing lullabies for the babies. Zendor and Gethyn took Anya and her friends on outings in the garden and around the city. One of the little girl's favorite places to go was to the waterfall deep in the jungle. She loved swimming in the cold water. Gethyn always looked for Adam and Eve, but she had not seen them since the day Zendor took her flying.

Their days were full. They had Bible school and church, and they always enjoyed listening to testimonies at the amphitheater. There was time spent with Gethyn's grandparents and other greats, and by then, Anya was enjoying the company of some of her own long-lost relatives. She even became acquainted with Viktor Borovsky, the kind peasant man who had carried her away from the filthy gypsy wagon where she had been tethered by her parents. The little girl comforted the lumbering man as he told her how he thought he was saving her life by leaving her on a nearby neighbor's doorstep and had not meant for any harm to befall her.

Little Stevie had taken a shine to Gethyn's daughter and had become a frequent visitor to their cabin as well as had Arie-Ann Tucker and Dolly Jemison. Although Gethyn had made many new friends over the years, she had formed a very special soul connection with Jace Covington. The beautiful titian-haired redhead with the heart-shaped face and her impish daughter spent a lot of time in his company. Anya especially enjoyed and delighted in visiting him at the royal stables where he helped care for the King's horses. When walking through the city streets, they stopped to chat with friends and newcomers alike; and in the evenings after changing into their white robes, they would summon the Lord. He was always faithful to meet them where they lived and would stay for as long as they wanted to talk.

One night during a visit, a week after Gethyn's mother had arrived, Jesus informed the young woman that her mother was ready to see her. Every day, there was a family reunion being held in the garden as new people were constantly arriving. Gethyn had been to dozens of reunions over the years, each time meeting at least one person related to her or Anya if only by a tenuous silver thread. After a while, the young woman had come to realize that everyone was related to one another. It was only a matter of discovering the connecting link.

It was hard for either Gethyn or Anya to sleep, so they rose early and dressed then said morning prayers before heading for the garden. They met Zendor at The River of Life and talked for a few minutes while eating choice selections of fruit. Once satisfied, they walked down the garden path and into a forest of conifers, oaks, elms, pines, and trees of other varieties. An intoxicating mixture of fragrances wafted through the air as they passed exotic flowers and plants until finally coming to the large clearing known as Homecoming Park. Every day, thousands of people converged there, looking for family members they may or may not have known in life. Today was no exception.

Music and laughter filled the air. People were rejoicing at being reunited with their loved ones, and everywhere Gethyn looked, she saw faces filled with joy. The young woman scoured the area looking for her mother, knowing that if she was ever going to find her she'd have to stand on Zendor's shoulders as she'd done when looking for her grandparents years ago. Her guardian picked her up effortlessly, and once situated, the young woman began combing the multitude of people searching for the one person she longed to see.

"There she is!" Gethyn and Zendor said at the same time. They had both spotted Amsul and knew Gethyn's mother would surely be with the enormous blonde angel. The celestial being waved, managing to catch Amsul's attention. Amsul waved back at them enthusiastically. Each group began making their way through the crowded park towards the other until at last they met in the middle.

All words failed Gethyn as she was drawn to the familiar soul essence of the one who stood before her. Likewise, the elderly woman recognized the daughter whose spirit had been carried away so many years before. Though housed in temporary bodies, they instinctively remembered the contour of the other's soul and fell into each other's arms. Neither wanted to let go, but they finally pulled apart. Their eyes feasted on one another as though ravenously hungry, and all the while their souls' thirst was quenched by drinking in the beauty of the moment.

"Oh, Mama, I'm so sorry for causing you so much pain and suffering!" Gethyn cried, a torrent of tears falling down her cheeks.

Tears welled up in the elderly woman's eyes as well, but they were tears of joy rather than of sorrow. She looked at her beautiful daughter with the heart-shaped face and admitted, "I thought I would die from the excruciating pain caused by your passing, Gethyn. There were many times I prayed for God to take me, and then I was angry when He didn't. Once the pain subsided, loneliness came and took its place. I don't know which was worse, but none of that matters anymore. This is a time for joyful celebration that has been a long time coming, so let's not waste a minute of it. We're together now and will never be separated again." The white-haired woman took Gethyn in her arms and held her as though for the first time, all the while stroking her long red-gold titian hair.

"Mama, there are others here I would like for you to meet. This is Zendor, my guardian angel," she said, looking at the angel she had come to love without question.

"Nice to meet you, Zendor," the woman said politely.

"Nice to finally meet you in person, Mrs. Fields," the celestial being responded.

There was a pause, and then Gethyn took Anya's hand in hers. "Mama, there is someone else I'd like for you to meet."

The young woman's mother looked down at the impish five-year-old child with the long dark red braids and blue eyes and smiled. She bent down, and she and the child came together like a magnet drawn to metal. The elderly woman hugged the little girl and kissed the tip of her nose, causing Anya to giggle.

"Why, she reminds me of you when you were a little girl," remarked the white-haired woman before giving the tiny child another hug.

Gethyn smiled and said, "Mama, I'd like you to meet Anya…my daughter."

References

Alcorn, R. (2004). *Heaven*
p. 11, 20, 29, 38, 39, 205, 311, 312, 334, 335
Carol Stream, Illinois: Tynedale House Publishers, Inc.

Christian Answers.Net: *Angels*
Retrieved April 1, 2011
p. 27, 50, 51
http://www.christiananswers.net/q-acb/acb-t005.html

Brown, B. (2012). *Daring Greatly*
p. 281
New York, New York: Gotham Books

Christian Angelic Hierarchy
Retrieved May 4, 2011
p. 77, 78
http://en.wikipedia.org/wiki/Christian_angelic_hierarchy

Danoff, B; Nivert, T; Denver, J. (1971, April). *Take Me Home, Country Roads*
HYPERLINK "https://en.wikipedia.org/wiki/Poems,_Prayers_%26_Promises" \o "Poems, Prayers & Promises"Poems, Prayers & Promises, RCA,
p. 1, 2, 3

Fitzgerald, H. *When a Sibling Dies*
Retrieved May 21, 2011
http://www.beliefnet.com/Love-Family/1999/12/When-A-Sibling-Dies.aspx
p. 306, 307

Foxe, J. (2004). *Foxe's Book of Martyrs*
p. 253, 254
Peabody, Massachusetts: Hendrickson Publishers, Inc.

Glazer, T. – (1963). *On Top of Spaghetti*
p. 293

KJV Study Bible
Grand Rapids, Michigan: Zondervan
p. 9, 21, 22, 30, 33, 38, 77, 78, 211, 212, 235, 257

Rankin, J., Tomer, W. (1882). *God Be With You 'Til We Meet Again*
p. 134

Recover-From-Grief.Com
7 Stages of Grief
Recovered May 20, 2011
http://www.recover-from-grief.com/7-stages -of-grief.html
p. 302, 303, 304

Rogers, A. (2004). *Dad's Who Shoot Straight*
Most Requested Messages CD
Love Worth Finding Ministries
Memphis, Tennessee
p. 148

Rogers, A. (1997). *The Mighty Meek*
Fruit of the Spriit CD
Love Worth Finding Ministries
Memphis, Tennessee
p. 244

Rogers, A. (1991) *How to Deal With Demons*
Dealing With the Devil CD
Love Worth Finding Ministries
Memphis, Tennessee
p. 152, 153

Taylor, M; Spivey, D: (1939). *You Are My Sunshine*
RCA Records
p. 196

The Bible Genesis & Geology
The Relationship of Flesh and Spirt
p. 122, 123
Retrieved April 12, 2011
http://www.kjvbible.org/body.html

The Order of The Angel's / Relijournal
p. 51, 52, 53, 54
Retrieved May 4, 2011
http://relijournal.com/religion/the-order-of-the-angels

Warner, A; Bradbury, W. (1860). *Jesus Loves Me*
p. 7

CPSIA information can be obtained
at www.ICGtesting.com
Printed in the USA
FSOW03n1408011016
25585FS